SOMETIMES YOU CAN HEAR IT COMING

Sometimes You Can Hear It Coming

STORIES FROM
THE RED CLOUD COOPERATIVE

Edited by
Jack Galloway

Red Cloud
COOPERATIVE

Copyright © 2008 by Red Cloud Cooperative
All rights reserved.

ISBN 978-0-9802221-0-4

Published by Red Cloud Cooperative
5105 Beard Avenue South • Minneapolis, MN 55410

Library of Congress Catalog Card Number applied for.

Art by Lois Severson

Book design by Sylvia Ruud

Contents

Preface	vii
Cross-Pollination ELAINE WAGNER	1
Nan BARBARA MARYSTONE	17
And I Married Her	39
The Lily of France Suit JULIE LARSON	48
Morning Chores STEVE CHAMBERS	59
At the Edge MARGARET SMITH	75
Promises LOIS SEVERSON	93
Wiltshire, England 1630 ANN CLARE SMITH	111
The Librarian JACK GALLOWAY ELAINE WAGNER	133
Ava's Story JOAN PORITSKY	163

Preface

I GREW UP JUST A LITTLE SOUTH OF THE MASON-DIXON LINE, in a time and place where stories were just part of the air around you. People communicated in stories that never seemed rushed. The time they took to tell was the time they took. You never saw anyone tapping their foot or looking at their watch, and you never heard anyone say, "Could you just get to the point?" I suspect you never heard that because oftentimes the stories might not exactly have a point. Or the teller might be figuring it out while she told the story, and that takes time. It also requires attention to detail and just the right language. So the stories I heard growing up often had language like, "Well, it was one of those hot days that just weigh down on you." And you'd hear a lot of phrases like "One thing led to another... and we ended up at... and after a while I...."

I have a sense that stories like those, that bring with them the slower rhythms and cadences of life lived a little differently, may have become anachronisms. Who has the time anymore to sit around while somebody wanders around the intricacies of some narrative that may or may not even be relevant to getting information more quickly and more condensed and more, well, to the point? And maybe that's alright. It's good, I suspect, to have a point, to have a reason to get out the door and get something accomplished. But I also think it's good to know that your life makes sense, that we're doing good things and taking care of the important stuff. That's where stories come in. An interesting story can take us outside our everyday lives and maybe give us a little different take on the world and the things we're up to.

We should probably be careful these days about giving too much weight and reverence to art. Please don't get me wrong, we need good art, in particular we need good stories that remind us of our common humanity, and of our individuality, two of the important components of American life. But once a story sets out to instruct us, it almost always becomes self-important and generally annoying and off-putting. Nobody likes to be instructed. Good stories may be concerned in some way or on some level with religion or politics or psychology, but those concerns, it seems to me, should be positioned somewhere well beyond the immediate goings-on of the work. A good work of prose should make you feel something. It should enlarge your experience of life and it should enhance your perceptions. You should feel like laughing or crying or screaming or blushing. It seems like a pretty straightforward proposition—introduce some characters, describe where they are, have them do some things to each other, and then wind the action down. But in reality, it is extraordinarily difficult to do it well.

The problem is, as Oscar Wilde said, "All bad poetry springs from genuine feeling." So the effort becomes finding just the right way to say it, and that's where the sweat comes in. To write well you have to hear voices and see landscapes with fresh eyes, and talk to characters who exist only in your imagination. It becomes necessary to engage the world differently. That, in turn, doesn't make the writer any more special or important than someone who is accomplished at any trade. In fact, the writer is often more of a nut bag than most folks. The craft just sort of requires a slightly off-balance weirdness.

Someone once described most writers as vain, lazy, and selfish. Fair enough, maybe that's true of most writers, but it doesn't square up with my experience. Most of the good ones I've worked with are engaged with the world in some way other than just as it relates to them. And they bring with them the work ethic it takes to write well, even if the housework gets a little backed up.

So these, then, are some stories from the writers of the Red Cloud Cooperative. We go by that name because we seem to share a certain affinity for Willa Cather, who spent time in Red Cloud, Nebraska, and watched and wrote as a way of life passed from the American landscape. We also like the name because red clouds on the horizon often signal changes are coming. Writers are often the types who pay attention to the horizon.

Most of these writers turned their hand to this work sometime after midlife, and I've been fortunate to be around while many of these stories took shape. I'm grateful for the experience, and I commend these stories to your care, because they belong to all of us now. Take your time with them, enjoy them, and don't worry too much about the point. Just look for the inner light within them, feel the emotional honesty, and listen for what you hear coming.
Cheers,
Jack Galloway

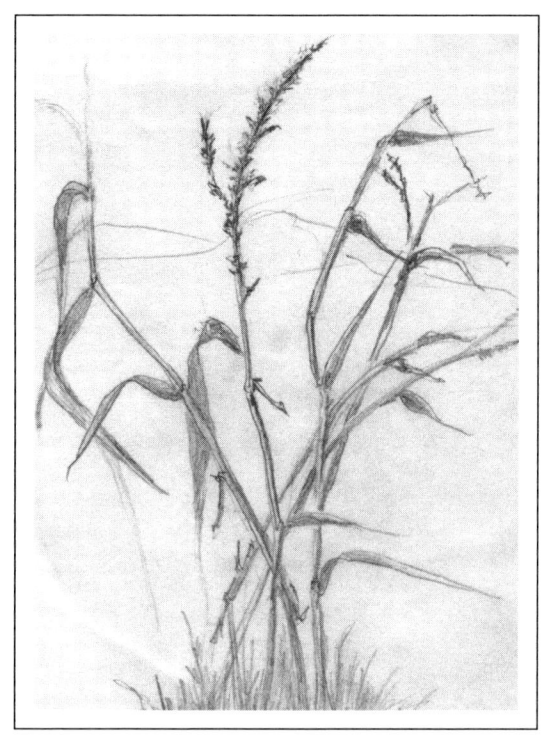

Cross-Pollination

ELAINE WAGNER

These days ELAINE WAGNER *divides her time between St. Paul and Los Angeles, a sometimes bumpy flight. Elaine loves bumps. They make good stories. And good stories send the writer and the reader on a bounce back up. Take heart, Lindsay and Paris, a collection of Elaine's best bumps,* Feeling the Distance, *will be available soon in your favorite Beverly Hills bookstore.*

This is the preface to Elaine's memoir, the tale of a widow on a bicycle going full speed ahead down a very high hill. There are potholes ahead, here and there a sudden curve, lots and lots of bumps. But off she goes, feet off the pedals, wind tossing her hair. She's going to enjoy a nice long coast before the next inevitable climb.

I'VE BEEN SPENDING A LOT OF TIME IN L.A. LATELY visiting my son in his new home, and one of the things I have learned is that a bird-of-paradise can bloom in a backyard with as little care as a lilac bush. I am a succulent when I am in California. Out here birds-of-paradise last much longer, like they are made of wax, orange and purple molded wax. Spring is too brief for Minnesota's delicate lilac. In Southern California, there are only two seasons, warm summer and not-quite-so-warm summer. And with every visit it seems as if I sprout another cactus blossom.

I feel bold when I am in L.A., like Desert, the little girl with a long black braid who lives at the bottom of a bluff in Doug's Lincoln Heights neighborhood. I met her at her birthday party. I watched this little birthday princess flit in and out of her celebration. She fluffed her dress, clicked her heels, and scooped up her candies. Then she stuck her finger in her cake, ran out and climbed on a new pink bike that was still a little too big for her. I watched her give the training wheels a good swift backward kick. I know exactly how she felt. She would find a way to get them off. Desert wanted to fly up and down her roller-coaster neighborhood. The wind would unbraid her hair. No one could catch up with her and tell her to watch out or be careful not to fall.

You don't tell a princess what to do. A princess may fall but you know she won't get hurt. I know how she feels because I was a lot like her when I was her age.

I knew I was a princess even though my parents' castle was rented and we shared our bathroom with the landlady. Every Easter Mom and Dad bought me a new pair of patent leather shoes. As I walked around the block watching them shine, listening to them squeak, I didn't see the grassless boulevards or the window boxes with no flowers. I didn't notice that the Victorian boarding homes needed paint. I had no idea they used to house just one family. I didn't care much for the sheets some mothers tacked on their windows instead of curtains and I thought black-and-whites cruised all neighborhoods every hour on the hour. I supposed every corner was like Dale and Selby, with Marlon-wannabees in leather jackets leaning against the stoplights, not noticing or caring when the light turned from green to red. And I had no idea my neighborhood would be labeled inner-city St. Paul less than ten years later. Maybe even sooner. You don't always see the changes when you are living through them.

I was Desert. I found adventure, even romance, in my tainted city block. The boarding house we lived in was to me a movie set, the side porch my Burt Lancaster balcony. I would scale the rail like a true swashbuckler on his way to rescue a maiden in distress. There was a wooden stairway at the back door. It had steps going up one side and down another. A stile, I remembered it being called in some nursery rhyme. I suppose I could have gone up and down either side, but I preferred to think there was some magic in playing by the rules. I still believe in magic although I've come to realize sometimes it happens when you don't play by the rules, whether it's life or bicycle riding.

Desert's training wheels make me think of passages. Protective parents attach training wheels to their children's growing up years. No one puts them on the years we spend growing old. The wise widow puts them on her own bicycle. There are a lot of potholes in front of her. Potholes that arrive as diminished dreams and lost loves. But the audacious widow swooshes down from the top of the hill with no training wheels at all, her feet off the pedals, the wind tossing her hair as she goes bumpity, bump, bump. She dings her bell to let the world know she is on her way.

I don't think I'll ding my bell. I'll give no warning as down I coast. I'll be a surprise to anyone who happens across my path. So we crash. If Desert isn't afraid, neither am I.

I am creative when I am in L.A., like Alex, the young woman who lives one door up from my son. Alex is a welder. She welds the curves and contours of nature into wrought-iron works of art. As I walk up her stairs, admiring a candleholder on one step, a birdhouse on the other, I want to go and do likewise. I want to see beauty in the world around me, capture it in words, interpret it and share it. Seeing her living on her own in a mortgaged house with a crumbling foundation, I feel as preoccupied with words as she is with shapes. I have stories inside me that want equal prominence, want to be seen, read, and felt by someone other than me.

Alex loves her house but it will always get less attention than her art. One of these days she will scrape off the old paint and apply a fresh coat or two. Sometime soon she will mend that broken window. She shores up portions of her foundation one commission at a time. She will get to it just as she will push that lank of hair off her forehead when her hands are free from wielding this torch. No matter, like her house her authentic beauty shines through.

Alex must be in her thirties, but as they say, today's thirties are yesterday's twenties. Her skin is young enough to need no makeup. Her dark brown hair and brown eyes give her face enough drama. Her pretty features become beautiful when she talks with animation. And she is always animated. She is small in stature but big in the impression she leaves. Men appreciate the curve of her busy little hips, the breasts pressing against her T-shirt. Her mother would probably say, "For God's sake, comb your hair." But since I am not her mother and her hair is no reflection on me, I don't mind seeing wisps of moist curls on her neck and around her forehead. I see a young woman too interested in what she is going to do today to spend time in front of the mirror.

She reminds me of a Greek olive with all those lovely little dents. They aren't blemishes to the olive connoisseur. Salt has ripened the olive to ready, set, eat. And the taste will last as long as the brine and brine lasts a long time. Alex looks good in her ripe years. And I sense a staying power deep down in her spirit. She isn't worried about externals, because everything is just fine inside. She doesn't fear change, because she has turned it to her advantage a number of times. Seasoned seems the word to describe her.

I am more the ripened peach. On my still downy skin there's a bruise here and there. But inside, I like to think, I'm sweeter than ever. But younger peaches have more shelf life left in them. You can take them home and watch them soften on your table. I need to be folded into a peach cobbler to look and taste as good. It can be done. I'm just not sure anyone else realizes that. I would really enjoy it if someone did. But that won't stop me from making the most of the rest of my season. I am not dead on the vine. Do peaches grow on vines? You know what I mean.

Anyway, Alex makes me look forward to those quiet times at my laptop. Some mornings I'm having so much fun, I forget to change out of my pajamas and put on some socks. My toes don't get cold till my fingers run out of words.

When I am in L.A., I am, like my son, open to people entirely different in experience and in dreams. Every other Saturday, Douglas volunteers at the Hippie Kitchen on a food line where he is the only blond head. I saw him offer a piece of buttered bread to a man who seemed to hate Doug for being on the serving side of the table. He threw the bread onto the dirt floor. He threw the next one and the next until my son shook his head no. There wasn't enough bread to throw any more slices in the dirt.

The angry man was teetering on a tightrope. If he fell, he risked being told he was no longer welcome. This would be his last meal with us. His rage could spread to the others moving forward in the line behind him. Lots of people at the Hippie Kitchen are on the verge. And no one could stop them if they lost it. Catholic Workers are as committed to nonviolence as they are committed to serving the poor. So the man thought about it for a while and then moved on to the red beans with cheddar cheese on top.

That same day, that same place, I met another man who was too happy for his circumstances. When he smiled, he glowed. And he smiled often. He gave me one of the paper orchids that decorated his backpack. I suspect that backpack probably cushioned his head on the nights when the shelters were full. An orchid may have been the first thing he saw when he awoke in the chilly morning mist, but somehow he could spare one of those flowers for me, white with a pink blush.

When he first walked across the courtyard towards us his arms were outstretched. He was shirtless, wore khaki shorts, and had that backpack over his shoulder.

"Hi, buddy. You missed dessert. We had cherry vanilla ice cream. Are you going to introduce me to your lovely lady?" He took off his baseball cap to reveal a crown of hair brighter than my son's. Golden curls repeated themselves on his tan chest and legs. The occasional cool spring breeze raised no gooseflesh. Not tall, he made a tall statement with his legs-apart stance. It reminded me of the musical *Carousel* and its hero singing about his boy Bill and his feet planted firm on the ground. The smile greeting me was as wide and proud as Darrell's ever was. His teeth looked even younger. There were no pipe stains. He was patting my son on the back. "We have a fine boy here." His smile went to his pale blue eyes. They were not pale blue because of lack of pigment, but because an inner glow seemed to be competing, shining through the color, surprising me with the sparks. "You should have brought your mom for lunch." He challenged Douglas's manners. "Get your mother a glass of ice-cold water and she can sit beside me on this shady bench and have a little snack."

I smiled back at Ray, who had somehow made himself the host of the Hippie Kitchen. He seemed to have no doubt of his right to play that role. He belonged here. He was happy to be here. I suspected he was happy to be anywhere, happy just to be, and unafraid, wonderfully unafraid.

On the drive home my son explained to me the philosophy of the Hippie Kitchen. Serve the poor, not because you want to make the world a better place. Serve the poor because it makes you feel better about yourself. Serve the poor because Christ told you to, when he said, "Whatever you do to the least of my brethren you do to me." But whatever you do, don't serve the poor for a "Thank you very much."

But then sometimes you get a paper orchid.

There are not many flowers in Ramona's life, real or artificial. Ramona is the mother who lives on the second floor of the duplex next to Douglas's house, and she doesn't have money for frills. Section Eight renters rarely do.

I can only imagine what she is up against. I will never know what it is like to have a different father for each of my kids. I have never felt the urge to stand on the porch of my new apartment and yell those kids back in the house, or "Damn you to hell!" full volume the latest man walking out without looking back. I do hear the fear in her screams, fear for her children, fear of the future, and I recognize that fear. I feel it more often than ever these days when Douglas calls home with tales of gang tagging or a gunshot in the night.

When I am in L.A. sitting on Doug's porch, watching Ramona on her porch, I can't help but feel her fear. Still, fear has yet to rob Ramona of her looks, although more often than not her bountiful black hair has a fresh-out-of-bed tangled look and her red T-shirt has so many wrinkles it looks like it dried in the wash machine instead of the dryer. Her eyes have never met mine. She looks away when I start up the steps to our hill. She looks down when she manages a smile to my hello. She looks at her hands just before she hides them behind her back. Seems she's been hanging by her finger nails way too long.

A lot of people come to visit Ramona and leave late, if at all—a lot of people who are hard to sugarcoat. Another woman with a couple more kids seems to have insinuated herself into the household. She is older, a few years further down the road of rough edges. Her hair has long since stopped being her crowning glory, clipped short, perhaps to minimize the gray frizzies. Her lack of waistline is camouflaged by an overblouse overblown with poppies. Her boys wear their baggy jeans low to ape hip-hop styles. And she, too, yells and sometimes curses her kids.

I'm not sure which men belong to which women, but four or five spend early evenings with their legs dangling over the porch railing or cross-legged on top of the steps or leaning in the frame of a door. The porch is close enough to my son's porch to see their tattoos, cryptic gang letters, numbers and symbols creeping out from under their wife-beater T-shirts. Doug tells me that teardrops record the years spent in jail. A tombstone is a murder avenged. I'm not sure if there is any significance to their shaved heads and if the gleam is from perspiration. Perhaps I am imagining it, but the musk from their armpits seems to be reaching the darkness of the porch where we sit, watch, and wonder. Just how many of their beer cans will be tossed into our yard? Ramona's children make a game of tossing the empties back and forth.

And then there are the cars that come every night making short, quick stops, exchanging few words, just maybe exchanging small packages. It's not hard to know what that's about and, as any mother would, I worry. But Douglas is comfortable in the social complexity of his neighborhood.

It's one of the deals you make with life and real estate. It's a neighborhood he can afford. And there are enough good neighbors working hard to reclaim it.

I've learned a lot from Doug's friends and neighbors, and I'm certain there's more to learn, some negative, lots positive, all surprising. I'm still trying to see it all clearly. I don't want to dilute the meaning or misinterpret the contradictions. I might simplify too much if I try too hard, too soon, and understand only halfway. It is important that I think the distance, feel the distance.

The average age for widows in the United States is fifty-six. That was me in 1995. I have spent the intervening years trying to get used to that fact. People might say that was long enough. People might say I need to let go in order to move on. That advice would be wrong for me. Darrell is a part of me now. Through the years the graft took, became strong, sturdy, and permanent. I no longer feel the need to say good-bye to Darrell, his dimpled chin and the gold hairs on his forearms. I can see and feel him forever and only be the better for it. It does seem that being transplanted to California is providing some interesting cross-pollination of feeling and thought.

Yesterday I said to my son, in front of his perfectly good kitchen cabinets, "You should paint them green, avocado green. Natural wood is nice, but not sacred, especially if it is thin, cracked, stained, and looks lame against your salsa red walls." Today the cupboards look brand-new. They belong in his southwestern kitchen. Douglas is pleased. And I am proud of my outrageous suggestion. Unfortunately, now the stainless steel sink looks really stained. Or should I say "fortunately." Doug and I have another challenge.

Sometimes I don't feel like I'm making a lot of sense, but I am making a difference. That's what L.A. is doing to me, for me, with me. It feels good. I want more. Maybe I'll even move here someday. Maybe I'll marry again, someone from here, a man like Hector, the absentee landlord of Ramona's house, who is suddenly less absent. Hector wears soft, wheat-colored shirts that bring out the bronze in his skin. He is all wrong for me, of course. Not even interested, probably. More likely, Ramona inspires his visits. She really needs a working doorbell and a good strong lock on her front gate.

And, then of course, she is one of those peaches still within her freshness date. No matter. No one here or in Minnesota need ever know that I was thinking such foolish thoughts, but I find myself hoping someone notices and appreciates when I return from the latest trip in glorious late bloom.

My mother would appreciate my transformation. She always understood me. She knew what to say to me, and when to say it. When I asked her about the facts of life and how to know what to do or not to do, her hazel eyes looked past me. "You'll know." She was too reticent to say more, but she was right. I did know. And when I asked her what to study in college, she laid it on the line: "Anything that will get you a job to make enough money to tell any man to go to hell, if you need to." And she was right again. I never had to deliver that message to Darrell. But Mom's "just in case" has served me well since his death.

Mom had my handwriting analyzed the summer I started college. The analyst saw intelligence and talent in my loops and spikes, but somewhere in those scribbles he saw romantic complications. "She will never meet her potential. She will choose love over ambition every time."

Mom challenged me to prove him wrong. "Give that class ring back to Ben and concentrate on your classes. Boyfriends can wait." But it felt comfortable and meant I belonged. Now that I think of it, Mother was another Alex. Both of them know it is important to have a love affair with your self first.

Men surround Alex like circling moons, not like the sun she needs to light up her life. I have met two of them. Jack, the guy who rents her downstairs, likes to meet on the steps and talk about his day. He was one of the first suitors to be rejected on the TV reality series *Married by America*. "Oh well," she consoled him. "At least you have thirteen minutes left of your fifteen minutes of fame." Sebastian is married in real life. He spends Saturday nights sharing a bottle of tequila with Alex, rationalizing, "It's kinder not to drink in front of my pregnant bride." He says his Welsh wife understands the needs of her Irish husband, knows she can trust Alex to send him home while he can still drive or put him up on the couch if he can't. Alex enjoys their company. And I'm sure she's had her share of more romantic entanglements. But they never stopped her from pursuing her passion, from making her own decisions, sometimes wonderfully rash, like making an offer on a fixer-upper without even going inside. She saw enough light going through its big windows, enough of the sun setting on its balcony and porches.

Alex and Douglas would make a perfect pair. He has her artwork in every room in his house, except the bathroom. And she is thinking, why not a sconce as a night-light. If they fell in love Alex would be permanently in our lives. Douglas would have just the kind of woman I want for him, passionate about her life, her art, and him. Douglas is passionate too. He has come all the way to California to pursue his dreams. I know, I know. It doesn't work that way. Mother may know best, but it's their feelings that spark the passion.

It's not too late for me to do an Alex. It's not too late to shake up my life. I might have published more books if I had not taken the baby track, if I had married a man who wasn't so much fun to play with. But doing an Alex means looking forward, not back, ignoring the clutter of life, or better yet, seeing its beauty and recording it as is. Have word processor, will write. I have already committed to do just that. Alex makes me rejoice in that decision more than regret the years I didn't commit.

I may still be tempted to crawl out of my creative cave and search for another Darrell to run away with. When I am in church I may look for white hair that curls around the ears the way his did. When I walk into a restaurant and feel someone looking at me, I may hope that someone has a chin that dimples like Darrell's. When I get an email from an old boyfriend I may wonder, "What if I tried someone new or someone I knew before? What if I dusted off those satin bedroom slippers with the white net puff balls and granted them twenty seconds more? That's usually how long Darrell let them stay on my feet."

Darrell and I had that spark. We ignited each other. And it burned bright through thirty-four years of marriage. The beginning years were the hardest. We had to find a place where an extrovert and an introvert could give each other energy and peace. He came to know I would always be there, sleeping on the couch to keep him company while he watched a midnight movie. I got all the alone time I needed in our quiet times: riding next to him in the car, humming to the music on the radio; sitting on lawn chairs at the cabin, watching fireflies light up the ferns.

I love you, Darrell. I always will. My light dimmed when yours flamed out. Now I feel this glow, even though I am more alone than I ever wanted to be. Maybe it's meeting Alex. Maybe it's the natural course of grief. When it's time, joy comes bubbling up to the surface. All I know is that I feel whole more and more often. Less and less am I half of something that once was. It's not a complete transformation. I'll probably feel this epiphany many times and think it's brand-new. That's the way it works. It sneaks up on you. You forget it. And then it sneaks up on you again.

My mom and dad had a more stormy marriage, not because he didn't love her, worry about her, and nag her when she forgot her gloves or crossed her legs in a short skirt. His rough hands were less than gentle when he tugged the material down. When mother was displeased with something I said or did, she would say, "You're just like your father." That was one statement I didn't want to figure out. I hated hearing her say it. I still do. I should figure out why, stand up to it. Sometimes a person needs to journey back to an old landscape to dig up some buried insights.

I have to go home soon anyway, to send out those invitations for my daughter Kristin's wedding. Curly Top might be interested in some of this wisdom I am so happily gleaning. Then again, maybe she doesn't need it. She is pretty much into her own story right now—the dress she will wear, the kind of flowers she will carry, what it will be like to live in her own home, how it will feel to have a new name. David insists she take his. It was right for me. Anyway that is Kristin's story. And I can congratulate myself that somehow, without knowing it, I passed on my mother's take on life. Kristin advanced her career before she chose to become a bride at the ripe, young age of thirty-seven. It means I'll be an older grandmother, but I can wait. It's so nice to have still another adventure ahead.

Guess that's where I am today, taking some steps forward and some back, in a journey that still fascinates, whether I go west or back to middle America, by plane or on a bicycle, consciously, self-consciously, or caught completely by surprise. I still enjoy being taken by surprise.

America surprises me. Living in today's America both challenges and perplexes me. I drive an SUV that makes me an independent woman in any snowstorm. I appreciate the fact that sensible shoes are now as fashionably styled as my old 4-inch spikes. I get a kick out of the fact that I helped vote in Kelly Clarkson as the first American Idol. I'm not so pleasantly surprised with today's four-door sedans. They all look alike—no fins, no whitewalls, no gleaming chrome. I don't understand why young men want to look like little boys in pants falling down their hips like wet diapers.

But it's not just pop culture that surprises me. So much of the light let into the Catholic Church during Vatican II is now being shuttered out. We can rethink the role of women in the Church but only so far. Homosexuals may receive six of the seven sacraments, and only if they are in the state of grace. Too bad. I was just getting comfortable being liberal. I was ready to give change some serious thought. I guess I'm still ready.

But I'm enough of a conservative to link sex with marriage, which puts me at a definite disadvantage in today's dating pool. And yet, when I think back, I wonder how it would have been to make love for the first time in one of those swept-away moments in the back of a '57 Chevrolet. Being carried over the threshold loses some of its passion when your husband is breathing heavy for all the wrong reasons.

A child of the 'fifties, I'm from what just might be the last generation to trump the generation before. We got more education. We landed better jobs. We bought, rather than rented our homes. And we prided ourselves at being the first generation to truly terrify our parents. We were, after all, the first rebels without a cause. No teenager felt the angst like James Dean, Natalie Wood, and us. Moreover, we were the first to dance to rock 'n' roll. "Work with Me, Annie" played over and over on our turntables. Mom and Dad probably thought all that moaning and groaning was about manual labor. We necked in parked cars. We got hickies. Most important, we were cool.

Cool meant swaying instead of bouncing when you bopped. If you were a boy you combed the front of your hair up and over into a pompadour. If you were a girl, it was a half bang with your right eye peeking through. You didn't go all the way and get pregnant. And you covered your hickies with a bandage so Sister Heaven Forbid could only wonder, and not condemn. There were rules to being cool. You only went so far.

Today it's all about breaking the rules, inventing and shattering new ones. These kids have to try harder. If you can't shock your rock 'n' roll parents with the beat and the moans and groans, you add four-letter words to the banter. Instead of combing your hair into an offending hairstyle, you shave and polish. Hickies are no badge of honor. You've just spent too much time in foreplay. Instead you pierce your belly button, your nose, and your tongue. Your tattoos are in places no one should see and then you let everyone see them. Young America today is my teenaged-America era squared.

Square. That's a fifties word too, something my generation definitely didn't want to be. Today there is another word for being cool, hip, with it, as well as its opposite. I'm not sure what those words are. But I am pretty sure that as soon as a person my age gets to know the word, it is so over. And that is not surprising. That's the way it should be.

Surprise is change. Change is being original. Original can be shocking. It shakes things free, things like yesterday's fears and prejudices. And even though it may not seem like it at the time, the really important things hold on tight. Once the dust of your generation settles you know who you are, with whom you want to spend the rest of your life, and what you would like to pass on to those who follow you. It happens whether you grow up listening to the Andrews Sisters or the Ames Brothers, the Four Lads or the Four Freshmen, the Beatles or the Stones, Jefferson Airplane or Three Dog Night, Prince or P. Diddy. Better stop now. I am past my era of expertise. But you know what I mean.

The question is, what does all this mean to me? Why has Los Angeles of all places brought new meaning to my life? Jack, my writing mentor, would say, look to the symbols. Desert with her training wheels, Alex with her sagging foundation, Ramona with her rough edges, Ray with his paper orchid, the man with the buttered bread. Off the top of my head I see adventure, creativity, risk taking, tolerance, understanding, and perhaps most important, making certain that I see the world in some way other than how it relates to me.

Desert is the child still within me. The horizon of my life is coming closer and closer, but there are still some hills and valleys in between to fly up and down.

Alex is my muse, inspiring me to ride the wave of my talent without looking back at that safe little house on the shore.

Ramona is all about making deals with life. A single mom, she accepts protection where she can get it, even if it's from a skinhead wearing a wifebeater T-shirt. A widow, I am every day finding ways to protect myself from everything from backed-up plumbing to a lonely Saturday night.

Ray and his paper orchid, the man with the buttered bread, they both remind me that I'm not the only one in this world with a story to tell. There are many people out there making difficult deals. Some shut down. Some gather in. Some even give away. In the pages ahead I'm going to explore these deals, mull over these meanings. I'm going to feel the distance between these people and me, between their stories and the rest of mine.

And I'm hoping that as I do, as I move out of myself and into others, I will have less and less of those blue times, those moments at the end of a day when I never stepped out of the house, or spent an empty evening watching *Dancing with the Stars*. I will always miss having someone looking over at me from the couch and sharing a Letterman laugh or laughing at me for saying something silly, but to him endearing. I still have this silly need to have someone watching me, applauding me, appreciating me. Sometimes I let Sean Connery do that. I conjure him up and have him follow me around and argue with my decisions or tell me that purple coat makes me look like a giant grape.

I know, I know. We are all born alone and we die alone and we should realize and make peace with that. I've made some inroads. I know I can manage Life. I've mastered Checkbook, Income Taxes, Mortgage Loan, Long Term Care Insurance, and now I'm doing a great job planning Daughter's Wedding. I can feel myself easing into old age where my love life consists of looking backwards remembering or far away into the future anticipating. There will be a reunion in heaven. I do believe. I do believe.

I can lock the door at night without really feeling afraid. Many nights I fall asleep without the TV babbling the worries out of my head. And growing older has yet to beat the passion out of me, one passion in particular.

I'm going to continue to write. I'm actually compelled to write. When I write I go on an adventure, and everyone knows an adventure of any momentum begins on your own. Harry Potter, like many heroes of children's books, is, you will remember, an orphan.

On a really exciting adventure, you don't even realize you're alone, or if you do it is part of the glorious challenge. I remember running into the cold Atlantic on our first vacation on Cape Cod. I didn't wait for Darrell to run in after me. I just ran. I couldn't wait to feel the waves push me forward and pull me back. I wanted to feel the foam on my legs and the sand between my toes. Oh my God, is that a starfish?

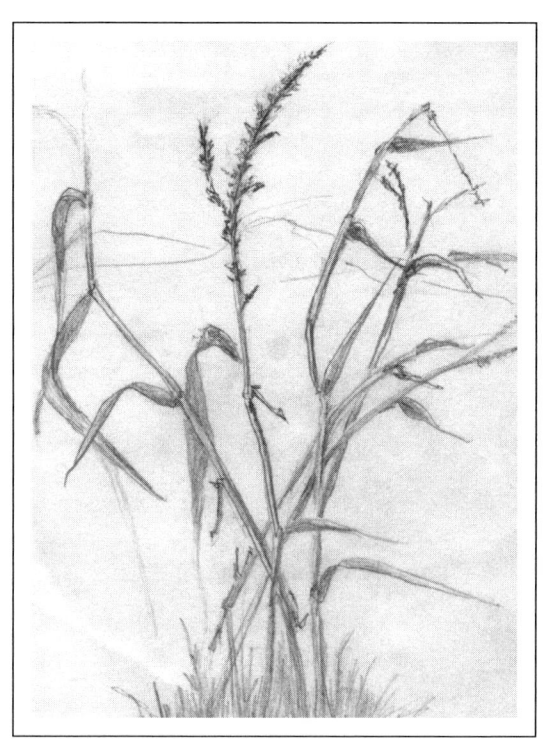

Nan

BARBARA MARYSTONE

BARBARA MARYSTONE *retired from a life of ease and relaxation in a high school English classroom. Now she learns about life in the real world by taking classes in literature and writing and spends her leisure time wondering if it would be okay to transform temporal linearity.*

In this excerpt from a larger piece, Nan Malone Carew, prompted by her work on a study guide for a young adult novel, considers the role of memory in her life. In the process she examines her feelings about how dissatisfied she is. Perhaps thinking will get her through this troubled time. Perhaps thinking may not be the way to deal with difficulties. If only things had been different in the past.

I HAVE TO GET THIS DOWN. Yesterday while I was at my desk at home in the middle of writing a teachers' guide for Lois Lowry's novel *The Giver*, I was back in the park in my childhood neighborhood. I was thinking of Jonas, the main character in the novel, and how hard it must have been for a kid to be the Receiver of Memories for the whole community. How could kids of today relate to that? I would have to come up with some pretty good questions to prompt essays from students barely in their teens.

My desk is in the attic of our house. The only windows in the attic are dormers at either end of the room, which spans the length of the house. My desk faces the east window. There is a blue leather Swedish recliner near the west window. Bookcases line the sides of the long room. Low bookcases tucked under the pitch of the roof on each side. Low was good years ago when we put them in, but now that my back is a little creaky, I might have to consider some other way to store my many volumes so bending won't have to enter into my decision to look for something. I once thought of having the floor carpeted, but while I pondered that I put down three huge braided rugs I found at an estate sale and carpeting never appealed to me again. The rugs are in shades of green and blue and made from real rags. I imagined women gathered into a rug-braiding bee creating these homemade beauties. The floor beneath them and around their edges, the attic floor, dark and rough, welcomed the teal, navy and olive colors that floated over it. The attic room sometimes feels to me like a ship. I can walk from the east end to the west end. The rugs keep me from slipping on the planks. It's an easy room to think in. The light is soft and diffused except for the lamp over the desk. Nothing is ever disturbed because no one uses the attic but me. When the children were little, I brought them up to nap or play while I worked, but that was eons ago. James never comes up. He has his own study around the corner from our bedroom.

This attic was a room of my own. It happened to be mine because I claimed it when we bought the house and after that no one ever wanted it or cared that it was mine. It is my workroom, of course, but it is like a womb for me, too, because I don't have to work at feeling good, feeling positive, feeling okay about doing nothing. The attic takes me in and protects me from whatever is outside trying to get to me. Even when I am not working, I return often. It never fails me. When I am in the attic, I feel like I am at home. Literally, that's true, but it's more than that for me. It has operated as a haven when I have needed one. More than once I have hidden in it, ignoring a ringing phone or doorbell. Lately, I have been sleeping here more nights than in our bedroom. I brought a bed up during my first pregnancy when my nighttime restlessness kept James awake. I could toss and turn up here without bothering him.

I feel unjudged in this room. The room is like another person who knows me well and likes me the way I am. I never have to pretend to anyone or to myself. When I am in the attic I often feel like I have vacated the world. That's kind of how I was feeling when I landed in Winesack Park. It was not the park of my drive-through just days ago. It was the park the way it was when I was young. I recognized the lampposts. It was a summer afternoon, but there was still a morning mist above the shrubs and bushes that indicated the outer edges of the park. The houses across the street looked like buildings in an out-of-focus photograph. This time I knew where I was, but I was a little thrown off by my clothes. I had on aqua pants and a matching tee shirt. It was an outfit from twenty-five years ago. I reached up and touched my hair. It was long and straight. I pulled a hank of it forward so I could see it. Very blond, not the dark hair I have today and no flecks of gray. I walked half a block to a clearing in the bushes where some steps led to the park playground. I had on athletic shoes and my right foot ached. No one was around. I went down the steps and sat on a bench at the edge of the playground near some swings, a teeter-totter and a sandbox. The swings were still and I could see the marks of the rake where the sand had been smoothed. I thought I should be afraid again, but instead I felt like I could go anywhere and do anything. I was blissful. It was the feeling I have when everything is going just the way I want. I put my head in my hands, closed my eyes, took a big breath and blew out. Slowly, I took my hands from my face and opened my eyes. And then I knew. I was in the past, my own past. My twenty-five-year-old self was remembering something. I was remembering something that pleased me and made me sigh with the knowing. Children appeared out of nowhere to occupy the swings and the teeter-totter. Two young mothers watched over toddlers playing in the sandbox with shovels and pails. I was overcome with a sense of well-being. I sat back and stretched my arms across the back of the park bench. The night before I had told James I couldn't marry him. Now relief flooded me. We were engaged for nearly a year, but had not yet set a wedding date. We had known each other since the second grade. We dated a few times in high school, but I think we would both agree that it was no romance. We knew each other well enough to be a convenient partner for a dance or party without having to commit to anything more serious. We went to different colleges so we saw almost nothing of one another until James came back to the city to the university to go to medical school. He called me, we became a couple, and then everything sort of morphed into marriage, jobs, kids, a house. It happened almost without my noticing. It seemed the thing to do so I did it. But this was different. I was in this past I hadn't lived yet. In this new version of my past, I broke the engagement.

It was like a dream in many ways, but the feelings were real. The place and the people were a little hazy, but I was sure about how I felt. I loved the feeling of freedom, the lack of responsibility I felt. It was a relief to have the marriage off and to feel so guilt free about it. And then I was back in the attic and I wanted to stay in that past where I was so happy and ready for whatever would happen next.

"Nan, are you up there?" It was James calling from the foot of the attic stairs.

"I'll be right down." I wanted to finish the work on the Lowry novel, but I was afraid I might slip back into my past and I had no idea how it happened or how long I was gone. I stood up at the desk. I must have been at the park for more than an hour. The sun, which was just at the corner of the west window when I went back, had wrapped itself around the front of the house and was laying itself out on the flat roof of the house across the street. I was now entertaining my own River of Memories. I didn't need the memories of the whole community. My own were burden enough. I put on my James-is-home face and went to see about supper.

I WALKED OUT OF WINESAC PARK and I knew exactly where to go. Up the hill, around the corner, and down the block. I stopped in front of a Chicago brick apartment house. It was out of place among the single family homes on the rest of the street. It was a building just blocks from where I grew up. I lived there when James started medical school.

I wondered whether I could get in the apartment. I had no keys with me. I looked at the building from the front steps. It had eight apartments. The front windows were flanked with white shutters in an effort to make it look homey. Bright red shocks of geraniums lined up across the entire front helped that notion and so did the brass hardware on the front door. I opened the door onto red-carpeted stairs and hallway. The aroma of beef and onions cooking was familiar. I knew instantly the smell came from the right front apartment of Catherine Larsen, a widow who had never learned to cook for one person. She offered her abundance to the rest of us who lived in the building. We all accepted her dishes, some of us who had little time to cook with more gratitude than others.

I walked to the end of the hall. There was a big brass 3 on the door. I tried the door. It opened; I stepped in and closed it behind me. I felt like I was trespassing, but I recognized the small purse and key ring on a table near the door. I opened the purse and took out the billfold. Among some credit cards I found my driver's license. I looked crabby in the photo, but it was me all right.

I looked out the back window at the yards across the alley and the tops of the trees from the park a block away. I swayed a little with the giddiness the feeling of freedom brought on. I opened the refrigerator and found eggs, oranges, lettuce, apple juice, two small T-bone steaks, a loaf of bread, a carton of milk, two bottles of dry sherry, and a six-pack of beer. I squeezed the lettuce. It was firm. I opened the milk. It smelled okay. So I could eat if I wanted to. And then I wondered if Mrs. Larsen would be knocking at the door with a container of beef stew.

I sat on the couch and picked up the *Time* magazine. August 19, 1985.

I really was in my past, but I had knowledge of my already lived future, too. And I knew what I knew earlier on the park bench: I had broken my engagement to James. I stood again and danced a little whirl in the living room. This was a second chance. I could do anything I wanted to. I wasn't going to marry James and live not-so-happily ever after. I could hardly wait. There could be so many choices. I felt like I did when I opened the menu at a new restaurant.

I had a little trouble opening the sliding closet door in the bedroom. It was stuck on the track, but I jiggled it loose, and hanging inside was the blue cotton cardigan I liked so much. I drew it to my face and inhaled. I ran my fingers across the sleeves of everything hanging and pulled open the drawers of the dresser. The smell of lavender danced by me when I fluffed up all the white nylon slips and bras and panties.

I laid out clothes on the bed and went into the bathroom. I undressed and turned on the water in the shower. When it was warm, I climbed in. I washed my hair remembering that it was long and when it was wet, heavy. I slid the soap over my body, enjoying how firm and upright my breasts were, *perky,* a novelist might have said. My skin was smooth and golden, and not a hint of backache when I bent to shave my legs. Everything was new, but I remembered it all. I thought about Jonas in the novel having to be the repository of memories for the whole community. Maybe it was possible. I was remembering without difficulty.

Out of the shower, I combed my hair and blew it dry. I drew up the hair in the front on each side and clipped it into a barrette in the back. I put on jeans and a pale blue shirt. I headed for the door, grabbed the little purse and the keys from the table. I set the lock on the door and ran down the back stairway to the parking lot behind the building.

The keys opened the door of a brown Honda Accord. I slid into the seat and sat a moment fingering the chain of the pendant around my neck. I remembered how grateful I was to my dad when he gave me his car even as I felt a little guilty for thinking it an old man's car. He had a stroke on Monday, offered the car on Tuesday, had another stroke on Wednesday morning, and died Wednesday afternoon. I looked down at the pendant. It was a simple gold heart Dad gave me for my birthday not long before he died. I've worn it ever since, twenty plus years, now.

The car started right away. I backed out of the parking lot into the alley and drove six blocks right to Bud's bar. I parked on the street. Bud's was a neighborhood bar with a reputation for the best steak sandwiches in town. It was early, about six o'clock, but the place was full and loud. The dark brown vinyl booths along the wall opposite the bar were filled and in the back a few tables were still empty. Several people surrounded the pool table to the left. There was the stink of stale beer, fried onions, and cigarette smoke in the air. It was a bad smell, but it was familiar and I felt like it was welcoming me back. The long bar was dark and shiny. Bowls of peanuts punctuated the top every three or four feet. I smelled the onions frying and heard the steaks sizzling, sending off a spray of grease to sail in the beery air. There were two empty bar stools. I took one of them.

Slim, the bartender, slammed both hands down on the bar. "Well, you have returned and we are glad to see you, Nan." His face was almost all teeth. They were smiling teeth and I was happy to see them again.

"Slim, it's good to see you. How have you been? And Teresa?"

Slim poured a glass of red wine and set it before me. I asked him once how he got the name Slim.

"Oh, Nan," he said. "My name is really John, but when I bought this place I thought the barkeep should have a kind of memorable name so I called myself Slim." I never heard anyone call him John. Teresa was his wife and business partner. She worked some weekends, but mostly she stayed home with the kids.

I took some bills out of my little clutch purse and put them on the bar. "No, no, Nanette. It's on the house. I hear you're getting married." He smiled that full-face smile at me.

"Well, that was the old Nan. The new Nan broke the engagement. The marriage is off." I raised my glass. It made me feel open and loose to acknowledge it.

"In that case let's celebrate your return." Slim raised the glass he always kept near for himself and we toasted.

I used to come to Bud's regularly after I finished school. James and I came a few times together, but after five or six times James told me he didn't like Bud's and didn't want to go anymore. I still dropped in now and then, but some months ago James asked me if I would please stop going to Bud's altogether.

"But why?" I asked. "Why do you care? You don't have to go." I felt like a little kid being scolded by a parent.

"I know, but I always know when you've been there. Your hair smells of onions and smoke and beer." He was studying at his desk in his apartment, a third-floor studio in an old house near the medical school campus. He turned from his desk to look at me, one arm over the back of the chair.

"What if I go there only when I am going to go home and shower before seeing you?" I was mad at him for making a demand like this. I snarled at him and even bared my teeth a little.

"Oh, Nan, it's such a scuzzy place. What's attractive to you about it?"

"I can't explain it to you. It's a neighborhood bar. I know the people there. It's friendly and it's safe. It's not scuzzy. I thought you liked the smell of onions and beer."

"The first time around, maybe, but not as perfume." He put out his hand to me. "For me?" his eyebrows went up. I took his hand. I hated these confrontations over such small stuff. He pulled me down to his lap. "I love you, Nan. And I only want what's best for us." His eyes pulled me in and I flowed right into him like honey. I thought it probably was the best for us if I cut off all those old habits. I'd soon be married and then I couldn't be stopping at the neighborhood bar anytime I felt like it. I kissed him with an energy I always felt when he talked about what was best for us. I was breathing hard. I longed to be fully a part of him and he always kept some part back. I kissed him again, pulling him against me trying to suck it out of him. He pulled back, but I pushed myself at him, opening my mouth and covering his. "Nan," his voice was muffled in my neck and hair. "Nan, I would love to keep this up, but I really have to study." He gave me a big squeeze like I was his teddy bear and set me on my feet, back on the shelf. I watched him turn back to his books. I wanted to be the one to fight *him* off, but it was always the other way around.

As I raised my glass to Slim's, I was not at Bud's Bar anymore, but in my attic sitting fingering the gold pendant heart hanging around my neck, looking out the window above my desk. I was a little warm, but otherwise I was fine. Just sitting there mindlessly looking out the window at the backyard trees waving to me. I knew I had just returned from the past, but I didn't know what triggered my return. I thought about what had happened. I was back at Bud's guilt free because now that James and I were no longer engaged I could go anywhere I wanted to. Although the place is still in business, I haven't been in Bud's since James asked me all those years ago not to go there anymore. I thought now about what a little thing it was. I have never been moved to go back to Bud's. And I can't think of any other place James has ever asked me to stay away from. I've gone out to dinner with friends over the years when James was working or out of town and he never questioned me about where I'd been.

I looked at the folder with the plans I'd made for *The Giver*. I had to call an illustrator for part of these lesson plans. I have a friend who saw the beauty of the novel and she agreed to do the drawing I need. Neither of us is much of a fan of science fiction, but this story has so many moral implications rising because it takes place in a fantasy setting that we got down to the exploration of those problems and enjoyed the make-believe landscape. The plans were almost completed. I closed the folder and stood up at the desk. I was beginning to feel like the person I was in Bud's Bar, young and free. I turned out the desk lamp and went downstairs to the kitchen. I had cleaned it up before I went to the attic, but when I went through the laundry room on the way to the garage, three piles of sorted dirty clothes rose up to meet me. I started the washing machine, poured in the detergent and dumped in one pile of clothes. I usually don't leave when the washer or dryer is running, but I didn't hesitate this time.

I felt an urgency like I had an appointment and I was running late. I backed out of the driveway and into the street with tires screeching. An old woman passing with her dog shook her finger at me. I waved at her and braked at the corner. I thought about taking the freeway across town, but I knew I could make better time on the city streets. I headed for downtown. The street was dry and the air felt new. Yellow daffodils barely out of their green leaf envelopes nodded from the front yards of three houses in a row. The drive through North Park was a mistake because the speed limit was twenty-five miles an hour. Keep it down, I told myself. This is no time to get a ticket. I saw a pair of runners headed toward me on the parkway path. Didn't they know they were going the wrong way? "This way," I said aloud. The parkway road curved and twined around the edge of the lake like it meant to slow me down. There was a parking area up ahead and my good sense led me to it. I pulled in and turned off the ignition. I was panting over the steering wheel. I got out of the car. I felt like I was one of the runners I had just passed. I leaned against the car and breathed heavily. There was a drinking fountain at the edge of the parking lot next to a big board announcing park activities. I took a long drink and walked to the edge of the lake wiping my mouth with the back of my hand. The lake water looked like shiny jet under the trees, like it meant business, but blue farther out in the lake and a little more willing to play. A few yards from where I stood there was a park bench. I walked over and sat down. I felt messy inside my head. I wanted to get in the car and drive on, but I also felt like that was a reckless thing to do. The water made little flip-flap sounds as it hit the shore. A car drove into the parking area behind me. A man and a woman carrying a Kentucky Fried Chicken box got out and walked to a nearby picnic table. I walked back to the car and got in. I backed out to the road and turned right as soon as I could to go back home. I drove around the block and wound up back on the parkway road heading the same direction I was going in before.

I had started this and now I wanted to see how it finished. I drove to the edge of downtown and then headed south. I didn't drive these streets very often anymore, but they were familiar. I drove by the apartment house where I had lived twenty-five years before. Two houses beside it had been torn down and other apartment houses built in their place. The street seemed cramped and the houses had peeling paint and broken screens. I turned the corner and after six blocks pulled up to the curb and parked beside Bud's Bar. Candy wrappers and cigarette butts littered the sidewalk in front of the entrance. A white computer-generated sign taped to the window announced the hours, eleven to eleven. I pulled open the door and smelled fried onions. The place was dark, the only light coming from neon beer ads and one window in the front that faced the street. There was an older couple seated in a booth near the rear. I was the only other customer. I looked for Slim behind the bar. A young man turned from scraping onions around on the steel griddle-top burner. I slid onto a bar stool. "Hi," I said. "I haven't been here for years. Is Slim still around?"

His name tag said *Slim*. "That would be me, but I think you're asking about my dad." His eyebrows went up.

"I must be. I'm Nan Malone Carew. I knew your dad years ago when I lived near here and came in often."

"I'm John Winter, but I became Little Slim and then Young Slim and then when Dad died about three years ago, just Slim. Can I get you something to drink?"

"Diet Coke, please." I pulled a couple of bills out of my jeans pocket.

Young Slim turned back to his onions for a minute and then put a can and glass on the bar in front of me. I shoved the bills toward him.

"On the house," he said. "In honor of your friendship with Dad." He smiled and I saw how much he looked like his dad.

I sat on the bar stool and sipped my Coke and watched him work at the griddle. There was a low light coming from under a wide hood over the stove. Every other surface was dark and without detail. I bent forward to see better and my pendant hit the edge of the bar. I sat back and took another sip of Coke, rubbing the pendant as I drank.

I put the glass on the bar and everything in my view shifted a little. Slim turned around and laughed, big teeth so white in that semidarkness. "Nan, what are you drinking? Is that Coke? Are you sick?" I bent forward toward the bar and my pendant hit the edge. I sat back. I started to touch the pendant and stopped as I realized that touching the gold must be what brings me back and forth between now and then. I looked down at the heart hanging from the delicate gold chain around my neck. "What's the matter? You lose something?" Slim was talking to me.

"No, I just hit my pendant against the bar. I didn't know what made the noise." The slide from present to past was so quick and quiet I felt like I was on the edge looking in.

"Is that Coke?" he asked again. "You want something stronger?" He turned to the onions he was tending on the griddle. He scraped them up with a steel spatula and flipped them over and spread them around with quick, practiced arm movements. And then he turned and smiled at me.

I DID THE REST OF THE LAUNDRY and made some brownies. I was licking the batter bowl with the rubber spatula and just being kind of glad the boys were gone and it was my turn to lick the bowl. I remembered thinking when I was a kid that it would be perfect to be the mom so I could lick the bowl every time. I put the bowl in the sink and ran hot water into it. Someone had given me Crabtree and Evelyn citrus-scented hand soap for Christmas, but I usually thought it too elegant to use when I was rinsing my hands every few minutes while I fixed meals. Now I squeezed some into my hand and made a foamy lather. The flavor of lemons and oranges unfurled around my head like welcome flags. "We're glad you're here, you deserve this luxury. Let us squeeze every aromatic drop of citrus out of this little dab of soap." I rubbed slowly and spread the foam up my arms and raised them so I could inhale the pungency they gave off. The smell was clean and sharp like bedsheets hung outside to dry. I felt a little transported and held off rinsing, massaging up and down both arms. Warm water was running from the tap and the heat from it rose around that little space where I stood making a miniature spa for me.

The phone rang and I started quickly to rinse the soap off, but before all the lather was gone I turned off the water and with my elbows leaning on the edge of the sink decided to let the answering machine take the call. It was James and I could call him back. I looked down at my dripping hands and bent to smell them again, hoping I could recover some of the feeling I had. I felt like an alarm had awakened me from a beautiful dream. I turned the water back on and rinsed the lemons down the drain. I dried my hands, covered my face with them and inhaled the memory of the dream.

I called James at his office. "Hi. I had wet hands so I couldn't answer."

"Why don't we go out to dinner? You choose the place. Reservations for eight o'clock, then I can come home and have a little nap and change clothes." I knew I could propose dinner at home and James would be okay with that, but he liked to go out now and then and I really didn't have any reason not to go. "Okay. Do you want a new place or somewhere we've been before?"

"Let's try a new place. You're good at picking places. Give it all you've got. And if we're too late for reservations anyplace nice will do."

"I'm on it." We hung up. I was usually on it for things like this. It won't be Bud's Bar, James, I thought and then felt bad for being mad at James for something he did more than twenty years ago because he thought it was the best for us. It seemed unfair to accuse him now and to do it without telling him. It was petty and mean and it made me feel small.

The scene was like one from a thousand movies. James and I sat across from each other at a table for two at Chez des Étoiles, a new place in a new development not far from where we lived. The tablecloth was brilliantly white and hung almost to the floor. We sipped Manhattans while we waited for our dinner. The table, against a dark wood-paneled wall, was set with huge European-sized silverware and clear crystal goblets and wineglasses. The house lights were low and there was a small candle lantern with a frosted shade on the table. I watched James sitting sideways at the table looking into his drink like he was separating the bourbon from the vermouth. He looked rested after an hour's nap. He had shaved again and the skin on his face was smooth and dark in the glow of the soft light. He wore a gray suit with a white shirt and dark red and gray tie. He looked up at me. "What are you looking at?" he asked, emphasizing the *you* in a playful way. He smiled and turned his chair so he faced me.

"You. You are very easy to look at." I took a sip of my drink and held it in my mouth a few seconds before swallowing. It made my head buzz. I set my glass on the table and laid my hand beside it. James reached over and covered it with his.

"Nan, you always say things like that to me before I get a chance to say them to you. You're the one who's easy to look at. You're my everything, Nan." His eyes welled with tears.

I leaned in to the table. "What is this about?" My pendant swung out from my chest and I drew it back. I felt like I had stood too fast and the blood didn't get to my brain quickly enough. I closed my eyes and leaned back and when I opened them, I was sitting at a Formica-topped table in the cafeteria of the medical school. It was a small table for two. The size never big enough for two cafeteria trays. The next table was piled with used lunch trays. There was a sanitary hospital bareness about the room like it had been prepared for an incoming patient. All the surfaces were smooth, mint green Formica or polished stainless steel. Eating here was like eating out of a can. James was sitting across from me. "What is this about?" I asked him.

"Nan, I know I said I would honor your breaking our engagement, but I have to talk to you some more about it. I know you don't want to hear it, but *you are my everything.*" He spoke the words deliberately, one at a time, emphasizing each one. He looked away and sniffed. He had asked me to meet him. It was about something important. I agreed. Here we were across from each other. "Can't you reconsider? Let's talk some more about it. I will do anything you ask. I'll change anything. Please, Nan." His eyes were bright with tears. He took a paper napkin from the holder on the table and blew his nose. It was four o'clock in the afternoon. He had worked all night and all day. He had hat head. His cheeks were pale and drawn in. He had a thirty-six-hour beard. He wore a wrinkled blue scrub suit with his name tag, *James Carew, MS IV.*

I sighed. "James, I don't think there is anything else to say. I don't want you to change. You are who you are. It isn't right, this marriage. I'm not ready. Maybe I'll never be ready. I just know that I can't marry you." I stood up and put my purse over my shoulder. James sat in the chair. He looked up at me, his cheeks wet with tears. He reached for my hand. I stepped back. "No, James. Don't do this. Make your own life. I did it. You can do it, too."

When I came into the kitchen, James sat at the table reading the morning paper, a steaming mug of coffee in front of him. "I have to go to the hospital in a few minutes, but I won't be long." He smiled at me and pushed his chair back. He wore a plaid open-collared shirt and khaki pants; Saturday rounds allowed more casual attire. His belt accented his trim form and I thought how perfect he looked, handsome and fit. He came to me and took my face in both his hands. "Thank you for last night, Nan. I love these quiet days and nights with you highlighted with an occasional dinner like last night." His face was inches from mine. He drew one hand down the side of my neck and kissed my lips softly, a kiss of gratitude. He took a breath. "Do you know how deeply I love you? Can you feel how one with you I am?" He kissed me again, softly, but with a lingering sense of desire, his hand traveling down the front of me, over a breast down the side to my waist where he pulled me in and nuzzled my neck. His breathing was hot and quick. He kissed me a third time and I could feel his satisfaction, his breathing slowed and he ended with a peck on my cheek. "Gotta run."

I took his chair and drank out of his coffee mug. The meal the night before had been excellent. James and I both ordered lamb chops, something I rarely prepared at home. They were served with a simple sauce and stir-fried vegetables. The wine was lovely and we even ordered after-dinner port. Everything was as it should have been. I played the part of the dutiful wife and I felt nothing. I was reeling from my last encounter with the past. Not *my* past, really, but that new past life offered to me in this strange way. James gave no indication that I had "gone back," as I now began to call it. After dinner we wandered around the development looking in a few shops, and then came home. I went upstairs to change clothes while James opened a bottle of port. When I came downstairs in my robe, he had two small glasses poured.

"Here, Nan. I poured you a port. Isn't this a great do-nothing Friday night? And I have nothing planned for tomorrow. How about you?" He sat in the big leather wingback chair near the cabinet where he kept the port. I ignored the glass he poured for me and sat on the leather couch set at a right angle to his chair. The room was lit with three lamps with dark shades so the light was low and the dark reds and browns of the room deepened and took on a velvety richness like newly opened plums and grapes. It was nearly midnight and I had been up since six. I yawned and stretched. James put his empty glass on the cabinet. As he stood, he offered me his hand and murmured low musical lulling sounds like he had tasted something especially sweet. He pulled me up from the couch and led me to the stairway, turning out the lights as we went along. He led me up the stairs. He said nothing. I let him lead me and watched his face, which in the pale light coming from the bedroom seemed to glow. I could see his profile in shadow, and the hollows in his cheek and beside his nose shone an eerie white. His hair seemed outlined in white chalk against the darkness. When we reached the bedroom, James was silent, but he untied the belt of my robe, and using both hands caressed my shoulders as he slid the robe off, letting it drop to the floor.

He made soft, easy love to me and I let him. I could tell it was an extension of his pleasure with the whole evening, that it was Friday, his nap, the Manhattans, the dinner, the port. It was like many other Friday evenings of our life together. There was a sameness about them like the pages in a blank date book. He slept then, breathing evenly. I watched the dark shape of my husband as it rose and fell almost imperceptibly. I turned to lie on my back and watched the moving shadow of the tree limbs on the ceiling made by the streetlight. I thought how like the shadow my life was, a little motion, some light, no color, like the shadow of a tree almost anywhere. My few ventures into my unlived past brought some interest into my life, but I couldn't be sure they were real. They seemed real to me. They seemed real to me in the same sense that the world of Jonas in *The Giver* seemed real. Like it was a sort of world inside a world where things could be more easily explained and living was uncomplicated. There were compartments for everything, not the least of which was memory. It was a life without color until page ninety-four, however. Ninth graders would love that little physical thing about the book.

As I wove this train of thought, I considered going upstairs to work on my lesson plan for awhile, but I was tired and the bed was warm. James wouldn't have cared if he woke and found that I had slept in the attic. He knew my work habits. I often went to bed after he did and he was used to my I-didn't-want-to-disturb-you reasoning. Time for lovemaking had no regulations. Since the boys were gone, James approached me whenever he was moved to and I rarely denied him. We could make love any time and anywhere in the house, but I became the initiator less and less as time went by. I was drawn in less and less, too. James never seemed to notice. It wasn't a hard duty for me, but it was a duty. It was all a duty, the meals, the laundry, the cleaning, the dinners out, and the smiling response to his invitations. It had become a role and I had my part down pat.

JAMES WAS IN HIS STUDY after dinner when I stopped to tell him I was going upstairs to work for a little while. "I have some things I have to look at before I go in tomorrow," he said. His mouth was turned down and he sighed as he turned to the papers on his desk. He had bought a new desk lamp, a shiny brass with a moveable arm. Now he sat with his papers before him, his arms on either side of the stack. His head was in darkness above the sphere of the lamplight, but his arms gleamed in the brightness of it. I had a momentary idea that his arms knew something that eluded his head. I could tell by the slump of his shoulders how tired he was. When I didn't leave right away, he looked up at me. "Did you want something?" he asked. I shook my head and started for the attic.

Of course I wanted something. I wanted to know what was happening to me. I wanted to know how I could be so dissatisfied with my life. I stopped on each step. I wanted my life to be different. Next step. I wanted bells to ring and whistles to blow. Next step. I wanted not just to want something, but to have it. Next step. I wanted to respond to something with an explosion. Step. I wanted to be turned inside out with feeling. Step. I wanted to fly. I felt like a jeweled necklace with one stone missing.

In the attic I took off my sweatshirt and threw it on the bed and when I turned around I was sitting in the waiting area of the Gatwick, England, airport struggling into my sweater. In my hand was a ticket for a short flight leaving in an hour for the small town of Rambleton. I had applied late for a two-week seminar on the Lake District Poets for high school teachers, so they put me on a waiting list. I never expected to get in. People never drop out of programs like this unless a relative dies or they have an accident. I had to scurry when I got a phone call from England that there was an open slot. A woman from Seattle broke her hip. I would be the only American enrolled. Everybody else was from England, Ireland, or Scotland. Ms Seattle had reservations at a bed-and-breakfast near Lake Windemere in Rambleton. I could have her accommodations. I was comfortable with everything. I had turned in my grades and summer-ized my classroom. I felt like I needed to be someplace where James couldn't reach me. He would understand a two-week academic course that kept me out of touch. I hadn't talked with him since the day I met him in the med school cafeteria. Tony Nilles, one of James' classmates, called and I told him I was leaving. He'd spread the word to James, I was sure.

I vowed not to think about James while I was in England. It wasn't so hard to forget about everything at home while I was in this new place.

I felt a kind of courage that was new to me. A sort of daring. An ability to do something on my own. Something different. Something without anybody to answer to. I could not stop smiling. I wondered why I had not thought of a trip somewhere before this. It was early afternoon in Rambleton. I felt the need for sleep that went with a nine-hour flight. I also felt the edgy glee of trying something new. I sat on the wide porch of the bed-and-breakfast. I looked over the railing at Lake Windemere just across the road. Gatwick was gray and misty, but here the sun glinted across the lake in eye-squinty sharpness. The house was at the rear of a long green lawn. Bushes of large white snowballs hugged the house. Lower, in front of them, yellow, orange, and purple blossoms burst out of the low fence containing them. From the side lawn just behind the house and up the hill among the trees I could see the upper part of the home of William Wordsworth and his sister, Dorothy. I felt like I was in the page of a guide to English poetry.

I'm not a really big fan of English romantic poetry, but I introduce it every year to seniors and we spend about a week on it. I was fast becoming a fan of this part of the country, though. The seminar began the next morning and in a couple of hours the participants would have dinner together in the town of Rambleton. I had put my luggage in my room on the second floor. I didn't change my clothes, because I wanted to take a look at the lake. I was reluctant to give up my chair, but I had to change before dinner.

My room overlooked the side yard so I couldn't see the lake. There was a double bed with a plain blue poplin bedspread. On the wall opposite the end of the bed stood a floor-to-ceiling armoire with claw feet and a round amber glass window at the top of each of the doors like eyes watching whatever went on in the room. The bathroom was small and cramped, but it was private. In front of the windows were a small table desk with a gooseneck lamp and a chair with a blue pad. It was the perfect place for a student. I peeled off my traveling clothes and took a shower. I was surprised to find a terry robe on a hook on the bathroom door and glad to wrap myself in it. I sat on the edge of the bed fighting the temptation to take a nap. The room was bright with daylight, which encouraged me to dress and get out.

I wore gray pants, a red shirt and gray blazer. Town center was not far. I walked in the late afternoon sun. The trees and grass seemed brighter and clearer than earlier. It was as though everything had been polished or the colors were high-gloss enamel. Even the pavement was a deeper black. I could see every imperfection in the cement sidewalk. Lettering on store signs was sharp and clear. I hadn't thought about home since I left.

The main street was narrow. One side was in shadow, those buildings with their backs to the sun. The other side was lit with the sun brighter than any I had ever seen that late in the day. The road presented itself like a path of good or evil. A good person would see right away that he should stay on the bright side. Another might take up the challenge of the dark side. There were people going in and out of the shops, a meat market, a chemist, a bookstore, a tobacconist. At the end of the main street, High Street, the road forked on either side of the Buswick Hotel. I waited for a car to pass before heading to the bookshop on the dark side of the street.

"You're from the States, aren't you?" I was wondering at all the unfamiliar titles and authors of the books arranged in the window before me. Her mouth was closed in a pleasant smile. "Are you here for the Lake Poets seminar?" Her hair was long, blond and straight. She was expertly made-up and her gray eyes drew me in. She was slim and dressed in a chic outfit of navy pants and blazer. She put out her hand. "Penny Meade. I'm here for the seminar, too." She smiled widely and her open mouth revealed a jumble of badly formed teeth that didn't go with the rest of her.

I looked quickly at her eyes and took her hand. "Nan Malone. And, yes, I am here for the seminar."

"I saw the list of people and noticed you are the only person from the States. Shall we sit together for dinner tonight?"

I hadn't thought about having a friend as soon as I arrived. I liked her immediately. "Thanks. I'd like that."

"Are you up for a before-dinner drink right now? We could have a little space to get to know one another." She took my elbow.

We walked to the end of High Street. On the way Penny told me she taught at a secondary school just outside Coventry. She taught the same things I did. Her teaching life sounded a lot like mine. We entered the hotel through huge double doors. The lobby was surprisingly small, but not at all disappointing. It looked like the set for a movie with Alec Guinness. The desk clerk, a short, bald man with a fringe of white hair, stood behind a dark wooden counter. There were a series of boxes on the wall behind him and a bell on one end of the counter. The clerk pointed out the bar to the side.

In the bar we sat at a small table near a wall of windows that looked out on the lobby. The glass was wavy and iridescent like oil on a puddle.

"Sherry?" I nodded and Penny ordered for both of us. The table was of dark wood. There was a small candleholder with a glass globe. The waiter lit the candle and set a thin cardboard coaster in front of each of us. There were a few men at the bar who were probably locals. The bartender bantered with them all. The ceiling was low and timbered. All light came from low lamps or candle lanterns on the tables. There was light coming from under the shelf of the bar that lit the work area for the bartender.

During the sherry, Penny Meade asked about my life at home. "Of course, I want to know about your professional life, but I would love to hear about what you do when you are not working. I long to go to the States. Go inland somewhere. I have a cousin who lived in Kansas for a year. If I go, I want to stay awhile. Maybe I could go to university, but I'm not keen on studying all the time." She twirled the sherry glass by the stem.

I told her I'd have a hard time telling her what I did in my spare time because I'd just broken my engagement to James. Her eyes grew wide at that detail. "Nan," she said, putting her glass on the table. "I just broke my engagement, too. We were to marry in autumn. I hate his parents. I couldn't think of having them in my life so I broke it off. I guess I didn't like John so much as I thought, either. My mum is beside herself. She can't fancy me a spinster." She laughed and then became serious. "What about you?"

"I'm not sure I know exactly. I just know it wouldn't work." I didn't want to talk about it. I hadn't thought about it for hours. I wanted to keep the distance. Penny seemed to pick up on my reluctance to talk.

"Let's head for the dining room. We're only minutes from the start of dinner."

The dinner was a surprise. The chef at the hotel was French. So was the menu. A filet mignon was preceded by the smallest cup of herbed split pea soup and accompanied by a potato gratin and a ratatouille of mixed vegetables. There were baskets of French baguettes, plenty of wine and dessert of crème brûlée. After dinner the director of the program, Trevor Simms, explained the agenda for the next day and excused us to get acquainted.

I stayed at the table nursing a glass of wine. Penny excused herself to talk with someone she thought she knew. The dining room was small with a huge stone fireplace covering most of the end wall. It was a real wood-burning fireplace with a fire tended by a man with large leather gloves. The tables had been cleared, but the bottles of wine and glasses were not removed. I filled my glass just as a man stopped behind Penny's chair. "May I join you?" He had his hand on the back of the chair. "I'm Jerome Cassidy." He pronounced it *Jerum*. He stuck out his hand.

"Nan Malone." I took his hand and invited him to sit. He had a glass in his hand. I offered to fill it. He smiled. "I'm happy to meet you. You're the only person in the program from the States. I'm the only person in the program with an Irish name, but I'm from London." His face was flushed. From the wine? His hair was long and curly in front and cut short on the sides. He wore a dark shirt, dark tie and a dark tweed sport coat with leather elbow patches. And black loafers of all things. I wondered if there were rules somewhere covering attire for male English teachers. Rules that called for strange colors and styles no one else would adopt. "Is this your first time abroad?" He leaned toward me a little.

"Yes, it is. I wasn't planning on coming. I was on a waiting list and was called at the last minute."

"You'll like the program. I've done others in this series and they really help secondary teachers." He nodded as he spoke.

"Where do you teach?" I asked.

"Oh, I'm in a boys' school run by Irish brothers in Kensington. I've been there six years. It's a good school." He kept on smiling. "I've a brother in St. Louis. Where're you from? Not Seattle, I guess."

"No, the Seattle woman broke her hip. I'm from Minneapolis."

Jerome was still smiling. "God bless her, she was probably an old lady. Only old ladies break hips. You're a fine substitute, you are." He raised his glass to me. He was kind of fun. Just listening to him was amusing. "Would you like something from the bar? We could go in there. Or have you been in the pub on the High Street? You should see a real English pub. Will we give it a try?"

And I Married Her
(excerpt)

The Lily of France Suit

JULIE LARSON

My mind is a playground. Characters of every sort from savory to unsavory keep showing up; most are uninvited. They rob my memory banks. They scramble fact and fiction, and I let them get away with it. What the heck, we need each other. No other writers want any of these characters, won't word them on their computers or word processors, not even on a legal pad with a ballpoint pen. Nevertheless, I cherish them. And so I let them mess with me. They climb and slide, jump and tumble. Then they feed my secrets and dreams back to me daring me to offer them to you. And so I do.

And I Married Her
A band of ruffians arrived one evening whilst I was doing the supper dishes. They roared up my driveway on a 1979 Fat Bob Harley Davidson and in a Ford F 350 pick-up-anything truck. Pete and Bessie Burns were riding the Harley and their son Tommy and his girlfriend Lurleen rode in the truck. The following is part of a longer yarn that they've been spinning in return for a place to sleep and a bit of bread—organic of course.

The Lily of France Suit
There are ways to get a yearbook and ways to not get a yearbook. You decide.

AND I MARRIED HER

When I'm oiled to the floor, I do what I can. I hunker down. When I've got a wild woman oiled down with me, lying in my lap sleeping, snoring like a lumberjack, I hunker down real good. I reach up from the floor where I'm trapped and yank the tablecloth out from under the salt and pepper shakers, sugar bowl, two or three coffee mugs, and a jam pot. Everything falls or spills to the floor but I pull the cloth so that it stays dry and un-sticky. I wrap it around me and my log-sawing lady and ease into the space between the seat and back of an overturned chair. I know I'm going to be here for awhile. Tommy's in his truck eating himself unconscious, slamming down Twinkies and Ho Hos. Stalling what he's going to do anyway—help us. My God, it's the Fourth Commandment. "Honor your father and mother." Tommy will not break a Law of God or a speed limit.

He'll eat himself to sleep and when he wakes up, I'll know. I'll hear it: the wrestling match, the contest. Tommy the good son tussling with Tommy the judge. He'll yell at himself, bang his head on the steering wheel, shake back and forth until the truck wobbles, slap the dashboard and then Tommy the good son will free us. Tommy our Dalmatian, our firehouse rescuer. One hour or three, what can I do but wait? Wait, watch my woman sleep, and remember... the day I fell in love with Bessie, Elizabeth Maloney, the day I married her.

Sixty-five years ago, my college graduation celebration. The kitchen was a battle station. My mother commanded like a general, sounded like a squawking hen. She had hired two neighborhood girls to help her.

"Marjorie, look, the plates and the silver must be exactly an inch from the edge of the table. This is no slap dap dinner. Ann, baste the chickens, slice the buns. Run, run girls. Hurry, scurry, go help Elizabeth carry in the salads."

Elizabeth Maloney delivered for the Maloney Family's grocery store. Mrs. Maloney catered for special occasions. Her specialties were potato salad, five-bean salad, creamed cucumbers, and pickled beets. My mother ordered every salad and relish Mrs. Maloney made. I was the first one in my family to graduate from college, and my mother had planned this celebration for four years, since my first day as a freshman. She was pride personified, walking and talking pride. At the beauty shop, the butcher shop, the library, her bridge club, the church women's club, she was a human sandwich board announcing: "MY SON IS A COLLEGE GRADUATE."

Marjorie, Ann, and I all went to help Elizabeth, Bessie to her friends, carry the platters and bowls in from the delivery truck. The way Elizabeth the mighty mite could crank that bulky truck around, back it up an alley, aim for the driveway, and land bull's-eye was a breath taker. And she did it in a skirt, the store uniform, a peach dress thing with white apron. Only, Elizabeth did something to her uniform. The sleeves puffed out and were trimmed with lace. The skirt was short, just under her knees, and it billowed around her unlike the uniforms worn by other employees: straight short sleeves with white cuffs and A-shaped skirts. She twirled and swished as she arranged the bowls on the table and then added garnishes: tomato wedges, orange smiles, olive eyes, and onion and almond slivers. And green stuff: parsley, lettuce, and maybe even grass, I didn't care. I was watching her arms. They moved with the grace and confidence of an orchestra conductor. A little red stuff here, some green there, back to red, more green, a sprinkle, a dash, a plop. The decorated bowls seemed to hum as her arms passed over them. I caught myself humming, hoping her hands would flutter over me. The kitchen was a cacophony of sounds: Marjorie, Ann, Elizabeth and I laughing, dishes clattering, oven door scraping, feet scurrying, my mother calling commands. This was a perfect day.

"Don't go getting all high horse yet, Pete my boy. Everything in your life is because of me. Your big fancy education has a lot to prove for what it costs me. I'd say right now you aren't worth the salt in your milk."

We looked like we had been playing statue-statue and my father had ordered us to freeze in place. The laughter, the clattering, the scurrying all stopped. The sounds evaporated like dry ice.

Elizabeth Maloney was the first one to start breathing. She stared at my father so intently they seemed locked in a stare down. Without breaking her focus, she stepped to the Frigidaire, opened it, and took out a bottle of milk. Then she lifted a goblet from a tray on the counter. She filled the goblet with milk and picked up a saltshaker from another tray. She unscrewed the lid on the shaker and poured the salt into the milk. She stirred the milk with her finger, licked it, and then drank the salty milk, every drop. She put the goblet down on the counter and wiped her mouth with the back of her hand.

"Peter Burns, you are worth all the salt in my milk."

My father was the first one to break the stare down. "Pete, get the young lady a glass of water, save her stomach from that concoction. And if I were you, I wouldn't let her get away." He smiled and left the kitchen.

With my father's exit the sounds resumed, the laughing, the clattering, and the scurrying. I hoped no one could see the turbulence I felt in my body. I contained an ocean. Internal waves rocked me back and forth. I steadied myself by looking into Elizabeth Maloney's eyes. Elizabeth Maloney's very, very blue eyes.

I don't know how she did it but as I was staring at her, worshiping her, she reached under her dress and began pulling at something. The she lifted one foot at a time and stepped out of that something. I was staring so hard into those very blue eyes, I didn't notice what she removed. She walked to me and put the pink something into my right pants pocket. I reached in and pulled the pink something out. For a second, I looked away from her to see what the pink something was. Underpants, lacy pink underpants. Elizabeth Maloney's lacy pink underpants.

"Marry me, Pete Burns. Marry me." Right there in my parents' kitchen, in front of Marjorie and Ann and my mother, she proposed. "You can keep the panties, either as an engagement present or a memento."

And I did. I kept her underwear. And I married Elizabeth Maloney that night. How could I help myself? While standing in front of platters of baked chicken and bowls of mashed potatoes, I had been struck by lightning. I felt like a Fourth of July sparkler sizzling, spewing bits of fire everywhere. I stepped to the middle of the kitchen so I wouldn't ignite my mother's celebration.

I squinted, blinded by my own light. My mother tugged on my arm.

"Peter, enough staring like a dumbstruck donkey, put more chairs around the dining room table." She seemed in charge like she had been a few minutes ago, but her eyes betrayed her. I had seen that look before: Mrs. Dunn's eyes, glazed with terror the day her dog Lambkin ran free.

"Lambkin is a lapdog. He wants to be carried and hand-fed. Don't you Lamby Pie?" Lambkin, a tiny Chihuahua, shivered for a living. He shivered and quivered and slept on Mrs. Dunn's bent forearm. He lived on her forearm. Then one day he escaped. Mrs. Dunn was fumbling for the keys to her front door and she set Lambkin down next to her on the porch, stood him there for barely a breath. In that breath, Lambkin discovered his legs. He shook them out, all four at the same time. He fell over. "Lamby, mom will pick you up in a sec, sweetie." Then Lambkin saw a squirrel. Lambkin was transformed. He may have looked like what my dad called him, a disgrace of a dog, but he felt like a pit bull. He stood, snarled, pawed the ground, and took off coughing and barking.

"Lamby, come back. You naughty fellow, Mommy is upset with you. Help, someone, help! Lambkin is loose, help!" I did the deed. I chased Lambkin down. He raced, I raced. He streaked across yards, tunneled through flower gardens, romped around vegetable plots, bolted in and out of the street a few times. All the forbiddens were his fruits. However, a dog that has spent his life on a forearm is not forearmed. In the middle of Mr. Johnson's tomato patch, Lambkin had a heart attack, or it sure looked like it. I picked him up. He was dead, limp as spent bread dough. I carried him to Mrs. Dunn. She looked at me the way my mother was looking at me now, with fright and sorrow. The kind of fright that shrinks pupils to pin pricks, the kind of sorrow that follows an irretrievable loss—haunting, panicked.

My mother's face glistened with sweat, sweat generated by terror. Here in her kitchen, her house, her domain, I was hatching. Chunks of my shell cracked and fell around me. A shell shaped so seamlessly, a dream smoothed so skillfully I thought it was mine. I lifted my arms, held them out in front of me. MY arms? I touched my face: MY skin, MY bones, MY eyes and nose and mouth. WAHOO, I shouted. MY voice? I laughed and I laughed, fascinated at the sound. I lifted Marjorie and then Ann and twirled them in joyous circles. They squealed. My mother re-barked her orders.

"Marjorie, Ann, collect yourselves, our guests will be here soon. You, Peter—the chairs."

"Yes, Ma, the chairs." Without my shell, I felt fluffy—the chairs feather-light. I lifted my mother. She felt no heavier than a balloon. I waltzed her into the dining room and set her down on one of the chairs. She was sobbing, she reached into my pocket for a handkerchief. "Ahhhh," she screamed. She jammed Elizabeth's underwear back into my pocket. "Peter, I don't like you like this. Remember who you are. You are Peter Burns, college graduate. You are the future Doctor Peter Burns. Now act like it, you hear me?"

Was she ordering or pleading? Neither. She was arguing for her dream, for her place, the mother of a doctor sitting front-row in the bragging mother's club, the Ladies Auxiliary. If I chose a lesser path, she would be banished. I was her ticket to preferential treatment: best seats at restaurants, blue-ribbon service at the grocery store, the butcher shop, the milliners. She leaned back against the chair, lifting her legs off the floor. She flailed her arms and legs in the air, thrashing like a June bug on its back, fallen and helpless. She screeched.

"Sam Burns, Sam come here. SAM GET IN HERE RIGHT NOW."

My father was out on the front porch smoking a mighty fine Cuban cigar. He was a mere five puffs into that roll of choice leaves when he heard her shrieks. He looked at the cigar and then bent his ear toward her squeals.

"Sam, I need you right now. HELP, HELP."

"Coming dear," he droned. He rested the mighty fine Cuban cigar on the porch railing, checked it for balance, and walked into the house.

"What is it, Pearl? I'm breaking in a new cigar, so this better not take long."

"It's Peter, Sam. He's gone crazy. I'm afraid of him. He pinched Marjorie and Ann on their backsides, polkaed them around the kitchen, and he tasted all the salads with his fingers. He went from one to the next scooping and talking, scooping and licking. Then he ran out and hid behind the delivery truck and when Elizabeth Maloney went out to get a bowl, he popped out, grabbed her, kissed her, hoisted her over his shoulder and carried her back into the kitchen. But the worst is he keeps laughing, loud laughing. Laughing like I have never heard from him before, wild dangerous hoots. Do something with him, Sam."

My father looked at me like I had never seen him look at me before. I was the horse that won the Belmont, his horse, the dark horse that came from behind and took the prize. This was the win he had waited for since I was eighteen. He smirked, he winked, he made clucking noises with his tongue. He and I now shared a wicked secret.

"So, Pete, what do you have to say for yourself? Better be as good as your mother says it is. I've got a good smoke going to ashes on the porch."

"How about giving me one of those cigars, Pop? And some bucks while you're at it. I'm taking Elizabeth Maloney dancing after the party and I want to show off. What do you say Pops, old boy?" With my requests made, I laughed my new throaty guffaw, tried to sound like a horse.

"No, no, this has to be a nightmare. Sam, stop him." My mother wailed and thrashed. Something diabolical was happening. The father and son who had lived together yet were as incompatible as oil and water, separate and insoluble, were cozying up to each other, smooshed together like peanut butter and jelly in a sandwich.

"Smoking a cigar? Going dancing with the trollop from the grocery store? No, Sam, not her. Not the trollop from the grocery store. If he goes, he will be the death of me."

My father's chest swelled like it had a bicycle pump attached to it. He embraced me. He patted my arms; he was puffing me up for the task ahead. He took a cigar from his suit pocket and shoved it into my hand.

"Dancing with Elizabeth Maloney, wonderful. You going dancing. Great day in the morning. C'mon, I'll give you a cigar-smoking lesson. My boy, you are on the threshold of greatness, yes sir you are."

He was more excited over my going dancing with Elizabeth Maloney then he had ever been over my dozens of straight-A report cards, my scholarships, and my pending acceptance to Harvard Medical School.

"But Peter, you don't dance. Never went to the prom or any school dances. You give your father back the cigar. Sam, feel his head is he feverish, delirious?" My mother with all her screeching had drowned out what my father was saying to me. She hadn't heard him and she didn't realize that both of us were a lost cause.

"He's fine, Pearl. He's ALIVE. Here boy, have all these cigars." He shoved three more into my shirt pocket. "Here's fifty bucks. Take Elizabeth

Maloney dancing. Do the town." Then he grabbed my arm and yanked me out to the porch. "Take twenty-five more bucks, Pete. Keep Elizabeth Maloney out all night, if you know what I mean." Once again he smirked and winked and made clucking sounds with his tongue.

"Gottcha, Pop."

"I'll take care of your mother. After the party, you and that little filly skedaddle, you hear? Go do what you gotta do to be a man."

"No underpants, the girl has no underpants, Sam. He can't go with her."

My father walked back to my flailing mother. "Pearl, calm down. That's an old vaudeville gimmick. Everyone knows about that one—the breakaway pants trick. They're kids having fun. We had a little fun in our day. Remember?"

"Cut that out. We were different. You didn't have plans for your life laid out like Peter does. Your mother didn't belong to the Ladies Auxiliary either. What will become of me, my standing in the community, my son mixed up with the grocery store trollop?"

There they were together, my mother the upended June bug clawing in all directions whimpering, and my father the inflated warrior smiling, savoring a vicarious score. And there we were, Elizabeth Maloney and me rattling, clattering our way south to Iowa in the Maloney Family's delivery truck. Before the first guests lifted the rapper on the just-installed Burns family crest door knocker, Elizabeth and I made our getaway. Elizabeth sat in the only seat in the truck, the driver's seat, her foot heavy on the gas pedal propelling us forward to our new life. I sat behind her on a crate filled with jars of pickled beets and fondled her pink underwear, the pink breakaway underwear. This was the perfect day.

THE LILY OF FRANCE SUIT

THESE DAYS, when I remember my high school graduation, I smile. However, I wasn't smiling on that day: May 20, 1960, the day my mother kissed Sr. Mary Thomas, our school principal. Was something wrong with my mother? Was she a fairy? Never did I imagine my four years at St. Gregory the Great Preparatory Academy for Young Women, situated in the hills high above Duluth, Minnesota, would end splattered like a dropped watermelon. Back then, my friends and I had our mothers figured out. If I were writing a play, my mother would be a stock character—a lot less stock than most mothers, but for me ninety-nine percent predictable. Ninety-nine percent mother dimensional. I could predict whether my behavior would provoke nagging, encouraging, granting or withholding permission, and even weeping. Sometimes she wept with pride, sometimes with frustration or exhaustion. However, I would have never predicted her behavior on this my graduation day. My mother was a book I had read a thousand times. I thought I had memorized every page. Yet I had missed this phrase, or sentence, or paragraph, this chink in her being. Perhaps I hadn't missed it. Perhaps I chose to ignore it.

I was stamping like a racehorse at the starting gate on Graduation Day. Good-bye St. Greg's, good-bye nuns, curfews, uniforms, girls, girls, girls. Hello freedom. Hello boys. Hello life. But there was a burr under my saddle, Sr. Mary Thomas's rule. No yearbooks handed out to students who had any outstanding debts. Damn her rule. My parents owed on my tuition. I wheedled, I guilted. I whined. I wanted that yearbook, my last yearbook.

"Jane, we know you're disappointed but we don't have two hundred and fifty dollars that we can pull out of the air right now. Your dad's been struggling at the station for months; gas wars are eating his profits."

They didn't have the money a month ago, or a week ago, and now on Graduation Day there still was no money for tuition and no yearbook for me. My mother was wearing her best suit though. She looked beautiful because she was beautiful and she knew how to be beautiful. This was no surprise to me. The other mothers in our neighborhood were Lucy and Ethel types, funny and comfortable. My mother was driven, focused, Scarlett from *Gone with the Wind*. The other mothers lived on the a.m. side of the clock, cooking and cleaning all day. My mother spent the a. m. hours sleeping and the p.m. hours waitressing. Her tips paid for that best suit and that best suit would help her get me my yearbook.

"This wasn't fair. I had done my part. I cleaned classrooms; I washed dishes, weeded gardens, worked off my board and room. You don't know how humiliating it's been for me, signing yearbooks, and not having one of my own for everyone else to sign." But she did know. My mother had walked to school barefoot, had taken coffee to school in my grandfather's discarded whiskey bottles because milk was for the little ones, and she had begged for the leftovers when invited to another child's birthday party.

"Go ask Sr. Mary Thomas," I begged. "She's in her office. She won't be able to say no to you. If you get my yearbook now, I'll be able to get a few autographs before everyone's gone. Please ask her. Promise her you'll pay the rest of the tuition this summer."

I wanted to shove her into Sr. Mary Thomas's office, shut the door, and not let her come out until she had my yearbook tucked under her arm. Why was she hesitating? This was the woman the whole neighborhood called Hot Rod Rosie. This was the woman who catapulted her Chevy down Emerson Street, fenders clattering, tires pounding in and out of every pothole, spewing dust, clogging lungs when she sped past. This was the woman who attacked the neighborhood boys with a lilac switch when she caught them stealing apples from her prize tree. This was the woman who hired a lawyer and won a five-hundred-dollar settlement when a pet macaw at the bowling alley wolf-whistled at her, causing her to fall and wrench her shoulder. This was the only woman on the block who shopped in Dayton's Oval Room.

What would Ice Woman Thomas do when challenged by an adult that didn't care a hoot about her rules? Here was a woman who wouldn't cringe when Ice Woman Thomas issued an edict. Who was this Sr. Mary Thomas anyway? Had she been born wearing a habit, ordering her parents about? Did she hold them hostage for infractions like she did us when someone blotted her lips on the 2nd-floor hall door? Ice Woman banned lipstick, forced us all to go bland until the criminal confessed.

January passed, then February, then March. Three months and no one came forward and no one was going to. We decided to finish the school year lip-naked. Sr. Mary Thomas thought she had us in a choke hold; we thought we had her in a full nelson, and nobody was going to the mat. We students were solidified, entrenched in our resistance. We were locked in our determination; rich girls and poor, gifted and not so gifted, we were united. Then Mary Thomas dealt the body blow that brought us to our knees. On April 1st, she posted her edict on the student bulletin board.

> Young Ladies,
>
> The culprit has not come forward. The lipstick blotter has not confessed. Therefore, no makeup, not a trace, will be worn by any student attending the Junior-Senior Prom.
>
> Sr. Mary Thomas, Principal,
> St. Gregory the Great Preparatory Academy.

She couldn't do this. Oh, but she could. Years of tradition were on her side. The prom was always held in the school auditorium—her turf. Our solidified resistance buckled, went down for the count. Sr. Mary Thomas walked the halls grinning like the wicked queen when Snow White bit the poisoned apple.

The Junior-Senior Prom was the IT event of the year. We started asking each other in November. Are you going to IT? We didn't need to say the word prom. We knew "going to IT" meant the prom. Girls attending an all-girls boarding school begged and bartered for dates. We swapped and traded brothers, cousins, even cast-off boyfriends. Sue Hansen was so desperate she asked Ollie the pot scrubber from the kitchen. He was only five feet tall and Sue, our tallest senior, measured six feet at the school physical in September. By now, early April, she might be even taller. But Ollie met the basic criterion, he was a boy.

Then there was the scramble to find a formal for every girl that had snagged a date. Some girls' families could afford a new prom dress, others couldn't. Several of us wore dresses that had been donated by graduated seniors to the prom closet. Others wore older sisters' gowns or borrowed bridesmaids' dresses from assorted relatives and friends.

The prom was always scheduled for the second Saturday in May and by the middle of April who was going with who had been arranged. After all there were other high schools in town and we did not have the competitive edge. If students in the other schools found out about Mary Thomas's edict we would be the laughingstock of all prom goers for 1960. And any males we had lured from other schools could turn skittish and run.

By April 3rd, we had a plan. The student body presidents—senior, junior, sophomore, and freshman—sent a communiqué to Sr. Mary Thomas requesting a meeting for ten minutes before dismissal in the auditorium. She agreed. She must have thought the sinner was going public. The sinners did go public. All two-hundred and fifty pranksters went public in unison. "We dood it. We dood it." We were having fun. We were a mob impersonating Red Skelton's Mean Little Kid. We held up tubes of pastel pink lipstick waving them while we owned up. "We dood it," we chimed.

Did Sr. Mary Thomas crumble defeated? Wither even a little? No. Sr. Mary Thomas laughed. She stood in front of us rocking back and forth. Loud guffaws blasted out of her mouth. She sounded like my grandmother watching Red Skelton do his Clem Kadiddlehopper character. My sister and I used to pray that our grandmother wouldn't have a heart attack while watching *The Red Skelton Show*. She laughed and screeched until her face turned red and then she gulped for air like a fish out of water.

Sr. Mary Thomas's face turned red but she didn't have a heart attack. She left the auditorium and we heard her laughing her way to her office. Each guffaw bouncing off the walls like a bowling ball hitting strikes. This was not what we expected. Was she going to turn the fire hose on us? Expel us? We stood silent, waiting. The dismissal bell rang. That was it. We were dismissed.

This was the most tranquil end of the year Sr. Mary Thomas had ever experienced since she assumed her principal-ness. Every day we expected THE PUNISHMENT. Every day we walked not ran to our classes and we were on time. We polished our shoes and we de-spotted our jackets and skirts daily. We ironed our blouses' sides and backs, not just the collars and fronts. No one forgot their chapel veil for services and no one fell asleep during services. When we passed Sr. Mary Thomas in the hall, we greeted her, we bowed to her.

We did wear makeup to the prom. However, we did not outline our eyes like we had practiced for weeks, painting our eyelids over and over until we had mastered the Elizabeth Taylor cat-eye look. Instead we imitated Debbie Reynolds; ponytailed and glowing, wide-eyed, the girl-next-door in 112 variations.

After the Graduates' Luncheon, Sr. Mary Thomas announced that she would be in her office if any parents or graduates wanted to see her. There was a short line. Mary Alice Shunk, Betsy Collins, and some parents. I knew what Mary Alice and Betsy wanted: Sr. Mary Thomas's signature in their yearbooks—goody-two-shoes types to the end. The parents, I wouldn't know what they wanted. I had enough challenges with mine to not guess what other people's parents were up to.

I placed my dad out in the courtyard where he could talk to other dads or look at flowers. Some instinct told me he would do more harm than good with Sr. Mary Thomas. I tugged my mother into the waiting line. I was so proud of her in her navy blue Lily of France suit with the crisp white collar. She wore the navy blue hat she bought at Gerner's in Minneapolis with some of her bowling alley settlement money. This hat with its forever brim and white silk rose resting across its width made my mother look like she came from Edina not Brooklyn Center. Every curl, every twist of her chestnut hair was calculated. Her purse and shoes matched. She wore white gloves. She was dressed to win.

However, winning is more than wearing the right outfit.

"Winning is how you present yourself, girls. Always look Put Together. No matter what, you are unflappable," was my mother's creed.

I remember the summer day Barney our milkman caught her standing in our kitchen wearing only a bra and a half-slip. He winked at her and made a clicking noise with his mouth. She had come home from work late the night before, taken off her uniform and nylons, and slid into bed exhausted. Did she gasp with embarrassment, try to cover herself, or hide behind the refrigerator? No, not her. "Just a minute, Barney," she said. She then stepped out of the kitchen, walked to her bedroom, grabbed my dad's robe, put it on and went back into the kitchen. "How about four quarts of milk, a pint of whipping cream, and a pound of butter?"

"Sure thing. Here you go. See ya Thursday."

After the milk truck rumbled away, she took off the robe, flopped it over a kitchen chair, and went back to bed. My sister and I whipped the cream, smeared it on graham crackers, and ate ourselves numb.

But today, in line, waiting to see Sr. Mary Thomas, she was cringing, rounding her shoulders, her head turned down. She was breaking all her own rules. Who was this woman? Was some alien trapped in her body? I stood next to her imitating a young sapling shooting up tall, reaching for the sky like she taught me. I stood up so straight I could have carried a fishbowl on my head. Unaffected, she stayed slumped over. I wanted to shake her but then what would the other parents think? Instead, I leaned against her hoping the slight pressure would wake her out of whatever goofy stupor she was in. It didn't. I left to get her a drink of water and when I returned she was staring, gawking at the other parents. If she had caught my sister or me gaping at people like that we would have been nosed into a corner and told to stare at the walls. I wanted to shock her back to herself. I lifted the cup, aiming the water at her. I stopped myself, remembering her admonition: "you are unflappable." I drank the water instead.

She huffed and she puffed. She wriggled and tugged. Gloves off, gloves on, gloves off, gloves on. She scratched at her neck, pulled at her skirt. She looked like my little sister did on Sunday when she was forced to wear a fresh starched dress to church. I continued to stand next to her composed, smiling my Grace Kelly smile, winning yet mysterious, as described in *Life* magazine.

Then it was her turn. Mr. and Mrs. Somebody, I didn't know who, stepped out. Sr. Mary Thomas slipped out of her office behind them. Unlike my tortured mother, Ice Woman Thomas oozed confidence. She reminded me of the nun doll my godmother had given me for my tenth birthday. Like the doll, Sister's face was frozen in a manufactured smile and her habit fell in graceful unwrinkled folds. The pleated wimple around her face was chalk white.

"Come in, Mrs. Ervin. Jane, are you coming?"

"No thank you, Sister."

She nodded, and then swept her arm toward her office, whishing an invisible path, which my mother followed. Sr. Mary Thomas shut the door. I looked around. No one was in sight, not up the hall or down the hall. I went to the keyhole. Although I had walked past this office hundreds of times during my three years as a student, I had never been summoned or invited inside. I had never dared to look into this inner sanctum. I didn't want to be noticed. I didn't want to be invited or summoned inside. Now here I was, Chicken Little of the senior class, looking through the keyhole of Ice Woman's office and I couldn't see a thing except Sr. Mary Thomas's black habit. However, I wasn't afraid. She couldn't do anything to me now. I had my diploma and I could live without the yearbook, but since I had guilted my mother this far she might as well finish her assignment. I turned the handle on the door. I could have been a safecracker or a cat burglar. I twisted the knob a centimeter at a time making no sounds, turning, turning until it wouldn't turn any farther. Then I pushed in and in while I leaned forward melting against the door. They didn't notice me. They were turned facing away from the door. I could hear my mother's voice, not the exact words but the murmuring sounds like I heard from upstairs in my room when my mother was talking to her friends on the phone downstairs. Her murmurs had distinct tones: rushed and excited meant gossip; whispery meant the listener had to swear to keep the information a secret; scolding, complaining meant some customer had stiffed her out of a tip; elation meant some drunk chump overtipped. The tone I was hearing now was a whine, the same tone I used when I wanted something I knew she would not agree to, like tickets to see Jerry Lee Lewis perform. I gave up. My yearbook was a fantasy. But before my mother was given the heave-ho, I leaned in to get the lay of Mary Thomas's land.

What a hangout Miss Nun had fashioned for herself. The back wall had two long, narrow, draped windows. The drapes like the walls were cream colored. This was the only room in the school, except for the visiting parlor, that had drapes. A huge painting hung between the windows. The wall to the right was floor-to-ceiling books. Two chairs were angled toward each other in front of this wall and on a small table placed between the chairs rested a collection of yearbooks. If only my mother could grab one and run. She'd have a hard time getting past Sr. Mary Thomas's desk though. The desk was smack dab in the middle of the room and it faced the door. I had never seen a desk like this. It was huge, a giant table with curved legs. If we had a table that big at home, the kids wouldn't have to eat in the kitchen for family celebrations. From behind this desk, Sr. Mary Thomas could intimidate a bishop. Maybe she had.

Where was my mother? I couldn't see her. Had she been Mary Thomased? Hashed? While I had been scanning the room, snapping mental pictures, my mother had disappeared. I jerked back from the doorway, rubbed my eyes, and then looked again. She was there. She was down on the floor, crawling around on her hands and knees rubbing her hands over the carpet. She could have been in a museum appreciating a work of art. I recognized what had captivated her. The carpet was one of those Persian things. My mother loved Persian carpets. I hated them. The only house I had ever seen one in was at a friend of my mother's who was old, real old, sixty at least. Those Persian things were for old ladies. What was wrong with her? What about my yearbook? All she had to do was turn on her boss voice and say, "I promise payment will be made," then take the yearbook and walk. Did she have a different plan? Was she going to bang her head under Sister's desk getting up, sue for damages, and get out of paying the tuition with a yearbook thrown in for good measure?

She didn't have any plan. She was being herself unpredictable, spontaneous. She was spontaneousing all over the stupid carpet; oohing and aahing, aahing and oohing. Her hat had fallen off. She didn't notice. Sr. Mary Thomas did. She bent down and picked it up. She sniffed it. My mother always dabbed a little perfume on her hats. She said it helped scent the air around her.

Whether it was the sight of my mother crawling around her office or the perfume wafting, circling her, I don't know, but Sr. Mary Thomas was grinning, sniffing, swaying back and forth from foot to foot. Should I run and get dad? No, not yet, something was happening here, something he wouldn't understand, something I didn't understand. Ice Lady was melting. The way she grinned and swayed and hugged that hat, Sr. Mary Thomas could have been Minnie Pearl in a nun's costume. I listened for her to break out yowling like Minnie did on the *Grand Ole Opry:* "Howdee! I'm just so proud to be here—holding this hat."

I absolutely positively did not know what to do. So I prayed. I believed in God again. The God I had outgrown a few months ago, I now pleaded with to do something. Send a thunderbolt or rain a thousand frogs on them. He didn't do either. He didn't do anything. My mother did the something. She stood up and she didn't bump her head. She smoothed her suit, patted her tumbled curls and reached to Sr. Mary Thomas for her hat. She was ready for business.

Sr. Mary Thomas wasn't. She was hugging my mother's hat to her chest. She smiled and hugged the hat tighter. My stomach lurched like it does at the top of the roller coaster that last second before a plunge. Then Sr. Mary Thomas tossed the hat on her desk and reached for my mother. I lost my breath. My mother leaned in to her. Sr. Mary Thomas took my mother's head in her hands, spreading her fingers on each side of my mother's face like she was holding something precious, porcelain or gold. She bent forward and sniffed my mother's neck, another place where my mother always dabbed perfume. My mother moved her head back a little exposing more of her neck. I inhaled again. I was ready for another plunge. Sr. Mary Thomas turned my mother's head until she was looking into her eyes, smiling into her eyes. My mother pulled away but that old Mary Thomas was quick. She pulled my mother's face to hers and kissed her. I gasped. Had the roller coaster crashed? That kiss wasn't any quick brush of the lips aunt-style peck thing. That kiss was intentional, purposeful—yuk, passionate even.

This must have been the day the roller-coaster attendant gave an extra go-around for free. My mother kissed Sr. Mary Thomas back. She reached up, grabbed Mary Thomas's face in her hands, and planted a smackerole right back on Mary Thomas's lips. This was not the Ice Woman meets Hot Rod Woman face-off I imagined. This was a combustion. I heard the snap, saw a flash. I remembered when I was seven years old; I found a box of kitchen matches in a cupboard. No one was home so I took them outside and ignited them, sometimes two or three at a time. I felt brave; I took five and struck them. The pop, then the flash startled me, blinding me like I was blinded now. I opened my eyes and neither woman was in flames or melted. Years ago, my five-pack of matches sent up what seemed like a mushroom cloud when I dropped it into the grass. Today there was no smoke and I had no words for what I had just seen.

My mother stepped away from Mary Thomas and reached inside her suit jacket into her bra where I know she kept a scented handkerchief. She pulled out the handkerchief, wiped a lipstick smudge from Mary Thomas's mouth, and then put the handkerchief in Mary Thomas's hand. This was either romantic or revolting. I had been warned several times that some girl or other had a crush on me. "Happens in a girls school all the time. The person you least suspect turns out to be a fairy chasing after you." Sr. Mary Thomas has a crush on my mother or is my mother after Mary Thomas? My heart was pounding so hard that I moved away from the door, closed it so they wouldn't hear me.

The door opened. My mother walked out. She looked at me sitting on the floor next to Sr. Mary Thomas's office but she didn't see me. Maybe I had to be invisible for awhile. "Mom, Mom wait." I stood up and ran after her. "Mom."

She turned and faced me. She looked like a painting left out in the rain. The sharp lines that had defined her were blurred. The brown of her hair, the blue of her suit, and the white of her collar were streaming into each other, leaking out of their boundaries. Her mouth was curved in a teasing, playful smile, the grin of someone who had just answered the 64 Thousand Dollar Question.

"Mom, Mom, what about my yearbook?"

"Jane? You want that yearbook? Go ask for it yourself."

Morning Chores

STEVE CHAMBERS

STEVE CHAMBERS *and his wife Helen are retired and challenging the ravages of old age with help from nine imaginative grandchildren. Although Steve has lived in the city nearly fifty years now, Helen says he's still an Iowa farm boy.*

Morning Chores *is a chapter from* Out to the River, *a memoir that explores life during the 1940s in Anderson, Iowa, a small farming community in the valley of the Nishnabotna River. This was a time of dramatic change in American life, especially on the farm, and gave young people like me unique opportunities to discover new challenges and possibilities emerging in our country. The soil was rich, the people fascinating, the skies magnificent, and the river mysterious. Old-timers passed on their frontier roots with countless stories.*

Each year brought challenges to our way of life: floods, drought, depression, war, disease, and the ever-changing cost-price squeeze my father worried might some day force us to the poorhouse. Yet, even when our crops failed, prices fell, World War II thundered on, and close friends got sick and died, we still had hope. If we applied ourselves in school, worked hard, followed the Golden Rule, and respected our elders, we would find a way to succeed no matter what the obstacles.

As I wrote my way through the events and realities of these times, I found myself swept into a sea of change. Giant new machines replaced horses, hybrid corn replaced open-pollinated, herbicides put an end to cutting weeds by hand, corporations pushed out family farms, and the information age beamed across America. With these and other changes, I realize now that a way of life was passing from the landscape, never to return as we knew it then. Yet at the same time, I feel the values of that time living on in the hopes and essential decency of most Americans. I believe Morning Chores, *which comes from the midpoint of the memoir, nudges into many of these themes.*

THIS PAST SUMMER, Jack and Anna helped me build paths through the woods behind our retirement house. It's a small woods; a narrow strip of native red oaks left by developers between our new subdivision and an older part of Mounds View. This woods has become my haven of chaos. Helen's too. Time disappears in its tangles of elderberry, honeysuckle, buckthorn, and wild raspberry. We gaze out from the living room, the porch, or the lower deck, our eyes following vines of woodbine and wild grape upward into canopies of oak where the redbirds and gray squirrels reign. Or we stroll along the edges where snarls of brush and tree limbs felled by forgotten storms bar entrance to all but the most adventurous. Other than hanging four small red lanterns and two birdhouses on outer branches and harvesting a few vines for wreaths and garlands, we've not disturbed this place. I've liked the sense of lurking at the edge of mystery, just peering in.

That all changed when our eight grandchildren started to explore. Jack and Anna were the ringleaders. Both of them have just turned five. For me, everything that matters in my life lurks in my grandchildren's sparkling eyes. If only my mother could be here with us. Young children's eyes fascinated my mom. She often said, "Those little eyes see everything." I remember her saying that about my eyes, not intending me to hear, and when I looked into the mirror I wondered what my mother saw in my eyes that I could not.

The idea of cutting an entrance into our woods came up during a family cookout in late July. We had gorged ourselves on brats, ears of sweet corn, and ice cream bars, then gathered around a crackling fire; adults drinking and telling stories while children roasted marshmallows, and dusk descended into night. The children played hide-and-seek, then discovered it was more fun to poke the fire with sticks and race with flashlights between the fire and deepest shadows of the yard. Every so often they stopped beside the woods and aimed their flashlights in. "Come out, all you monsters!" Jack yelled in his Count Dracula voice. "We'll capture you!" others screamed. And sure enough, sticks and chunks of wood became monsters hunched against the ground, and shadowed leaves became ears, faces, and scary hands creeping through the brush. The children dropped to their hands and knees, squiggled forward with great caution, grabbed their prey, raced for the fire, and threw their victims in amongst the crackling flames: sticks, chunks of bark, and coils of vine. "Take that you monsters," they screamed.

But the woods were deep and dark, the fire burned down, and soon all the monsters disappeared. "Please, Papa," the children yelled to me. "Help us get in there. We have to find more monsters."

"Okay, okay," I answered. "You're right. Why don't you come back next week? I'll help you make a path."

As it turned out, the very next day, when older children were busy with friends and younger ones were taking naps, I picked up Jack and Anna and we went to work. "Let's start there," Anna announced. She pointed toward a mass of golden grape leaves, her clenched lips and hazel eyes poised for action. "That's the prettiest spot, so we have to start there."

Jack hesitated, the blues and greens in his eyes dancing with mischief, leaping through other possibilities. "Nooo, let's start over there." He nodded toward a pile of rocks barely visible behind an elderberry bush, rocks I had gathered when the builders dug out the basement for our house.

"Let's cut through both places," I yelled, "Anna's first, then Jack's." We clipped and sawed branches; kicked soft, decaying soil to form our routes; pulled dead branches into place for borders; and made a maze of paths reaching all the way to metal stakes with flags that marked the rear corners of the property. "Just look at all the places we can go!" Anna yelled. In and out we ran, several times, then found a battered bench under the porch, placed it in an inner clearing, and took a rest, the three of us sitting side by side, admiring our work and deciding where to make more paths.

"It's really big in here," Anna said. "Once we get inside." Her eyes darted from tree trunk to tree trunk, found a shaft of light, and followed it upward to the treetops.

"It's so quiet," Jack murmured. "Are the monsters scared of us?"

"They're just resting," Anna answered. "Are they like us?"

"Noooo," Jack said. "They're dead. But they come back to life at night. Let's make more paths for them to play on."

Later, Grandma, parents, cousins, and other friends came by to explore our hidden world. At each showing, Jack and Anna made our paths more perfect. They moved branches, clipped twigs, kicked sticks and leaves aside, and taught us exactly how to yelp when we ran around the curves. Then dusk arrived, and all our work disappeared into the dark and silent majesty of woods. All ready for the monsters to come out and play.

Now it's late October, and I'm preparing the plants and soil to rest until another year. I've learned it's best to clear away only the scruffiest of the dried stems, leaving most to stand all winter as reminders of seasons past and as heralds of seasons yet to come. I divide sedum, hosta, lily, and gay feather plants to fill in gaps, spade the soil a final time, plant tulips and daffodils, and run the hose at the base of each large bush and tree, at least half an hour for each one.

Several times I step into the woods and walk a few feet along the path, soothed by the sound of water gushing from the hose and a light breeze against my face. I feel the hard work and excited shouts of the children on the day we made this path, my thoughts break free, and I'm five again myself, back in the village of Anderson in Southwest Iowa. The feel of the shovel in my hands pulls me along, and once again I'm riding with my father in our Model A, driving north on the dirt road from our house at the edge of Anderson to our eighty-acre farm beside the Nishnabotna River. We lived in town because our farm was flooded nearly every year. "You're a good worker, Bub," Dad says. "I couldn't get it all done without you." I know from his excited voice and light blue eyes beaming into mine that he really means it. It doesn't matter now that, for a good long while, I probably was more trouble than help. Dad was patient, I learned fast, and by 1943 when I was five, he could depend on me to feed the livestock, turn the windmill on and off, harness the horses, and chop weeds out of the corn and fencerows with my own corn knife.

The world I grew up in was very different from today, especially farming. Back then, big operations weren't necessarily worth all the extra worry, and we took our time to be sure expensive new equipment like hay balers and corn pickers really did make you more productive. Why buy four-row tractor equipment when you could do a better job with two-row planters and cultivators behind a team of horses? I remember old-timers gathered down at the Anderson Store, predicting it wouldn't be long before bigger tractors and equipment would push horses and half the farmers off the land. "Just won't need as many of us," they all agreed.

But nobody in their wildest fantasies would have imagined how it's all come about—in just two generations. Just the other day I got into a conversation with a young farmer from western Minnesota. He was excited about his new thirty-two-row planter. It has computerized controls that include a global positioning system to keep rows perfectly spaced and straight as an arrow. Most amazing, it senses the end of the field approaching, automatically turns itself around, and heads back with the next thirty-two-row swath. "It's a snap to set," the farmer said. "I just sit in the air-conditioned cab and enjoy the ride. But don't get the wrong idea. Modern farming is one helluva cutthroat business. The profit margin is so narrow you have to farm several thousand acres just to make enough to pay expenses. That's why we need innovations like my new planter to be more productive. They usually pay for themselves. Not always, though. A lot of guys go under. Farming is a real balancing act, hanging out there on the margins."

Our eighty acres took a lot of work when I was young. Today, it would be about six rounds for a thirty-two-row planter. But though Dad dreamed of adding another eighty acres to our operation, hopefully up in hill country safe from floods, we got along just fine, especially during the War years when farm prices were okay. Smaller farms meant we had a lot of neighbors. We admired each other's operations, stopped to visit, and pitched in when a neighbor had a job that needed several sets of hands: threshing, putting up hay, castrating young bulls and boars, and erecting new barns, cribs, and sheds. We worked shoulder to shoulder, got the jobs done, and formed friendships that lasted all our lives.

That world now is gone, pushed aside by financial pressures to be more and more efficient, leaving what feels to me like a robotic world. When it's time to plant or harvest, computerized machines suddenly appear. For a couple of weeks in both seasons they charge across the fields around the clock. They finish their tasks quickly, then disappear, leaving a deserted land. Cultivating growing crops, such a big part of what we did when I was young, has disappeared completely, replaced by herbicides now spread by sophisticated attachments on the new planters. It's all one operation now. And even though farms are so much bigger today than when I was young, one farm now where there used to be thirty, there's not much work for human beings. Just plant and harvest, then work at other jobs or go on vacation. You don't see farmers out there working on the land.

This enormous change hit me especially hard a few months ago when we took some of the grandkids on a drive through Iowa. Emma, a second grader with a trip-journal assignment, wrote: "Iowa is green and beautiful, but it's empty. Unless you're in a town, you don't see any people." Alas, I'm afraid Emma is absolutely right. Very few people are needed on today's sophisticated farms; certainly no five-year-olds pitching in to help their parents. In my seventy years, I've been blessed with many lucky breaks, and one of the best was growing up on a small family farm where I was useful when I was very young. I regret that my grandchildren, whose parents rush off to work at computers in a sophisticated office, have no idea what they've missed.

I remember announcing in my first grade class that I could harness a team of horses all by myself. "You cannot!" some of my classmates shouted. But I really could, and Rock and Rowdy, our team of dark grays, made it easy. They stood patiently while I threw the black leather straps and shiny rigging up and over their shaggy backs, and they lowered their long necks so I could work the leather work collars up to their shoulders. It took me a while to sort out all the straps, but when I had it all just right and snapped the double trees to the harrow, they snorted approval and leaned forward, anxious to get moving. I climbed onto the rusty iron seat, flicked the reins with a click of my tongue and a *gitty-up,* and off we went across the field, the harrow smoothing the soft silt from the river into a perfect seedbed. "Bub, you really have a way with horses," Dad said.

While I jiggled along on the harrow, Dad marched behind cranking the handle of our seeder, a canvas apparatus that hung against his chest like a modern-day baby pouch. For bigger seeds like oats, we borrowed Uncle Bill's wagon seeder, and Dad let me ride in the wagon using a pail to keep the hopper full of oats. But Dad said legume and grass seed was too tiny and too expensive to risk wasting with the big seeder. I liked to watch Dad adjust his pace and crank speed as he marched along, seeds shooting to the soil like swarms of microscopic bees. Every so often he stopped to give a particular spot an extra crank or two. He was determined to sow exactly the right number of seeds over each square inch of the field. When he was finished, he motioned me to give the field one more light harrowing, enough to cover the seeds with a quarter inch of soil and not a bit more.

A couple weeks after sowing, we walked through our new field marveling at the tiny filaments of green and silver emerging from the soil. Dad grinned and laughed out loud. "Boy did we get a good do. I think every seed germinated." Sometimes he paused, gazed up across the valley, and added, "This is what the world must have been like on the first day of creation."

Dad taught me to recognize the different varieties of legumes and grasses when their first shoots emerged. If Dad wanted a hayfield, he sowed alfalfa. If he wanted pasture, he sowed red clover because it was a biennial and would make good pig pasture for two years. Then it would give way to grasses for cow pasture. After a couple years of grass and cow manure adding nutrients to the soil, we plowed it all under and planted corn. Cow pasture had to be pure grass because cows could founder if they gorged themselves on alfalfa, red clover, or other legumes. Every year there were stories of farmers making that mistake and finding their cows flat on the ground, legs sticking straight out, dead as doornails.

We stepped carefully along the edges of new seeding, not wanting to crush webs of three-leaf clover and wisps of the new grass. Thick scents of humus and nitrogen hung in the air, assuring us we soon would have rugged plants strong enough to withstand heat, drought, hard freezes, and trampling hooves of hogs and cattle. Soon we would have windrows of alfalfa hay curing in preparation for the haymow, and clumps of mature grasses swaying in breezes that drifted through the valley. "New growth like this is a miracle, Bub," Dad said. "Anyone who denies there's a God in

Heaven needs to walk through a field like this." I remember him nodding down to me, a twinkle in his eye. I nodded back, and we kept walking, side by side.

Of all our jobs, my favorite was morning chores, especially in the busiest seasons when my dad got up before the sun and there was time for me to help before school started. I begged Dad to take me along, and he usually did. I'd be snuggled in my sheet blanket, drifting through dreams of horses, the river, the War, and a thousand other things, the images flashing with strange shapes and colors I barely remembered five seconds after I woke up. I'd be walking or running somewhere, pushing against a strange tug on my shoulder, a tug that refused to stop, insisting I open my eyes. I'd blink into dim light and see my dad's face just above me, his eyes bleary but perking up when our eyes met. He grinned and I felt myself grin back. Nothing mattered except being with my dad. "Hi Bub," he whispered. "If we hustle, we'll have time after chores for breakfast with Aunt Mabel and Uncle Bill." I feel those moments in the core of who I am, and realize so much was going on besides just learning how to farm.

I jumped out of bed, pulled on my bib-overalls and work shoes, and in a few minutes we were in the Model A, headed up the bottom road. Some mornings, pitch black blotted out the world, defying even the headlights from our car. It felt like we were driving off the edge of the earth. Sometimes the Milky Way hung in ink blue sky, reaching toward other stars poised above the eastern hills. Cool valley air rushed through open car windows. "Faster, faster," I yelled. I liked to stick my hands out the window and feel them fly with the breeze. Sometimes I stuck my head out too and imagined I was flying on a rocket.

After about a year of helping Dad with chores, I could do everything except milk the Guernsey cows. I dumped oats and black supplement into feeding bunks for the horses, pitched hay into mangers for the cows, tossed ears of corn to the sows, checked the feeders where the market hogs ate, and cleaned the water troughs. By my seventh birthday, Dad let me try milking when all my other chores were finished. He nailed one piece of two-by-four on another to make a stool the right height for me, and before long I could milk a cow about halfway, squeezing the rubbery teats with every ounce of strength I had, aiming white squirts at the bottom of a silver bucket. By my eighth birthday I could almost finish a cow, but not quite, and had to get up so Dad could squeeze out the last few squirts.

I think the cows appreciated the dawn as much as Dad and me. They nudged me with their white, bristly, damp noses when I released the wooden stanchion bars to turn them loose. They turned slowly, as if waiting for good instincts to kick in, their enormous eyes gazing through the gloom of the barn toward wispy morning light outside. They reared their heads in approval as Dad poured the morning's milk into ten-gallon cans and slammed the steel covers tight with the heel of his hand. Satisfied we were taking good care of their milk, the cows processed outside, pausing to gaze through the haze toward the river. They stomped and snorted. Then, tails hanging straight down, they formed a single file and headed east across the lot toward the pasture where they would graze and make more milk.

As we did our morning chores, Hilltop Farm gradually emerged, breaking through darkness and wisps of fog rising from the valley floor. It stood half a mile west of our farm on a the highest hill above the valley. For my branch of the Chambers clan, it was the home place where our generations often gathered on Sunday afternoons. Harlow Chambers, my great-grandfather, mined silver in Colorado in the 1860s, brought the money back to Iowa, and bought this land, three hundred and twenty acres running west from the river, across the flatland and up into the hills. He built his homestead at the crest, using lumber from the sawmill he operated with his father, Ezekiel. Respect hovered in the voices of my father, mother, and other adults when they talked about Hilltop Farm: respect for Harlow's accomplishments, for the beauty and fertility of this land, for family stories that unfolded here, and for Aunt Mabel and Uncle Bill who lived there now. "I thank my lucky stars," Dad said, "to have inherited eighty acres of Grandpa Harlow's farm."

Even when it was pitch black, I felt the presence of the Hilltop as I hurried with my chores. For some strange reason, I didn't like to look up there when it was hidden by the dark of night. So as I carried buckets of feed out to the livestock, I held my eyes in the valley, turned in the general direction of the river. Only when all the chores were finished, our last cow milked,

Dad lugging two ten-gallon cans of milk to the Model A, light spreading overhead, was I ready to gaze up at the hill. It was high and long, stretching as far as I could see from north to south, Hilltop the highest point in the middle. Sometimes Hilltop Farm blended into the western sky as if it had just arrived from a different world with the first rays of the dawn. Other times it nestled into the slope, outbuildings hiding in haze, the fresh whitewash of the house and barn shining through the gloom. I couldn't wait to get up there and look out over our farm, to pick out the white dot of our house at the north end of Anderson, and to follow the tree line of the Nishnabotna River till it disappeared in haze far off to the south.

As we drove across the bottom and up the hill, Dad's voice floated through the car like a hillbilly guitar easing into ballads. Sometimes he was happy; sometimes sad. The Model A's engine kept a steady beat in the background. He talked about problems with our farm and jobs he'd be doing later in the day. When things were going well, he told family stories, especially about Uncle Bill and my Grandpa Sam being partners, farming the land they and their sisters inherited. All four sisters lived away from Anderson at that time and were happy to rent their land to their brothers. Bill and Sam also bought the Anderson Store where Sam took the lead because he had a business head. Bill was the first to marry and start having kids, so they agreed he should live on the farm. Sam lived in Anderson, where he could keep an eye on the store and deal with salesmen.

A couple years later, Sam built our house at the north end of town and married my grandma. They had just one child, and then Sam died suddenly of meningitis when Dad was five. Dad's eyes got spooky when he talked about it. He stared at me, then out across the fields. "Thank the Good Lord I had Uncle Bill after I lost my dad. There's no way I'd have made it this far in life without him."

One particular summer morning stands out in my memory. I was about seven. The sun had just peeked above the horizon, and shadows still stretched across the fields as we headed west across the valley. I'd just watched our cows disappear into the shadows as they trudged out to the pasture. Hilltop had a strange look that morning; the house and barn seemed to rise up from the hill while the outbuildings and lots hung below, crumbling into nothingness. I sat on the Model A's torn front seat, pushing my feet against gunnysacks filled with oats, my chest pounding like a trip-hammer as Dad talked about his father dying. Steel cultivator shovels jiggled beside me on the car seat. I picked one up and twisted my fingers around its sharp edge. If my grandpa died when Dad was young, maybe Dad would die when I was young. How could a person's life suddenly be over like that? It wasn't fair. I wanted to jump out of the car and run, yelling up at God not to make my father die. But then I looked over at Dad, his hands like heavy ropes on the steering wheel. He looked back at me, I forced a smile, and he grinned back. His eyes gleamed into mine like they did every morning when he woke me up, and I knew he wasn't going to die.

Whether it was breakfast time or later in the day, Uncle Bill always saw us coming and waved as we turned in and putt-putted up his driveway. Usually he was coming from the lots and barn just below the lip of the hill, a lariat or halter in his hands. Sometimes he was working on his rusty red Farmall tractor or stepping out of the garage with a wrench or grease gun. Or he'd be at the well, one foot on the wooden curb, gazing out across the valley and the cornfields. He said no view in all the world compared with the view from up there, especially when the lines of willow and maple trees along the river changed colors in the sunlight, and the distant hills beyond the river rolled on forever.

"Good morning, Paul. Top of the day to you, Master Steve. Magnificent morning, wouldn't you say?" He held his black, curved pipe in one hand and tipped his straw hat or striped overall cap with the other, a twinkle in his light blue eyes. A tin of George Washington tobacco peeked from the bib pocket of his overalls.

"Mornin', Uncle," Dad answered. "Steve milked two cows this morning. Got all but the last four squirts."

"Then he's earned his breakfast. Mabel just called out that it's ready. Have a cup of water first, and we'll go in. This cup's good and rusty. Water always tastes best from a rusty cup." His voice sounded like Mr. Roosevelt's. Dignified, yet smooth and friendly.

His buddies nicknamed him "Buffalo" because he hunted buffalo out west with his father, Great-grandpa Harlow. I always thought there really was a certain buffalo look about him, even though he was tall and slim. Maybe it was the way he planted his feet squarely on the ground and looked you directly in the eye.

"Will you men get your rear ends in here? Everything's getting cold." It was Aunt Mabel, standing at the porch door, hands on husky hips, her face red and jolly. Of all the good cooks in Fremont County, Aunt Mabel was the best. Everyone agreed. Even her oatmeal was worth a twenty-mile drive. It teased your tongue, delicate and smooth, a distinct oat taste but sweeter than other oatmeal, like she'd mixed in flower blossoms.

Much as I liked the oatmeal, I liked Aunt Mabel's fresh rolls and homemade jam even more, especially her elderberry jam. And she cooked side pork so every morsel tasted like real meat, not cracklings. Dad and Uncle Bill loved it too, and taught me to dip it in oatmeal.

Sometimes my mother joined us for breakfast at Hilltop Farm. To make it in time, she had to rush through her morning chores for the four schoolteachers we boarded. Mom usually ate with a certain delicacy, but something about Aunt Mabel's yummy side pork made her dip it in oatmeal and gobble it down like the rest of us. Sometimes she giggled as she slurped the oatmeal. She always had a notebook in her dress pocket and was forever asking Aunt Mabel for cooking tips and writing them down. Mom told me once that her Aunt Mill and Lula Penn had been her best cooking teachers, but Aunt Mabel was even better. Uncle Bill thought Mom's cooking notebook was a great idea, and urged Aunt Mabel to teach Mom everything she knew. "Gotta pass that knowledge on, Mabel. Helen's turning into a fine cook, thanks in part to you. But now those daughters and daughters-in-law of ours, they're something else again." He shook his head sadly.

If we weren't in a rush, Dad and I did dishes while Uncle Bill chattered with Mom and Aunt Mabel. This was the best time of the day. Chores were finished, our bellies were full, and we had the whole day to look forward to. Jokes just bubbled out, especially from Aunt Mabel and Uncle Bill. She called him a fool for doing most of his farm work with horses and mules. He needed to modernize, she insisted, and buy more equipment for his old tractor. Even if he was partial to his horses, he owed it to their son Don to have a good tractor operation set up when he came home from the War. Uncle Bill tried to change the subject, and accused her of wasting time on too many putsy things around the house. She should spend more evenings sitting with him out by the well. They laughed as they argued, and when they got up from the table, one of them would say, "Would you ever have believed a woman and a man could be as happy as you and me?"

They teased about how they met. Uncle Bill called her a "city girl" because she grew up a police captain's daughter in South Omaha. She called him a "young ruffian who needed a dose of civilization." The friendship started when Lizzie, Uncle Bill's older sister, moved to South Omaha with her husband and two daughters and became friends with the Glovers. So in 1902 when Mabel Glover, still a high school girl, was looking for a good-paying summer job, Lizzie arranged for her to be cook and housekeeper for her widowed father, brothers, cousins, orphans, hired hands, and whoever else happened to be staying at Hilltop at the time. Mabel was an instant hit, especially with her skill in whipping the menfolk into shape. By the third summer she and Bill were together every chance they got. "Quite a story how you and I got sweet on each other," Uncle Bill mused.

"Friends is one thing, Bill," Mabel said with a grin, "but you were absolutely out of your head that night you proposed. We were just young kids."

"Well, it only took you half a second to accept," he shot back. Their eyes came together, serious now, his voice soft: "I wouldn't be worth a plugged nickel without you, Mabel."

Years later, one of their daughters told the part of the story they left out when they told it in front of me. Two days after their engagement, they took the train to Omaha to tell Captain and Mrs. Glover and receive their blessing. The parents were delighted. Uncle Bill thanked them for accepting him into their family and added, "I feel very fortunate. You two have raised quite a daughter."

"That she is," Captain Glover answered. "I'm sure you realize she has lots of spirit. She'll keep you on your toes. But then you've got plenty of spirit yourself. You two make a fine couple."

"Well, I'm the fortunate one. Mabel has a quick mind, treats others with respect, and, as you indicate, is full of the dickens. And her cooking is out of this world. In fact, just the other evening I said to her, 'Mabel, after the fine supper you've just cooked, I want you to know you're welcome to crawl into my bed anytime you want.' We thought about that a while, and decided we'd better get ourselves up here and make sure you approve."

When we had the breakfast dishes washed and put away, one of the adults would announce, "Let's go stand by the well a few minutes. I'm not quite ready to take on the day's work." This was my signal to race outside. I dashed through the porch, banged the screen door open, took two jumps down the sidewalk, and landed on the well curb. I liked to grab hold of the iron pump and swing myself toward the valley while the others caught up.

We stood there side by side, three generations, sweaty, muscles a little sore from our first duties of the day, gazing at the wondrous scene unfolding across our valley. My mother usually was the first of us to gasp out loud. Suddenly, like we were seeing it for the first time ever, the sun suddenly popped up from the horizon, sending streaks of red and orange through the clouds. If conditions were just right, shafts of gold danced across the land. As we watched, the sky softened into baby blue, and the land responded with gleams of ivory, rose, brown, and every shade of green.

It's been sixty years now since those mornings when we gathered at the well on Hilltop Farm. Yet I often feel I'm there again, especially when I walk along the paths I made with Jack and Anna. The oak trees of our woods in Minnesota become maples and cottonwoods, and I'm beside the Nishnabotna, its strong brown current flowing past our Iowa farm. To the west, towering above the flat fields where I used to work beside my father, the highest hill marks the spot where Great-grandpa Harlow's well and buildings used to stand, before new owners tore them down. Rich scents from another harvest fill the air, and where I stand among the trees, brown and yellow leaves tumble gracefully to the earth.

Some mornings as we stood up there gazing out across this valley, the sun suddenly burst up and over the horizon with such intensity that our cows and barn, even the windmill, disappeared into a silver sea. I blinked and squinted, but couldn't see a thing.

"Just be patient, Master Steve," Uncle Bill instructed. "Your eyes will adjust. I'll show you."

With a nod his eyes met mine. Then he closed his eyes and turned, directly into the sun, angles of his long face relaxed despite the glare. He stood like that about a minute. "Now watch," he said. "Make a very tiny squint, hold it a few seconds and let the light ease in, then open ever so little more.

Then again. And again." As I watched, I sensed my own eyes adjusting with his, a hint of light blue appearing through his lids—eyes from all our generations.

I squinted, blinked, peeked at my uncle's eyes, and squinted again. Gradually, the world below began to reappear; tan dots of cows spreading over a light green sea of pasture that splashed against a darker sea of corn. Just beyond, tall blurs of maples and cottonwoods marked the river's course. And the river flows on through the valley it has formed.

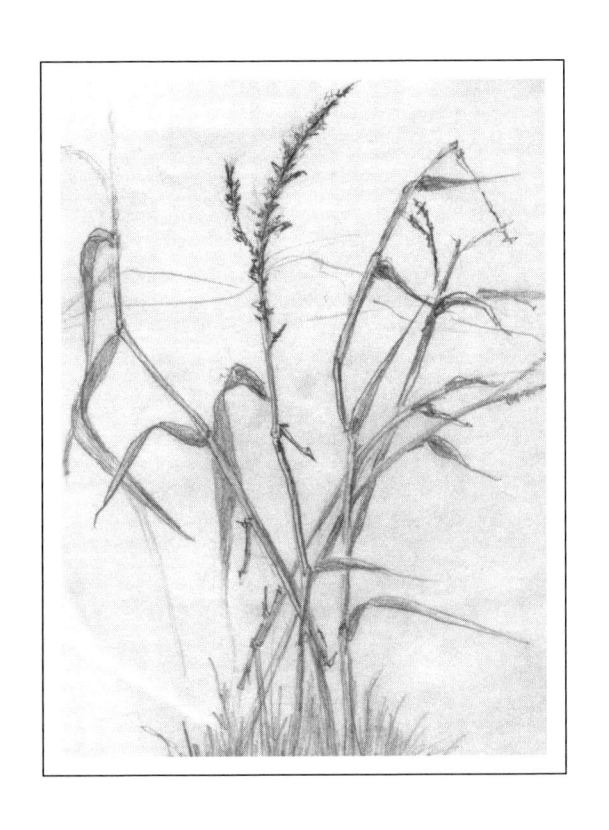

At the Edge

MARGARET SMITH

MARGARET SMITH has been having a contest with a younger member of this writers' group to see who can forget the most. Now, at the age of eighty-five, Margaret has discovered that most of those things are not worth remembering after all. On the other hand, Margaret says she will never forget her many years working in the peace movement and for other causes and candidates, including her own unsuccessful run for the Minnesota State Legislature.

This memoir is based on an event at the Weisman Art Museum in the spring of 2000.

T̲his morning I'm on my way to the kitchen. The first thing I'll do is open the curtains and let in the new day. As I move past the table and reach for the cord, I remember that I have been opening and closing these curtains every day for forty years. It is such a simple act, pulling the cord to open the curtains and see the morning. It is so familiar, so comfortable. This simple ritual has become a thankful reminder of our rootedness in this lovely, familiar place.

These curtains have been here as long as we have, but I have no interest in redecorating. There is no reason to throw them away and buy new. They are just right for my kitchen and for me. They have an intriguing Oriental design of plum blossoms and Chinese calligraphy that makes me think of faraway, exotic places. I love those little mind-voyages out of my kitchen. When I first saw this colorful print in a fabric store, I bought the material without thinking twice, and I still love it.

Thinking about living here for forty years does make me stop and wonder. Eventually we will have to sell our house. I worry that potential buyers might be turned off by the mismatched colors of my kitchen appliances. I tell myself that whoever buys this house will probably rip out the kitchen and put in whatever is new and fashionable that year.

These days I have stopped talking to my husband about selling this house now. He designed it and watched it being built. It has become part of us and our lives, and we love living here. From time to time I do worry about what would happen if one of us got sick or became disabled and could not climb the stairs to our second-floor bedroom. That makes me think about how hard it would be for me to do all the sorting, packing, and moving that might suddenly become necessary.

A few years ago some of our longtime friends moved to a senior condo. I listened to their enthusiastic descriptions of their easy, maintenance-free life in their condo. I repeated these stories to my husband. "We've got to admit we're getting older. Wouldn't it be wonderful to have everything taken care of for us?" I asked, using my most persuasive voice. "Maybe we should think about moving to a condo." My husband laid down the book he was reading and listened to me describe the advantages of condo life. Then he grinned at me and said, "You'll have to go without me. I'm not moving out of here until I am carried out in a box." We both laughed. After all these fifty-seven years of living together, we don't even want to think about living without each other. We plan to live here until we decide we are ready to call it quits. Then together we will move on to the next stage. At least, that's what we have in mind. We'll work out the details later.

My husband is ninety-three, still full of energy and drive. He still teaches one economics course each semester at the University. He is a serious man with deep, compassionate concerns about the problems of our world. When he was growing up, his mother often said to him, "You can't solve a problem by fighting about it." That made a deep and lasting impression on him. It led him into a lifelong search for peaceful ways to solve problems.

He looks much the same as he has always looked. He is a man of medium height, with dark hair that is now finally graying. He usually wears a serious expression in public, but in private his sense of humor delights me, as we laugh and joke together. His face has a few wrinkles, but he does not give the impression of being an elderly man. His brisk walk and active, challenging mind are those of a much younger man. Although now slightly stooped, he engages life with vigor and audacity. Just ask any of his students.

I, at eighty-five, am more and more aware of how much I have changed. My hair used to be a shiny dark brown. It was thick and soft, and curled easily, but it is now mostly white, very thin and limp. I can't do anything with it, so I simply wear it cut short. In the last few years, I've been surprised to find some of my most valued possessions—my eyesight, my memory and my hearing—simply fading away, like color photos left out in the sun too long. I am helpless to stop their silent, mysterious disappearance. It feels like a thief in the night has stolen my most precious jewels. Sometimes I am angry at this fading away of myself when I feel so young. Other times tears rise in my eyes as I feel the approach of old age. But occasionally an old Sunday School song from my childhood pops unbidden into my mind. Then I hum the part I remember: "...there is a joy, joy, joy, joy deep in my heart, deep in my heart, deep in my heart today." Often I have to remind myself to tap into that joy, but it's there, ready to flow through me, lifting my spirits and chasing away the blues.

After all these personal losses, I ask myself what is left. Let's see. I still have a good grip on my sense of humor. I rejoice in the memories I have left, and the family and friends who surround me with love and care. On the whole, I am a very fortunate woman, but I am surprised by two things. I am seven years younger than my husband and I am still surprised that he has more energy than I do and that I have more white hair than he has.

I go into the kitchen and pull the cord. The curtains slide open, and the outside world appears. It often reveals a rosy sunrise behind the line of oak trees, their long, early morning shadows streaking across the lawns.

My view from the windows shows me only a small piece of the world, of course, but I know the rest of it—our big, beautiful planet—is out there, waiting. I smile a little to myself, thinking of some special places I love. Today I am not thinking of visiting any of those places. Today I am content to glance out at the nearest suburban backyards and check the weather.

My mood often changes depending on what I see when I open the curtains. A gleaming new layer of snow and ice coating every twig is a fairyland delight. The roiling purple and red clouds of a November sunset stir my fantasies.

Today, in the middle of April, I am simply hoping for a heavy downpour of rain. The dry grass and shrubs and trees are desperate for a big drink of water. The world will look so new and refreshed after a spring rain.

My husband and I like to eat lunch at the table by the kitchen windows. This week we watch the pair of mallards that return every spring, like clockwork, to the pond next door. Our neighbor's large back lawn has a low area in the middle and a pond forms there from the runoff of melting snow or from a heavy spring rain.

Last week we had snow, this week we have a pond, and the two ducks appear, waddling quietly out of the little woods in the back. We both delight in our closeness to this bit of wildlife, and we watch together as the mallards peck through the grass or glide slowly across the pound. We like the male's glistening wardrobe of brightly colored feathers, and I question the unfairness of the female wearing such drab colors. But Mother Nature apparently knows what she's doing. The ducks seem to enjoy the pond. We wonder what they think when their pond slowly disappears into the ground.

Yesterday their peaceful world was interrupted by an intruder. Mr. and Mrs. Duck were pecking in the grass, about twenty feet apart. Intruder Duck, decked out in his finest feathers, strolled casually out of the woods and toward the pond.

He stopped. Mr. and Mrs. Duck both stopped pecking and looked at him. Intruder Duck moved a few steps toward Mrs. Duck. Mr. Duck moved several steps toward Intruder Duck. Intruder stepped a little closer. Again Mr. Duck moved toward him. Each time Intruder Duck moved closer to Mrs. Duck, Mr. Duck stepped closer to him.

We were fascinated, almost holding our breaths. I have to admit that I didn't really see this drama with my own eyes, because my eyes now see very poorly. My husband described the ducks' activity to me and I saw it with my mind's eye, which is still sharp and clear. Mrs. Duck stood absolutely still, watching both of the male ducks. I wondered if she was trying to decide which one she would choose. Intruder Duck waited a few more minutes, looking steadily at Mrs. Duck. Finally Intruder Duck made one more effort and got too close. Mr. Duck ran at him, quacking loudly. Intruder Duck turned and walked back towards the woods.

From that moment on, Mr. Duck stayed close to his ladylove, never leaving her side for an instant. We actually breathed a sigh of relief.

This morning I open the curtains and am surprised to see heavy gray clouds pressing down on us, darkening my whole world. I banish the dark in the kitchen with a flick of my finger. Instantly light blooms, filling the kitchen and reflecting off the windows. Unlike my iris and peonies, which need the long, dark season to rest and to prepare for their time of blossoming, I need light every day. When shafts of bright, white light pour through my windows they fill me with delight and renew my energy, A day full of light seems full of possibilities. I feel cozy and safe in my bright kitchen, with the calendar promising spring and long hours of daylight.

But when I close my curtains at night I know the darkness is out there, pressing against my windows, hiding the unknown. Even when I was a child darkness made me uneasy. Now darkness in the small hours of night, when I am seeking sleep, often brings thoughts of regret, missed opportunities, and mistakes I have made.

I need to get out of this dark mood. I pick up yesterday's mail and begin to sort it. I flip quickly through the flyers and ads, tossing them into the wastebasket. I am going so quickly I almost miss the pale lavender invitation card. I pick it out of the wastebasket.

The card announces: "Give Sorrow Words: Passages of Grieving. A Reading of Original Prose and Poetry." The reading will be at the Weisman Art Museum, on Thursday, April 26, at 7 p.m. I look at the card again: "Give Sorrow Words, a Reading." I've been working at being a writer off and on for many years and I've come to appreciate what a precious gift words can be. Perhaps these writers can inspire us to speak our own feelings more openly, to give our own words to our sorrows and joys and longings. I look at the names of the writers who will read and recognize one of them. His wife, Nancy, died from cancer at the age of 50. He will read from "Love Letters," a collection he has written to Nancy since her death.

Nancy was a special friend of mine, the most spiritual woman I have ever known. I am eager to hear his love letters, to share in the memories, perhaps to feel her spirit there with us. For a few minutes I wonder whether I really want to listen to the other readers' stories of friends dying with AIDS or cancer, because I know I will start to cry. I feel tears rising in my eyes now, just thinking about all that pain. But perhaps many of the people around me will also be crying. I decide not to worry about it. Besides, there is no way to hear the "Love Letters" to Nancy without also listening to the other readers. I hope I can learn something about expressing feelings from these writers. I walk to my desk and prop up the lavender invitation card next to the phone, where I will see it every day. I don't want to forget it.

I am eighty-five years old, and I need to prepare for the endings that lie on the road ahead of me. I had always hoped that anticipating how to deal with shock and trauma would soften the sorrows that come to us. But thus far in my life, it seems to me that nothing can soften the devastation of a loved one's death. I have also discovered that is not the end of it, that the pain from remembering the unfinished business of life grows even stronger as years pass.

As I sit there my mind roams out and away, back into the years, and I think of my beloved older brothers, Joe and Bill. The memories pour in and I can't sit still. I have to move, I have to get up and walk around to deal with the ache that fills me. I can hardly believe that they have both been dead for so many years. So many things were left unsaid, left undone. For many, many years I believed that "Words should not be spoken unless they are true, kind, and necessary." In the face of those three rigorous tests, I had left unsaid many important things. I had never even told my brothers I loved them. I hold my head and rub my face with both hands. My tears start to flow. We were playmates and good friends when we were growing up. I admired them and looked up to them, following their lead in everything we did. But by the time we were in our late twenties we had scattered across the country, deep in our busy lives, and growing apart in our interests.

Always in the back of my mind there was a belief that sometime soon we would all get together for a great reunion. Perhaps we would go, together with our own families, to the annual Guthrie family reunion on the Riggs' farm in southeastern Ohio.

I imagined it would be just like old times. The day before the reunion we would make the five gallons of homemade fresh peach ice cream just like Mother always made for the family reunion. I remember Mother peeling and cutting up baskets of fresh peaches. She put the peaches, milk, cream, and sugar in a metal canister that fit inside a yellow wooden tub. Next she inserted the metal dasher, with its four blades, into the mixture in the canister. Then she put on the lid, and fitted the crank into its slot on top of the canister. Then we packed chunks of ice and rock salt around the canister, filling the tub up to the top.

I remember that Bill and I took turns at working the heavy metal crank as it turned the dasher blades, constantly mixing the ingredients. As the ice melted, Joe added more ice and salt to the tub. When I was a kid, I always believed the rock salt was used to keep the ice from melting too fast. Now I know that the salt and ice water together formed a freezing mixture around the metal canister, cold enough to freeze the ice cream. When it began to freeze and the cranking got hard, Joe and Mother took over that work. Finally, the mixture had been transformed into smooth, delicious ice cream and we got our reward! Mother removed the handle, took off the lid of the metal canister, and pulled out the dasher, with some ice cream still clinging to its blades. Mother would not allow us to lick the ice cream off the dasher. Instead we scraped it off with spoons, battling to get our share. Then the lid was put back on the canister and ice and rock salt packed into the tub again. The tub was put in a cool area in the basement with a covering of old blankets to keep the cold in until the next day.

The yellow tub always rode to the reunion on the floor behind the front seat, with my brothers and me on the back seat, squirming to make room for our legs and for the tub. In my memory it was always a bright, hot day in August when we loaded up the car, crossed the bridge into Ohio, and headed north on a road that followed all the bends and curves of the Ohio river. In those days it was at least a two-hour drive on poor roads before we spotted the sign for the tiny township of Raccoon Island. In a few more minutes we drove up the gravel road to the Riggs' home, spewing a cloud of dust behind us, and waving gaily to all the others on the porch and the lawn. Children playing in the barn and hayloft saw our cloud of dust and came running to find out who the new arrivals were. They clustered around the men lifting the ice cream tub out of the car and carrying it to the shaded back porch. They set it down next to a washtub containing a fifty-pound block of ice covered with a heavy piece of canvas. As the day and the heat wore on, more ice and salt were added to the tub as needed.

The big picnic dinner would not be served until mid-afternoon. The adults spent their time sitting on the porch or strolling across the lawn, chatting with relatives they had not seen or spoken to for at least a year.

The house was set on top of a small hill, giving us a pleasant view of the cornfields across the road and the river beyond that. A huge oak tree with two swings hanging from its lowest branches stood where the ground dropped away sharply, giving swinging youngsters the delicious sensation of flying out into space.

Even though I was busy with the other girls, I remember noticing that many of the men and women seemed to be waiting to speak to my Dad, Dr. Joe. They hung around near him, talking, in groups of two or three. Whenever one person finished talking with him and walked away, someone else hurried up to Dad for his or her private conversation.

In those days most of the men and women who came to the family reunion were farmers, who might not have seen a doctor from one year's end to the next. My Dad was one of their own, because he also grew up on a "poor dirt" farm in southeastern Ohio. Somehow he and a friend had gotten on a train to Baltimore in 1902, and found their way to the medical school at the University of Maryland. Dad always enjoyed telling us how those two farm boys walked from the train station to the medical school. There someone directed them to the office. They each laid down five dollars on the wood counter and Dad said, "We've come to go to medical school." Now he had his M.D. and he was back, eager to help anyone he could.

On this day the men and women at the family reunion could talk to Dad without having to spend hours on country roads driving to his clinic. Playing nearby with the Riggs girls, I could hear the gruff worried tones of the men as they described their aches and pains. I could see the women whispering to Dad, their eyes looking down in embarrassment as they forced themselves to ask their private questions, their hands twisting together.

I could hear Dad's low, reassuring talk with the men as he tried to diagnose and to encourage at the same time. I noticed he always clapped the men on the back when they had finished talking. When a woman came up to him, hesitant and unsure of herself, he took her hand and smiled gently at her. Sometimes he asked about her children while she struggled to compose herself. They usually walked away smiling, reassured, even when Dad had told them to come to the clinic, maybe spend a day or two in the hospital.

Dad took time to go with the men and boys to the barn to see the horses and the tractor, and out to the fields to look at the crops. Other than that, he spent most of the day talking with individuals. Dad told some of them they should come to the clinic for an exam and one of the newfangled X-rays.

For others he recommended a medicine. He understood their struggles to survive and never talked about payment for his advice that day. When any of the farmers came to the Guthrie Hospital, they always brought something for the hospital kitchen, a ham or bushel baskets of freshly picked corn. The wives brought their preserves and jelly, or freshly gathered eggs, and, occasionally, for my mother, a handmade quilt.

Mother had never lived on a farm. Her father had been a high school principal in a small town in West Virginia and her artistic mother made pottery in her own kiln and painted lovely flower designs on china. But Mother knew how to work. When she was a girl, her mother taught her how to keep house, to cook and sew, and to preserve food. It was taken for granted that these were essential skills for girls, to prepare them to take care of their future families.

I remember Mother spending most of her time at the reunion in the kitchen with Mrs. Riggs, enjoying her bright, bubbly personality, as the women got the dinner ready. Mother also had a great talent for organizing, for seeing that everything was done perfectly and on time. I imagine she simply walked into the kitchen and started organizing all the food brought by the Guthrie women. I remember platters of pickled watermelon rind and loaves of salt-rising bread. There were piles of fried chicken, sliced hams, corn on the cob, tomatoes, rolls, watermelon, cookies, pies, and cakes, all topped off with our peach ice cream.

I popped into the kitchen occasionally, to see how the dinner was coming along. I also learned to get out again quickly, so Mother wouldn't see me and put me to work.

The day ended with the long drive home and sometimes a flat tire on an isolated stretch of the gravel road. That meant that Joe crawled under the car and placed the jack under the rear axle. Then Dad cranked up the jack, hoisting the rear of the car about a foot off the ground. Then Dad and the boys took off the flat tire and put on the spare. Sometimes the spare tire had lost some of its air, so the boys got out the hand pump and pumped more air into its inner tube. Then they forced the tire onto the wheel, getting their fingers pinched in the process. It was at least an hour or more before we were on our way home again.

The quiet dusk came on. By the time we had gotten home the stars were out, their fascinating constellations lighting up the sky. I never tired of studying the night sky, finding the Big and Little Dippers and the North Star, Orion, Arcturus, Cassiopeia's Chair, and all the rest of them. I felt as though I knew all about those brilliant constellations because I read and reread the ancient myths for which they were named.

Even now, on summer nights I walk out onto our second-story deck, lean against its white wood railing and search the night skies. Nowadays there is nothing to see, unless the moon is out, or a dot of fast-moving light swings by on its way to the airport. I long for my glittering stars and complain to my husband about the blanket of light pollution that is hiding them.

Sadly, my hoped-for family reunion of adult brothers and sisters never happened. The years came and went like ghosts flying with the wind.

My brothers and I rarely saw each other, all of us so scattered around the country and so immersed in our busy lives we never made time for a reunion of the whole family. We always thought there would be another time we would all be together, but it never happened. I wonder what were the last words I said to Joe and to Bill. Probably just "See you!"

How I wish I had thrown my arms around each of them and said, "I love you." I find myself wondering if there is any way to heal that emptiness and regret. Now that Joe and Bill are gone, the regret is more poignant than ever. Instead of disappearing as time goes on, that ache comes back at odd times, when I least expect it. I look back and wonder what kept us from sharing our feelings. It's true that in those days the rules for polite conversation were strict. Any expression of intimate feelings in public was unacceptable.

In our family there was not much conversation at all, except as we children chattered to each other. Dad did talk about his cases at the hospital, but that did not lead to much conversation until my brothers got older and became interested in Dad's medical practice. Mother was a woman of few words, frequently emphasizing orders to us kids about how to do something. As I got older, I wondered if Mother was holding something back, because so often her lips were pressed tightly together. I can only guess at what it could have been.

It is time for me to go to the reading at the Weisman. I leave for the "Give Sorrow Words" program on one of our loveliest evenings, fragrant with the fresh, sweet smells of summer. On the way, my clear view of the twilight sky delights me with its wonderful blueness beginning to darken into dusk. Pink and rose clouds ride low on the horizon, edged with golden light pouring from the sun setting behind them.

The Weisman is the art museum on the Minneapolis campus of the University of Minnesota. It is an unusual building, as it presents two distinct personalities. The east side faces the Minneapolis campus and shows a demure, matter-of-fact reflection in red brick of the other University buildings around it. The west side, sitting on a bluff that looks down on the Mississippi River and across to the West Bank campus, is a wild, stick-in-your-eye, I'm-desperate-for-attention collection of pock-marked, shiny aluminum curves, angles, domes, scrolls, corners, twists, and turns. When its irregularly placed lights turn on at dusk, the face of the Tin Woodman from Oz seems to appear on the west side of the art museum, floating in the night sky. He is keeping an empty eye on the barge traffic moving down the river below him. The Scarecrow and the Cowardly Lion are nowhere to be seen. I find the meeting room on the second floor of the Weisman and am surprised to see the seventy-five chairs quickly filling up. The invitation says this reading is presented in conjunction with an exhibition from The Smithsonian Institute called "Hospice: A Photographic Inquiry." Perhaps many of those gathering here are people involved in local hospice programs.

I find a seat in the second row of folding chairs and look around the room. I glance cautiously at nearby faces, wondering who has come to this reading. I try not to stare, then I realize no one will pay any attention to me. In the last few years my hair gradually turned white and announced my passage into the dreaded Land of the Older Woman, the Invisible. Even though I am friendly, active, outgoing, and love to laugh, many younger people, store clerks, waiters, and others look through me as though I am invisible. I wonder if I behaved the same way when I was young, when I could never think of myself as getting old. I wonder if this happens only in America. Friends who have traveled there tell me Hawaiians celebrate, revere, and honor their elderly. All of us oldsters would appreciate being treated like that. Even a smile, a pleasant "Hi," a recognition that we exist, would brighten our day.

I look around the room and see all kinds of people. All ages are here, all shades of skin color, all kinds of dress from formal business suits and ties to T-shirts and pierced lips. What a wild variety of faces and ages. I smile to myself at some of the extreme statements on the T-shirts, and think about the pleasure those young people derive from such challenges to us oldsters. I have to admit I'm concerned about the pierced lips, pierced ears, pierced fingers. Self-mutilation has usually been a sign of religious frenzy or mental illness. I hope it is neither of these, that it is merely an extreme form of youthful rebellion.

Only one thing is missing in this room. In this art museum, there is no art on these walls for us to enjoy. I am here a half hour early, and I would have liked to have some art (other than the T-shirts) to look at. But I see we are not in one of the art galleries. We are in a smaller space that has been created with temporary walls, partitions on rollers. Probably it is easiest to move the partitions around without anything attached to them.

Facing the audience, on a low platform, are four chairs and four microphones. The four writers come in and take their places. One after another, they read their moving words, remembering loved ones suffering through prolonged deaths from cancer and AIDS. The "Love Letters" to Nancy are tender, passionate, and heartrending. Most shocking, because it is unexpected, is the death of one writer's son. Her only child, he was killed in a rescue mission on Mount Rainier, where he was working as a junior ranger, a summer employee. My heart aches for the reader, the mother, as I listen to her describe the numbing phone call from the ranger station. The officer reported that her son and another young man, both less experienced summer workers, volunteered to try to rescue two stranded climbers at night. When they were at 13,200 feet, before they reached the stranded men, a sudden violent storm swept away the two young men. They fell 1200 feet down the face of the mountain. The officer said her son's body was so badly broken, his face so mutilated, that the chief ranger, in his kindness, recommended that the young man's body be cremated and the remains shipped home to her. In the shock and confusion of the moment, she agreed that was the right thing to do. She reads of her pain and her persistent regret that she was not able to see her son, her only child, once more, not to touch his body ever again.

There is not a rustle in the room. Only the reader's voice stirs the silence. Then she stops. Sorrow packs the room, expanding like a pool of water that is freezing solid. No one can move. We sit like carved ice sculptures, frozen in our grief for her.

In the stillness, my own restless dead begin to move before my eyes. I see my dead father, lying in his open casket at a funeral home in my hometown in West Virginia. I had received the phone call about his sudden heart attack less than three days before the funeral, and my family and I had a difficult, exhausting trip to get there in time. I rested my hand on the edge of his casket as I looked into the face of the kind, gentle, patient, loving man who had been my father. I wondered if he understood how much I admired and appreciated him. Tears rose in my eyes and I had to grab the edge of the coffin as a wave of faintness swept through me. Perhaps young people will never appreciate their parents until the young ones have gotten married, or until they have reached middle age or even not until after their parents have died.

I thought of all the years after I was married, when I couldn't seem to find the time to write letters to my father. Now I am so sorry. I never intended to neglect him. It just happened.

Now my children say, "Why didn't you just phone him?" I try to explain that I did phone home for occasional brief talks, but in those days a long-distance phone call was expensive, and rarely used except for emergencies. They don't really understand because they are members of the cell phone generation.

I say good-bye to Dad, and join the rest of my family where they are sitting. Mother has been greeting friends as they arrived, and she now sits down with me. She is dry-eyed, as I expected. She never wants to show her emotions. Perhaps that is the only way she can cope with them. The only one in our small family group who might be crying is my brother Bill, who spent his life as a doctor working with my father at his hospital, and knew him best. Bill is sitting with his head down and one hand shading his face.

I bring my thoughts back to the present, to the readings we have just heard. In some profound way all of us in that room shared in the healing power of writers reading aloud the words of their sorrow and their survival. We are no longer frozen in our seats in a quiet, listening room. We burst into applause for four survivors who have shown us strength and resilience.

Everyone moves, talks, starts down the hall. I join the crowd heading for the galleries to see the hospice photographs. Men, women, and children flow in and out of rooms lined with photographs of faces: they are the faces of hospice patients, caregivers, relatives, and friends. The photographs are tender, sad, honest, sensitive, full of love. Sometimes there is a note of joy, as in the delighted smiles of two little girls, leaning against their grandmother's bed, who are pleased to have their picture taken. They are not aware that death hovers close to them.

We move slowly, caught in a knot of people who start and stop, start and stop, wanting to move on but captured by each image. Each stop is a challenge to look into the eyes of a patient, perhaps a child dying of cancer, or a young man with AIDS, or an elderly woman who is reduced to skin and bones. At each stop we feel a continual admiration for the caregivers who tend their patients so gently, for the family and friends who are with them, for the courage of the patients themselves.

All around me handkerchiefs are coming out of pockets and purses, wiping the tears, wiping the sorrow. Many visitors are volunteers at hospices, or are professional caregivers, or are people whose dearest relatives and friends have died in a hospice somewhere. Many times in their lives they have looked death in the face. Yet here they are, again, to look into the eyes of the dying and to pay tribute to the spirit that loves and comforts them to the end.

At the end of the exhibit, I step out from the last gallery into a large hall, and find I am alone for the moment. Confronting me is a huge artwork, centered in a large open space. I look up at two enormous sails, or wings, made of a mottled gold material, with curving and ribbed panels that are almost translucent. They remind me of oddly angled sails on small boats plying the Nile or the Yangtze Rivers, or, more appropriately, the River Styx, that gateway to the other world.

Enclosed between the sails and resting on the floor is a pedestal holding a container of water. A pamphlet tells me this is a participatory artwork, titled "Casting Off the Unspoken Words." I pause to consider my own unspoken words.

The pamphlet describing the artwork invites me to use the specially treated paper to write about my feelings, either about the exhibit, or about a painful loss in my life, and then to cast off my own unspoken words by dropping the paper into the water. The pamphlet promises the words will float off the paper and disappear. I wonder if this can really help me find closure. Or whether this is just a magic trick, something about the graphite in the pencil lead not adhering to the special paper. I want to know! Eagerly I look around for the paper but there is none. I am so let down and disappointed. I shake my head and mutter to myself as I continue to wander around the exhibit, hoping to find some paper that I missed the first time. The crowds of people at the exhibit tonight must have used it all up. I leave immediately, feeling there is nothing left to see or learn there.

In an hour I am home again, sitting alone with my disappointment in front of our cold fireplace. I recognize now that the tears shed when Joe and Bill died were not enough for healing. Now I need to find another way to send on the words I feel. I pick up a piece of ordinary paper and a pen; I hesitate between memories. Then quickly I write a few words to Joe. It is not enough for everything I wish I had said to him before he died, too young, two thousand miles away, with that terrible cancer on his spinal nerve. The note does not say enough but it says the most important thing, and that will have to do for now. I am eager to bring these words to life and send them out into that other world. I pick up another small piece of plain paper and think about Bill. He, too, died of cancer. I write the same message that I wrote to Joe.

I hold the two pieces of plain white paper in the cup of my hand for a minute, reading aloud the words I have written: "Dear Joe, I love you so much. Margaret Ann," and "Dear Bill, I love you so much. Margaret Ann."

Slowly, silently, a strange warmth creeps into my palm and fills my hand. I am startled by this unusual, unexpected sensation. It feels like it is a response to my two messages, before I have even sent them.

I close my fingers to hold that warmth close to me as I think about Joe and Bill.

"Kneel always when you light a fire," I have been told. So, with some effort and with a match in my hand, I kneel down in front of the fireplace.

It is spring, so the hearth has been swept clean of all the ashes from the winter's fires.

I lay my messages to Joe and to Bill on the bricks. I light the match, and touch the flame to the two papers. They both blaze bright for a few seconds, then fall into a tiny pile of ash. I kneel there watching the ashes settle down. Two wisps of smoke float up the chimney with a faint aroma of burning paper.

My words are at the edge, on their way into the mysterious other. In this moment I am filled with a sense of love and healing that eases my regret. Sorrow slowly begins to give way to acceptance and finally I am at peace with myself and my memories.

It has been a long journey. Sorrow and regret cling to us in ways we do not expect, their pain staining the fabric of our everyday lives. That stain will taint our lives until we deal with it, acknowledge it with our own words of sorrow. Then we will find acceptance and peace, the most precious gifts of all.

Promises

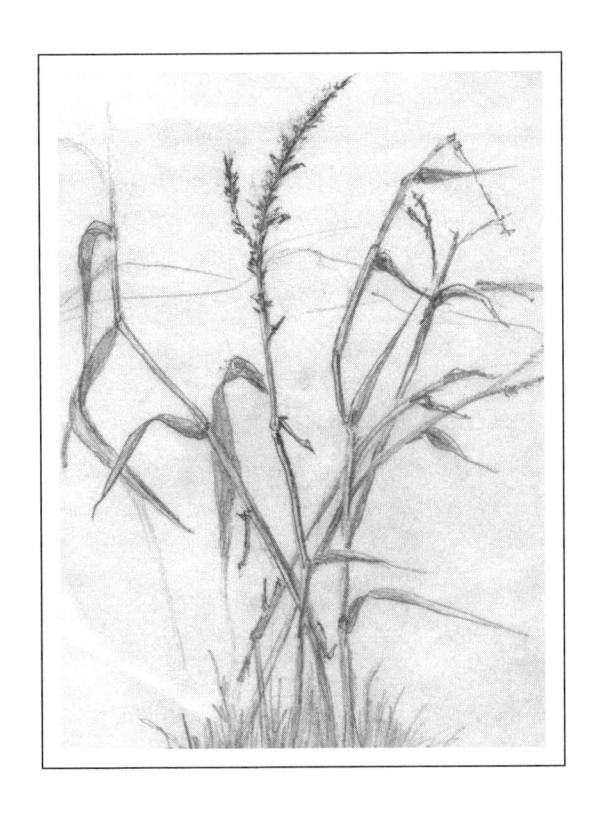

LOIS SEVERSON

I used to write for money, lots of money. I actually begged for this money from foundations, corporations, and governments. In those days I thought the begging was noble because I believed I was saving women's lives; like Scheherazade I had to be persuasive and always timely or meet a cruel fate.

Now I spend hours writing stories that come from my memories and my imagination. I am able to sit here as long as it takes to journey through the twists and turns of my story. I can start a pot of stew and write while it is simmering and the winter sky is slowly darkening. Nora is snoring comfortably at my feet, reminding me that there are no longer any fateful deadlines.

It is autumn on a small farm near the Saint Croix River Valley. Jessie is eighty years old. She has been struggling to keep the farm going since her husband John died, but she stubbornly refuses to leave. A stranger (Kenneth) walks onto her land looking for work. He has been sent by one of Jessie's neighbors to help her with the fall farm work. He stays on in a small cabin near Jessie's farmhouse.

A storm begins the day after Thanksgiving. It blows and howls about the old house for two days. Late on the second night, Kenneth is led back to the house by Jessie's anxious dog Nora. He finds Jessie lying on the floor close to death from what he believes is a heart attack. Kenneth, who has served in Viet Nam as a medic, is able to keep Jessie alive until help arrives. While Kenneth sits beside Jessie and waits for help, we find out that he has lost contact with his own family since the war. He has lived a lonely life tortured by memories of the war and has drifted from place to place, never settling down with a family of his own. Now, with Jessie so close to death, he is suddenly afraid of losing her and the contentment he has found in this peaceful place.

K ENNETH CAME QUIETLY INTO THE DIMLY LIT HOSPITAL ROOM and when he saw Jessie's face, he felt a sudden stab of fear. Her eyes were folded closed like dusty moth's wings and her face was placid as still water, as if all the pain of eighty years had been smoothed away. He looked anxiously at the monitor above the bed. The bright jagged lines still moved up and down and told him that that her heart was still beating, but somehow he felt it was only a faint whisper of what she really needed. Finally, he let go of a deep sigh and eased himself into a chair to wait and watch over Jessie for as long as she might need him. Slowly he tried to lighten the gloom that was still clutched in his chest.

After awhile Jessie opened her eyes. She searched his face as if she didn't know who he was. "I..." her voice caught before it left her throat, "I've been..." She struggled again for a breath and said no more.

"Jessie," he paused and wondered if she knew who he was. "I'm here now, to take you home." Jessie heard Kenneth's voice as a low comforting rumble in her ear. "I brought your dog with me too." He went on. "We have been here most of the night waiting for you. I wanted to see how you were, and hear your voice." He stopped and took a deep breath. "Well, the nurse told me you needed to see me."

Jessie's eyes followed the movement of his lips. She frowned a little and looked puzzled at what he was telling her. "Nora, here?" she tried to ask, but her voice didn't make any sound.

Her eyes were the deep clear color of a newborn baby's and she looked slowly around the room as if she was seeing it for the first time.

"I had to put Nora back in the truck for awhile, you know they don't allow dogs up here much." Kenneth smiled at her, "But she was so quiet.

You know how good she minds, and I guess she was wanting to see you too."

Jessie listened to him and tried to understand. She felt the rough comfort of his voice and she could smell the cold winter smell on him as he leaned close to her, wet wool and tobacco smoke and maybe some wood smoke too, all blended together with Nora's familiar odor.

"I finished plowing the driveway. We shouldn't have any trouble driving back in there, to your house. I cleared it all out in front of the barn too." He paused and wondered what to say to her. "When you got so sick the other night," he coughed when his voice caught in a rough spot in his throat. He swallowed and patted the back of her hand. "The state highway trucks came in and plowed the driveway during the storm, to get you out to the hospital." He saw the image of her lying on the floor where he had found her in the dark house, cold, as if she were already dead. He reached across the hospital bed for the blanket and pulled it up to her chin. "Well Jessie, you don't need to worry now, everything's real good back home."

Jessie heard what Kenneth said to her and wondered why she didn't remember any of it. But when she felt his warm touch, and felt the cracked sores of his frostbitten hands, she knew him. She remembered how it had felt then, when he pushed his warm breath into her, and how he had demanded that she live and claimed her as his own. When Kenneth saw the spark of recognition in Jessie's eyes, his chest ached with gratitude. He wanted to put his arms around her and leaned closer, but he pulled back when he saw the wires that tethered her to the machine. So he took her hand and gently stroked it between his hands.

Jessie's eyes dropped closed again. She felt her father rubbing the cold winter out of her hands. It always burned like sandpaper when he did that. She could see the deep worry lines on his forehead when he leaned down to her to examine her face carefully for signs of frostbite. But when he saw her rosy cheeks he would smile. His eyes seemed to float toward her like blue balloons when she looked up through the little lenses in his glasses. It was usually dark by the time she came in from sliding on the snow-packed hills, and the kitchen would be steamy with the rich meaty smell of stewed beef. Jessie's feet felt cold from the snow that was packed inside of her overshoes. When her father pulled them off, she heard the ice chunks as they bounced and clicked on the worn linoleum floor. While her father held her wet wrinkled feet in his lap, he rubbed each foot so hard that it throbbed with pain when the blood rushed into her toes.

She could hear her mother's worried voice from where she stood by the stove, "Don't be so rough, Hans, you are hurting her."

Now, Jessie heard Kenneth's voice close by, "I've cut a tree for Christmas. It's a real beauty, Jessie. It's one of the Norways. This one has a straight trunk and it's about ten or twelve feet, I'd guess. I will have to rig up a stand, the trunk is so thick." He paused. "Well, Ariel is here now and Rose is on her way. They will both be here for Christmas after all and…" his voice trailed off. "Christmas is only three weeks away. You will be home by then Jessie and it will be just as you planned it, with your daughters, and you will get to see your granddaughters for the first time." He leaned over and covered her cold hands with his. "Jessie?" Her eyes are still closed and he doesn't know if she has heard him.

Jessie felt her hands getting warm. They tingled when Daddy cupped them with both his hands and blew his warm breath into them. Then she whispered, "Daddy there is snow in my overshoes."

Kenneth moved to the end of the bed and felt Jessie's ankles for a sign of blood moving through her veins. He rang for the nurse to bring a heating pad and held both hands on the soles of her cold feet while he waited. He wanted to stay with her long enough to hear what she wanted to tell him. And so he waited and listened for her voice even though her eyes were closed and she made no sound.

He watched her mouth as she tried to form words that were barely audible. After awhile he began to understand some of what she said.

Now, she seemed to be repeating something that John was saying to her. "Jessie, don't ever leave it. Hold on to the land."

Then she answered him. "John, all this time I have been listening for your voice. Now I can hear you," she smiled. "I have been waiting here in the cold autumn wind," she paused for a breath, "waiting under the falling leaves for your touch. Now I feel your warm hands." Her cheeks were pink now, and her skin was moist. "I am here." Kenneth saw little drops of tears gleam in the light as they seeped from under her eyelids. He leaned closer to wait for her next words.

"Jessie, what do you want to tell me?" Kenneth spoke close to her ear. She opened her eyes and looked across the room. He looked into her eyes. "Is there something you want me to do for you?" He waited. Her eyes were locked on his eyes and seemed to nod yes. "Oh, Jessie I will do anything. I..." he leaned closer. "The time I have spent with you. I have learned things from you, I can't explain it Jessie. Ah, you have changed my life."

"Don't let them sell it." Jessie's soft voice is clear now. "If Ariel or Rose won't stay there, either one, then..." She paused and said slowly, "I promised John. I promised him before he died that I would never sell it. I would never let the developers tear open our land and rip out all the old trees, our woodland, and leave the birds and all the wild things with no place to hide."

Kenneth held his breath and tried to understand what she wanted him to do.

"We decided, John and I, a long time ago, after Ariel and Rose left. We didn't know if they would ever come back and settle here again. The land would go into a trust, if they never came home to stay." She reached for his hand. "You, Kenneth, if you love our place the way I do..." She stopped and closed her eyes. Her felt her hand tremble in his like a frightened bird. "I've known for a long time that they wouldn't claim their inheritance but I pretended that it wasn't true." Jessie sighed and her voice was weaker. "I want you to go now and find the papers in the cabinet, in the basement under John's workbench."

She waited for a breath again. Kenneth bowed his head and squeezed back the choking hot tears. "Kenneth, I want you to promise you will stay this time, stay long enough to get the papers to the executor, now, even before I'm gone." She closed her eyes and Kenneth looked at the monitor. He saw that her heartbeat was faint. She whispered, "It's all there in a big envelope, you will see it."

Kenneth leaned forward and rested his chin in his hand and rubbed the rough stubble on his chin with his thumb. She trusted him to take care of her most precious possession, to help keep her land fruitful and abundant for years to come. He wondered if he would be able to keep his promise to her. As he thought about what Jessie had asked him to do, he remembered a promise he made to his mother when he was a boy. It was many years after his father and mother were divorced. He was probably about fourteen, almost fifteen, and it was just before the start of his summer vacation.

He had told his mother that he was too old to need a babysitter. "I'm big enough to take care of myself, Ma. Don't worry about me so much." He stood slouched in front of her with his thumbs hooked in the back pockets of his jeans. "Jeez, you treat me like a baby or something."

But he saw that worry line between her eyebrows again and he knew she wasn't convinced by his promise to stay out of trouble. "We'll see," she said. "We will see if you can keep your nose clean like grandpa said. He needs your help. The floor on our deck is rotting. It has to be torn down and rebuilt and Grandpa can't do it alone." She searched his face, waiting for his response. He thought, "Oh shit, how am I going to get out of this," looked straight into her waiting eyes without blinking, and nodded yes.

He remembered that first day of summer vacation. He woke up to a golden spring morning, to the high sweet shrieks of the little kids playing next door. There was the smell of apple blossoms that blew in on a breeze pushing its way lazily through the window. He sat up on his elbows and squinted at the bright sunlight that flooded into his bedroom. His cheeks were still smooth and rosy and his big feet stuck out over the end of the bed. He flopped back down, clasped his hands behind his head and smiled as he counted the days and weeks that still lay ahead. The whole fuckin' summer to be with the guys, he thinks. To play baseball, and after, when it got dark, hide out down at the creek. While they were there in the woods, nobody could find them and they could smoke and drink beer or booze, or whatever they could take from home.

It was very quiet in the house that morning. He listened for the sounds of his mother making breakfast, the soft clinking of dishes and running water, but there was no sound except for his dog's snoring nearby. He heard the phone ring. He unfolded his long legs slowly and hitched up his pajama pants that slid back down on his narrow hips as he stumbled down the hall. He picked up the phone, nobody there. He looked at the clock on the stove. It was almost eight. He knew his friends wouldn't call this early, so it must be his mother or probably his grandpa to tell him he was on his way already. "There goes my summer," he thought as he rummaged in the cupboard for some pop tarts, punched the toaster, and stomped back to his room.

He reached for his cut-off jeans and pulled on a wrinkled tee shirt from the bottom of his closet, grabbed the hot pop tarts and juggled them in one hand while he opened the door into to the garage. The big dog squeezed through the door with him and nearly pushed him off the steps. He heard the slow crunch of tires on the driveway.

The dog recognized the sound and barked. Kenneth didn't need to look out the window. He knew who was there. He grabbed his baseball mitt from the careless pile of gear on the floor and ran back through the house to his bedroom window, pushed the screen out, climbed out and ran down the hill toward the creek. The dog was close behind making anxious squealing noises as they thrashed through the rough brush, but she stopped long enough to wolf down one of the pop tarts that Kenneth had dropped. He sat down on a rock and watched the smiling dog paddle around in the cold water while he chewed on the dry pop tart. When she climbed out, she shook cold water over him. Kenneth watched her roll on the muddy bank of the creek until she had covered her white bushy fur with black slime. Now, we are both in trouble, he thought. His shoulders slumped as he rested his chin in his hands. He wondered how long he would have to wait. The sun was hot on his back and he squinted as he watched the deep woods across the creek, looking for one of his friends to show up.

Two weeks later he was on a train headed for Des Moines to live with his father.

Kenneth remembered that and could see himself on that day as if it were a dream. He stared out the window of the train as it rolled past the Iowa farm fields and he heard the iron wheels click past the rows of new green corn shoots that had just sprouted in the dark earth. He wore the White Sox hat his father had sent him, and carried his mitt with him. He had two duffle bags filled with his gear in the overhead rack. When he had packed the bags, he threw in his hockey skates. Maybe, he thought, there would be some indoor ice. Even if he couldn't join a team right away, he could keep his game sharp just in case. His father told him to bring his baseball glove because they were going to hit some balls around. Kenneth wanted to show his dad how sharp his hitting and fielding was now after so many years, and he promised they would probably get down to Chicago to see the Sox play before school started.

It was late afternoon when he got off the train in Des Moines. He could hear his footsteps as they echoed in the cavernous granite building. He looked around and noticed that there were not many people, except for a few who stood at the counter waiting to buy tickets. He noticed an old guy slouched against a marble column with his hands in his pockets. He wore a dark baggy suit and watched Kenneth as he dragged his duffle bags across the polished floor and pushed them up against one of the rows of wooden benches. He sat down to wait for his father and squinted up at the domed ceiling where afternoon sun filtered weakly through the smoke-stained windows.

He wondered why his dad wasn't here yet and if his train had been late or maybe, he thought, it had come too early.

He heard a gravelly voice ask, "Hey kid, can you spare two bits for a cup of coffee?"

Kenneth looked up at him, but couldn't think of what to say, so he looked down at the floor. "Well, how about a cigarette, ya got a butt for an old man, eh?"

"No, I'm not old enough." He hung his head and mumbled, "Ah, I don't smoke. Sorry." He kept his head down so he wouldn't have to look at the man again.

"Yeah, I bet you wouldn't pass one up if you could steal it, eh?" The man came close enough so that Kenneth felt his sour breath on the back of his neck. He turned his back to the man and looked up at the big clock that hung in the center of the station. It was almost five o'clock. It had been over an hour since he arrived. The hollow space in his gut tightened into a fist. He shivered with fear when it grabbed him. He wondered if his dad had forgotten that he was coming today.

He heard a shuffling sound behind him. He thought the man was gone, but there was still a musty smell nearby. He was afraid to look back, so sat without moving for a long time.

After awhile he got up and dragged his gear across the smooth stone floor to a bench closer to the bank of doors in the station entrance and sat down again to wait for his father.

When his father came through the revolving door, it was after six o'clock. He was moving fast. He wore a short-sleeved white dress shirt and khaki pants. He was red-faced and the top button of his shirt was open. The knot of his tie had been yanked halfway down to his belt. Kenneth stood up and raised his hand palm up when he saw his father's eyes scanning the few people left in the station. "Hey Kenny." He ambled toward him, a sidewise look, his head tipped, still unsure, but then, "My God kid, have you gotten tall. You must be playing center on your basketball team, huh?" He punched Kenneth hard on his upper arm. "Got some muscle there too," and he pumped his forearm up and down. He hoisted the biggest duffle bag onto his shoulder and grunted. "Whad'ya got in here, rocks?" He was moving fast toward the doors, bent over a little with the weight of his load. "Come on, we got to hurry, I'm parked in a no parking zone."

Kenneth saw that there was a girl sitting in the car. His dad waved his arm toward her. "That's Linda, ah, she's your step-sister." He motioned to Kenneth to hurry into the back seat. "That's why I was late, had to pick her up from her softball game." He looked back and grinned, showing his big square teeth, and then Kenneth remembered that one in the front was a fake. It had fallen out once a long time ago when he was a little kid.

His dad had told him it got knocked out when he was hit in the mouth by a hockey puck. "Never back off when that slap shot's coming at you Kenny," he told him then. "You gotta skate like hell right at it and block it with your chest or it will hit you in the mouth for sure." Dad had grinned and showed Kenneth the black hole where his tooth used to be. "Don't be afraid of it, you can't back off, or it'll getcha right in the chops."

When they got to the house he stopped the car in the driveway and said, "I gotta drop you two here now. I'm an hour late to pick up Gloria from work. Boy, is she gonna be mad." Then he turned to look at Kenneth, "I figure you and Linda will get along just fine. She's a good kid. Just about your age too."

Linda helped him drag his stuff into the house. She was tall and looked pretty strong for a girl. She showed him the room they had fixed up for him in the basement. "Dad said that you would probably like it better down here, more privacy, you know."

He nodded, "Yeah, and I bet it will be cool in the hot weather too, our basement is."

Her mouth turned up at the corners and her eyes looked like she was laughing. "OK, Let's go up and find something to eat. We have lots of TV dinners."

She stretched her long legs and raced up the stairs two at a time. She opened the freezer and asked, "Let's see, what would you like? We have fried chicken and French fries with peas and carrots, Salisbury steak with mashed potatoes and gravy with green beans, roasted turkey and..." She kept pulling boxes out and handed them to him. "That's OK Linda, I like green beans and hamburger steak. It's my favorite."

While they waited she turned on the TV and set up the trays. She asked him if he wanted a cigarette.

"Won't your mother be coming home pretty soon?" He was worried. "We'll catch hell if they find out, won't they smell the smoke?"

"Naw, don't worry, my ma smokes like a chimney and dad doesn't care. Besides, they won't be home until real late."

"Where are they? Does your mother work overtime, is that why they will be late tonight?" He felt let down now and he wondered who was playing right field for him in the ballgame back home.

"It's like this almost every night. They like to have dinner together, and be alone I guess. You'll get used to it, it's better than when they're here."

"Hey, do you want to go to a party tonight?" She smiled at him. She had beautiful teeth, big and very white, and deep dimples. Actually, she was pretty nice-looking, he thought.

"Well, what do you say? Do you want to go or not?" She got up to put away the trays.

"Well, I guess so, if you think it's all right." He wondered what kind of party it would be and what kind of clothes he would need to wear.

"It'll be fine, lots of kids, a good band, and no parents. You drive, don't you? It's a ways out in the country, in a barn. We get to use it all the time, whenever we want."

"Well, I guess, but we don't have a car, so how?" he stopped, confused about what she wanted him to do.

"Oh, no problem, we'll take my mom's car. It just sits in the garage all the time anyway. She'll never know if it's gone." She got up on a chair and reached for some liquor bottles in the back of the top kitchen cabinet. She held out a half-full bottle of vodka to him. "Here, help me with these. We have to bring some booze to the party." She handed him three more bottles and took another that was almost empty.

"Not a good idea, Linda, they'll find out for sure. Then we'll both be in trouble."

"No problem," she held her thumb on the side of the bottle to mark the level, then poured half of the vodka into an almost empty bottle of white wine and filled the vodka bottle with water to where it was before. Then she did the same with Dad's Christian Brothers brandy, then some Windsor Canadian whiskey, and topped it off with a bottle of Tia Maria that she found way back in the cabinet.

"Jeez, are you gonna actually drink that rotgut?" He looked at her and said, "Well, maybe just a beer would be fine for me."

"What's the diff? If you get high that's all that matters. Let's get ready."

By the time they left it was almost dark. Linda drove because he told her that he didn't have his driver's license with him. She just said, "That's OK, I know the way. Anyway, I'm used to driving mom's car." Kenneth figured she knew he was lying, but she seemed so easygoing that probably nothing he said would bother her.

They drove out of the city on an old two-lane highway, not far from the freeway that went from Des Moines to his dad's house.

It seemed like they were going east, but he couldn't tell for sure because the moon had not risen yet, and the sun was gone, leaving behind only a dim memory of the day that still hung suspended above the shadowed barns and farmhouses. The car windows were cranked down and he hung his arm out the window against the door while the warm air made a balloon up his sleeve.

She didn't say much, but every so often she smiled without turning her head and then he smiled too, because just being out there, going down the road with her, feeling the cool damp breath of the turned-up earth on his skin and hearing the rhythm of the slapping tires hitting the mended cracks on the old concrete, was all the good times he thought he ever needed.

When the last light had drained from the sky, Linda turned on the headlights and they drove down a gravel road for awhile, through swarms of little frogs who were caught in the light of the high beams as they leaped and dived from out of the ferny wet ditches along the side of the road. It was not long before she turned off the road, the car bounced heavily onto a culvert that passed over a drainage ditch, and she drove between two rotting posts draped in tangled barbed wire that used to be a gate.

It wasn't real road, just a hayfield with worn tire tracks that were only visible as far as the headlights beamed.

She didn't slow down much. He felt the rear end of the car slamming down hard into the ruts and he heard the rustle of weeds scrape against the sides of the car and the sharp sounds of twigs exploding like firecrackers under the weight of the tires. He remembered the sweet smell of newly mown clover blowing into his face. After about a half a mile they came to a small grove of maple trees. She made a wide sweeping turn around the grove, churning up pebbles that pinged and rattled hard against the undercarriage.

On the other side of the trees loomed the skeleton of a huge sagging barn. Some of the roof was missing and the rafters showed up like black ribs against the rising moon. She drove the car under the trees and parked. It looked like there were at least twenty cars there already.

Linda reached into the back seat for her hat. It was a white rolled-brim Western style with a silver buckle on a black suede band. Her pale hair looked silvery in the moonlight. It was knotted into a ponytail just below the hat brim and it fell almost to her waist. When she turned to get out of the car, he noticed the stray curls of damp hair that were sticking to the back of her neck. He followed her toward the barn and watched her step carefully from side to side to avoid stumbling on the narrow rocky path. Her high heeled boots and tight jeans made her legs look even longer.

He was wearing a brown buckskin hat of his father's. When Linda had tried it on him and stood back to check him out after she adjusted the brim, she smiled and said, "Hey Kenny, you are totally cool in that hat, with your pretty brown eyes and curly black hair. She hollered, "Oooh eeeeh ya, take a look at that dude." She laughed and clapped her hands. He wore his best pair of jeans, but he had to make do with his old beat-up tennis shoes.

He heard the deep thrumming sound of the bass guitar tuning up. The piercing squeals of the loudspeakers obliterated the soft rustle of the night and even the shrill waves of metallic music from the crickets could not be heard over the noise coming from the barn.

They stopped inside the door of a huge shadowy room that was open to the dark sky. It looked like a cave to him. Dusty amber light glowed from the smoke-blackened oil lamps hung from the posts on each side of the barn.

Linda stepped inside and looked around for someone she knew. She smiled toward the group of kids that were clustered in front of the bandstand and paused. Her feet were planted wide apart, thumbs hooked into her belt, her hips were easy and slung forward. Kenneth stood beside her and waited for her next move. What he saw when he looked across the room seemed unreal to him. It was like being in a dark theatre and watching a Technicolor movie.

Everyone looked so glossy bright, and each seemed to have a role to play in the movie. They all knew their parts and they always moved smoothly together.

No one looked out of place. He knew they would always be like this no matter where they were. Each would play the same part and never be aware that there was a missing piece, a character that never appeared in the story. He looked down at his worn tennis shoes. The sole on his left shoe was loose and might even start to flap if he tried to dance. His jeans seemed too short. He jammed his fists deep into his pockets and pushed down hard to make them longer to cover up his shoes. He moved closer to Linda and then slid behind her where he could look out over her shoulder and not be seen.

He heard a loud whistle and high yell that sounded like a yodel, and a barrel-shaped guy with a curly red beard grabbed Linda in a bear hug and swung her high, "Whoo eeee, look who we got here, our Linda baby." His face was flushed and sweaty, he danced away with her and she stood on his shoes while he turned and wheeled light as air around the huge room.

Kenneth felt that without Linda he was under a spotlight and he moved away into the shadows.

"Go Davy go," the crowd yelled and circled around them. They clapped and stamped with their hard metal heels; while the guitar strummed, they sang, "It was late last night when the boss came home, A-askin' 'bout his lady. The only answer that he got, She's gone with the Gypsy Davy." They surged onto the floor holding hands, pulling each other in one snake-like movement into a circle, shouting in unison, "She's gone with the Gypsy Dave."

Kenneth stood frozen, unable to turn away. It was like a silent movie, and as it flickered he saw her briefly, in and out between the jerky silhouettes of the dancers as they moved past the lighted bandstand. He saw that her hair had fallen loose and when she twirled, it floated around her head like a filmy curtain. He saw that when they danced, their legs seemed tangled somehow. He saw how they moved apart then merged again and then at the end, how Davy leaned over her, his thick arm held her so close that her head was thrown back and almost touched the floor. Her mouth was stretched wide and he couldn't tell if she was laughing or screaming for help. He tried to imagine himself holding her that close, so close that she had to bend backwards, almost down to the floor. What if he dropped her and had to carry her from the dance floor?

He wondered why Linda had brought him here, to a dance. Was he supposed to ask her to dance with him? Could she tell that he didn't know how to dance, had never even been to a dance before?

He heard a thin mocking voice close to his ear. "Hey, Slim, you new around here?" The warm breath from the voice touched the nerves on the back of his neck.

"Where'd you come here from?" Kenneth didn't move, pretended he didn't hear.

"They must have a whole lot of floods back there, where you live, hey Slim?"

He knew what was coming next. He reached back and carefully smoothed down the fine hair that was tickling on the back of his neck.

"Seein' that yer wearin' those brand new haigh-water pants here, now. Ye musta bought 'em special. Just to show off to that gal out there. Heh?"

Kenneth wanted to get out of there, to run, to lose himself outside, hide in the woods. But now, he thought it was probably too late. He heard them laughing, sniggering. Were they behind him or beside him? Without moving his head, he slid his eyes to each side trying to see if anyone else waited for him to make a move and maybe see what they were carrying.

He saw Davy climb onto the bandstand and get behind the drums.

The noise from the band cranked up to play "Peggy Sue" and right away the dance floor was mobbed with dancers who swelled and spilled out over the edges. Clots of churning couples whirled past. A girl, lost from the sweaty grip of her partner's hand, flew out of control and he caught her as she bounced into him. A breathless "sorry" wafted back to him as she twirled away. He strained forward to see through the dancers. Where was she now, he wondered, now that Davy's on the bandstand. He felt a soft tap on his back, smiled and turned quickly, expecting to see Linda.

"Hey, Slim, ye're not bein' friendly. Now, you need to make frien's here when ye're a newcomer, while ye're waitin' for that little gal that's outside in the back." He had a small girlish face, a snub nose, and cornflower blue eyes with pale eyelashes. There was blond fuzz on his upper lip and his red Kewpie-doll mouth smirked as he offered his hand to Kenneth.

Kenneth saw that he was trapped inside a half circle of guys that looked ready for a fight. He figured that he was going to have to take a beating. He glanced over his shoulder for a way out. "Don't look around for that gal, Linda, to hep you outa this, she's got a bigger fish to fry than you." Some of them laughed and yelled, "Yea, she'll jest throw you back in the river, boy."

Kenneth took Kewpie doll's hand and smiled. His heart was pounding in his throat. Sweat trickled, sticky air pressed in on him, he swallowed and tried to say something casual.

"Hey," he croaked and smiled again. He could see there wasn't a chance to get out through the door and run. He knew he could outrun just about anyone and these guys wouldn't have a chance; once he broke out into the open, he'd lose them easy, but there were too many people between him and the door and more were coming, curious and waiting. He turned fast and broke into the crowd on the dance floor. The dancers reached out and grabbed his clothes and others pushed him. He half-fell on them as they pushed him back and pounded him on the back and shoulders. Two guys grabbed his feet and dragged him across the floor into the bright light in front of the bandstand. He heard girls laughing and shut his eyes tight and tried to keep the tears back. One big heavy guy straddled him and unbuckled his belt. The crowd was clapping, while the others yanked his pants down to his ankles. He tried to roll over, but they held his feet so hard that every move bent them farther back. Then he heard the mocking voice again, "Well why don' you turn tail and run away. Let's see how far you can run now, you skinny little puke."

The band stopped playing.

Linda's voice came through the crowd, "Get your sorry ass off'n him Johnny Turner, you big jackass." The crowded room got quiet and some started to leave.

Linda strode into the middle of the circle and stood with her hands on her hips, "You, Billy, you goddamned moron, you're too stupid to be ashamed of yourself, but the rest of you, what the hell is your excuse?" They shook their heads and started to say, "But, Linda." She cut them off and shouted, her voice hard and angry. "This is my brother and you treat him like this?" They all were silent when they heard her words. They let go of Kenneth, who wouldn't open his eyes. He covered himself with his hands.

She raged at the crowd, "Don't any of you shitheads have any sense, but to stand here and let this happen." She knelt down next to Kenneth to help him up, then, up at them, " You all get the hell out of here, haven't you seen enough?"

Kenneth had rolled himself into a ball. His knees were pulled up to his chin, his eyes closed. She leaned over him, took his hands and tried to pull him up. He was rigid. "Kenny, please get up. I'll help you. Let's get out of here, we'll go to the car, now." She wailed to the almost empty barn, "Will somebody please help us, we need some help here." Then Davy came on the run with a horse blanket and covered Kenneth. "I can carry him Linda, if he would just straighten out, I can carry him on my shoulder."

"I'm real sorry about this, Kenny." Davy whispered, "I'll turn off all the lights. Everyone has gone now. No one will see you." Kenneth opened his eyes and looked around. Davy looked around on the floor and picked up Kenneth's pants and underwear, rolled them up and tucked them under his arm. Then he took him by the hand and said, "Let me help you now. Linda's gone to get the car." He gently pulled Kenneth up onto his feet. Davy pushed his face close and asked in a low voice, "Are you ready?" Kenneth looked down at the floor and didn't answer, so Davy wrapped the heavy blanket around him, stooped down and pushed his shoulder into Kenneth's stomach, and grunted when he hoisted him up onto his shoulder.

Then Davy stood up slowly and shifted Kenneth's weight once for balance, before moving slowly toward the door.

Linda waited in the car by the barn door. She had all the windows open and heard the sounds of the girls' high bubbling laughter, car doors being slammed, and the roar of old truck engines being gunned up. The happy shouts of "call me in the morning" and "don't forget the barbeque on Sunday" floated back to her on the soft night air. And then it was quiet, except for the music of the crickets. After awhile Davy came out with Kenneth hanging over his shoulder rolled up in the horse blanket. The moon was bright and it lighted up Davy's wild red curls with a lemony glow. Kenneth's bare feet dragged on the ground in front of Davy's hunched body. He stooped into a deep knee bend and eased Kenneth down onto the back seat, then pushed his knees up so his feet would clear the car door.

Davy tried to tug the blanket further down over Kenneth's knees, but he had it clutched over his face. Davy sighed and patted him on his arm. He brushed and picked at the hay-flecked old wool as he whispered, "Oh, that's OK Kenny. You'll be all right now." Davy pulled off his shirt, wiped the trickling sweat from his face and draped the shirt carefully over Kenneth's legs so it covered his feet. He folded Kenneth's jeans and underwear on top of his tennis shoes and patted him once more. Then Davy stepped back, signaled a hand up goodbye to Linda as she turned the car around and pulled out toward the road. He stood alone and watched the red glow of the taillights as they bounced up and down through the meadow. When they were out of sight, he walked slowly back into the empty barn.

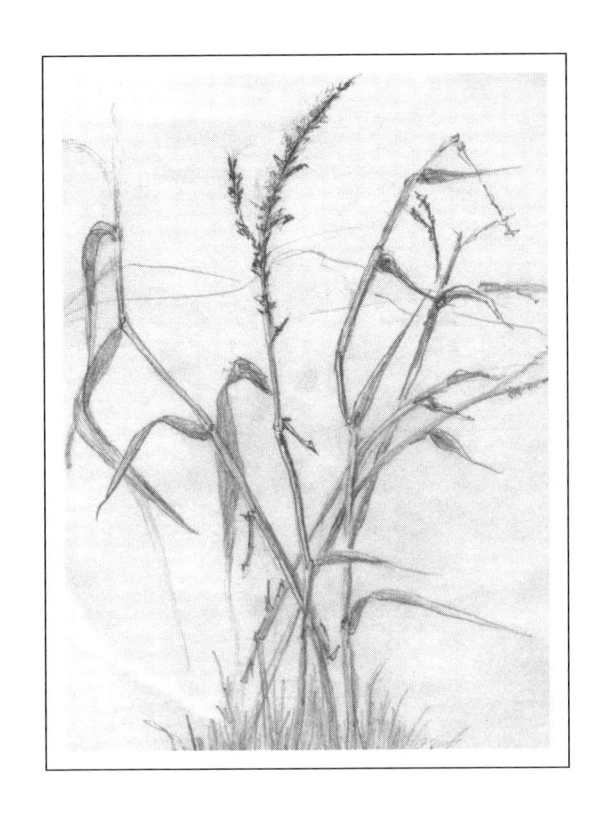

Wiltshire, England
1630

ANN CLARE SMITH

Wiltshire, England—April, 1635

The following story is selected from an ongoing narrative of the emigration of the young Woodman family from Corsham, Wiltshire, to the Massachusetts Bay Colony in New England. Edward and Joanna, his expecting wife, with their sons, Edward, 7, and Jonathan, 5, are joined as they approach and cross the Great Salisbury Plain on their way south to their port of departure, Southhampton.

ANN CLARE (WOODMAN) SMITH, CSJ, *calls herself an immigrant as well, having come to the Midwest from Down East Maine's Atlantic coast. A direct descendent of the progenitor immigrants, Joanna and Edward, and of an Irish mother who came directly from County Clare, she is allowed a certain confusion of identity, having her two feet in such different and conflicting camps. Her tale is factual, based on a genealogy published in Boston by a cousin in 1874.*

THE TEAMS CAME TO REST under the river's trees and the family tumbled out. The wagon, with the crofters from Arthur's holding, drew close behind and soon everyone left the two Edwards and began to walk the footpath toward the village square.

After seeing to the horses' needs with his father, young Edward asked: "Papa, this is a good time for us to speak, is it not? The others will not hear and the animals cannot tell. Shall I relate to thee my thoughts about this Chippenham town where we are stopping?"

"Aye, son, it is time for plain speaking. Rid thy mind of its burden."

"You know, Papa, I am older than John and I am the eldest brother of all the children yet coming to this family. This will be true forever, Papa, will it not?"

"Aye, aye, young Edward, I think often of this and know how well suited you are for such a responsibility. But our time is short, lad. Think thee thou might find words now, or soon, for what you are wondering?"

"You are right, Papa, it is truly a wondering," he said, shifting his stand and gazing away to the west side of the river, "I am wondering if it can be that we are going to pass so near to our home and not turn by once more…to…well… you know, to check on things."

Gripped by the serious demeanor and pluck of this confrontation from his namesake, Edward took off his cap and placed it on the lad. He knelt on one knee before him, took his hands and said:

"My son, I must confess that your mamie and I were hoping neither you nor John would reckon this. It is true; we are but a good canter from Corsham. But did we not say all of our farewells a scant day since? Have you a mind to worry our hearts anew, before there is any time for healing?"

Eddy looked into his father's eyes and whispered: "Not everyone's heart, Papa, just yours and mine."

"My son, what is thy true quest? What troubles thee?"

"Papa, I am afraid I shall not remember my homings. Already they grow dim. How shall I tell my brothers and sisters this story if I forget my memories?"

After a long pause, his father spoke: "Edward, little man, think thee can sit saddleless with me for a league and a roundabout?"

"Oh, Papa, yes! I am very able to do this; I am certes of it!" the child said, embracing his father and taking the hand he extended. In haste they secured a fresh mare and made their excuses privately to Archelaus. They crossed the river and, with only a rope for bridle, cantered off westward toward Corsham, wearing identical grins and bouncing their heels against the roan's sides.

It was not until they reached Devizes that Edward found an opportunity to talk with Joanna and to tell her about the sudden excursion to Corsham. He sent the children off to the old farmers' market with the two crofters and, while Archelaus checked out the woolens, he and Joanna strolled about the bustling hamlet. They followed along the high street to a sheep lane that meandered its way back to the common where the wagons and horses waited. As they walked, they grew silent. Joanna tightened her hold on her husband's arm and spoke softly: "Edward, these minutes alone are precious and will not often be ours in the days we voyage. I would speak to thee from my heart."

"Aye, my wife, and doubly dear for the glimpses we share of our land in these days will be the last. I, too, hold thoughts I desire to share with thee. Wist thou to speak first, my dear one?"

"Edward, I do. We have tumbled through these past days with such a haste my heart scatters and leaps unbidden in directions I would not. Can we not together steady our humours during these last miles and arrive at the sea of one mind?"

"It is my fondest wish, Joanna, and, in the light of our expected increase, my heart's one desire. I have been thinking as we walked and stored away these sights and sounds of Wiltshire."

"Oh, my darling, yes, and the scents, the scents Edward, we must never forget them."

"Aye, the scents, too, and the damp and fog and the rains of spring and early summer, and the dew on the young lambs shining like gems of morning... these we carry close, my love, never fear. I could as soon forget them as I could forget thee and our lads. But, Joanna, I want you to know before we take another step that as willing as I am to turn my back on all here, I am in no mind to turn it on thee. You must be as ready as I for this venture or we go not one jot further. Knowest thou this?"

"My love, I know if I asked it, thou wouldst return home with me and the children to Corsham. But this I shall never put on thee. We cast our lot as one, and so it will be. My heart breaks because we are leaving, but it would break anew if we were not. You are more to me than all of this, my Edward, and I fancy my place at your side," she said with a sudden gleam in her eye and the makings of a smile gathering on her lips.

In reply, Edward crushed her against him and kissed her with so unlikely an abandon that she erupted into gales of laughter and pulled him along toward the common. The excitement eclipsed in the morning by departure, emerged once more amid the bustlings and flurries of facing toward Southhampton. The great port loomed as an exciting goal, shrouded in an aura of the unknown and the final. But first, they must face the Salisbury Plain that lay ahead ten miles distant like a giant causeway tracing a path to the sea. Its crossing if, God willing, uneventful, would consume the best hours of the afternoon.

Joanna knew the men were carrying arms; it had been planned so from the start. And, indeed, they were required on shipboard. Nevertheless, it shocked her to see them removed from hiding and displayed for all to see. She corralled her boys and settled them at a distance from the wagons with lardy cakes and a bit of watered ale.

"Master Woodman," she called, "may I not have a word with thee before we depart?"

"Might it not bide, Joanna? I take not to losing any time just now. Daylight will see us into Salisbury only if we leave on the non. Can not whatever vexes you be settled while seated and moving forward, my..."

"I am not vexed, my dear Edward," she interrupted with spirit, her cheeks coloring in betrayal of her words. "The lads and I would not delay our company; I would but know if there is aught to fear as we go onto the Plain."

Without responding, Edward lifted John into the carriage through one door while Joanna and young Eddy stepped lively through the other.

"Papa," John asked, beginning to cry, "is crossing on the great Solsberry plain going to hurt us?"

"*Salisbury*, John, say *Salisbury*," corrected Edward.

Whereupon, Eddy jumped up and squeezed in beside his mother and the frightened child, embracing him and turning to square up to his father.

"Papa, it is the guns, do you not see? You told us nothing about having them in the wagons. To see them now gives us a proper startle."

"My son, you are in the right and I the wrong. You and John are fine lads with your eyes wide open, and it is best if you know what is happening. And I owe an apology to your mother as well." He took his wife's hand and said, "I regret not alerting you, Joanna dearest, to the need for caution as we cross the plain. Letting our weapons show is but an announcement to anyone we meet that we are prepared."

"That is all well and good, my husband, but being prepared must include each one of us, *n'est-ce pas*? If I, or either of the children, is by happenstance confused, we can not be of help or grasp the need presented to us. We must know your intent when you prepare to address any threat. We need direction from you, and from Archelaus. This is all we ask."

"Yes, my dear family, and you will, indeed, have it, I swear."

"No need to swear, Papa, " noted young Edward, "it is enough to have understanding among us. See," he said, trying to embrace his brother, "even little John is feeling happy again!"

"Stop," shouted John, pushing him away. "I hate kisses, I'm not a baby!"

Joanna and Edward exchanged quick smiles and Eddy let out a roar and shouted to his uncle to go faster.

The next few hours passed with no untoward incident. Save for the loss of a forward wheel on the baggage wagon and the arrival of several more parties destined for the seacoast, all went well. Moreover, the brief respite gained by the mounting of a new wheel was welcomed. Joanna cast herself prone on the fresh spring grass under an old oak while the boys shadowed the men in their task, querying their every move.

"Mamie, look," shouted John anxiously, "we will be last, we will be last." Opening her arms to the child, Joanna replied, "Yes, my sweet babe, we shall. Does that not settle well with thee, little one?"

"But, Mamie, we shall not see; we shall not see anything, just the backs of the wagons. And there is something else that will be bad, also, but I'm not of a mind to speak it out loud to a lady. You are a lady, Mamie, are you not?"

Joanna picked the lad up and, laughing, swung him around and around until they both were tipsy. Preparing to remount, she said to the men, "Well, Edward, Archelaus, we seem to have a small matter needing attention."

"Not so small, Father," interrupted John, staggering to his feet, "it could become very displeasing and I have thought of a s-s-solution already. Do you want to know what it is?" he asked, hopping around on one foot and holding his nose.

"Whatever, John, just steady on and wist it out of thee! And why ever are you pinching your nose like that, soon you will be gasping and wan. What? Out with it this second or I will toss you into that tree yonder and leave you here!" Edward blustered.

"Papa," laughed John, honking through his nose, "the tree might be a good idea once the sun cooks up the horsey pies right before our carriage. My thinking is to wait until the others are well away before we follow. Do you not agree, Papa, this idea is a good one?"

"Son, you are becoming much like your brother and soon we will be rife with captains, but the idea is sound. May hap a dip into the larder might be another good idea, John laddie; you and Eddy help your mother now and we shall have an early sup."

"Good, Edward, I agree. The sun is holding and we have only to follow the river hence due south, and the road is fair traveled, making our time short," Joanna responded.

"Fine. Then Uncle and the men will rest the team and take them to the river. Step to, now, I am of a sudden that hungry I could eat a goat!"

Their journey south and east from Devises skirted the eastern rim of the plain and brought them once again to the banks of the Avon flowing south to Amesbury and thence, in another eight miles, to Salisbury. Edward did not reckon the plain itself difficult, but knew travelers crossing it were prey to the many ills of isolation—mainly, the wandering hordes of thieves and brigands and the mustering ruffians who made up the footsoldiers of the king's men. The plains were bivouacking grounds for them in times of unrest at court.

Archelaus and Edward had talked long about their prospects before departing Malmesbury, but avoiding the plain was equally undesirable. Well armed, four men should suffice before any threat. The route chosen also afforded them the advantage of avoiding the center of the plain and following a fair-traveled route. With good fortune, they would reach Salisbury well before sundown.

"Brother, the trail is pleasant and we are well fed, we need take care our senses not betray us," Archelaus shouted down to Edward, as the team ambled along at a lazy walk.

"I shall join you, brother, and trust our conversation to keep us lively. There is much to discuss and plan before the voyage. Our provisions must be reckoned anew once we reach the port and details of our accommodations are not yet final. It is at our peril if we leave anything to chance. Do you not agree?"

"Aye, indeed I do. We trust only ourselves, and even then, I shall check carefully on thee, my lad," chuckled Archelaus, giving Edward a stout jab with his elbow.

Joanna smiled to herself and pulled the boys to either side of her on the facing bench. "Look now, the two of you. We must cover the two sides and watch for any sign of movement. It is a pleasant enough day and the plain appears serene; for this reason, we need be mindful. What say you to this?"

"Mamie, yes, yes, yes," answered Jonathon bouncing with excitement, but Edward fell silent. Reaching to touch his brother gently, he gave Joanna a somber glance and said, "This is a true responsibility, is it not, Mamie? Would you not say?"

"What are you thinking, young master? Does it affright thee that troubles might come to us?"

"Oh, no, Mater, I know the crofters are hearty and brave, as are Father and my uncle. My thoughts are with John. Me thinks him wee for so earnest a duty. Is he not apt to fidget and fret ere we have a furlong behind us and attend too little?"

"I see that thou hast a full-born suggestion in that busy head," said Joanna, trying not to smile. "What is it?"

"I would to watch myself by the west window, Mamie, and John can best be between us, watching where he would."

"Ah, so be it, Eddy lad, hop over and we'll talk no more."

"Unless we must, Mamie?"

"Yes, child, unless we must and I pray we may be silent until the first glimpse of Amesbury."

"Amen, Mamie." Amesbury, a quiet town of little commerce, tucked itself snugly into a loop of the Avon with an air of grace and contentment. Sheep grazed in the outfields and laborers tended corn patches already well grown. The old village seemed timeless, as settled into the rich earth as its abundant oaks and willows.

Archelaus pulled the lead team close to the riverbank and gave his brother a knowing nudge in the ribs before jumping down to care for them. Edward laughed with relief and gathered his "watchers" down to rest in the cool freshness of the spring shade. When the bustle of everyone finding a fit footing subsided, Edward drew the men aside to rest by the water. Speaking low, they conferred about their plans. Archelaus knew they were a scant lope from the henge of giant stones. He had passed them by many times on his marketing forays to Salisbury. Why not take the lads for a look? Young Edward, at least, could mayhap fondly remember such in years to come.

"Aye, and here the young'un comes nigh. What say you, Eddy, are we rested enow, or have you some new-thought wisdom to share."

"Papa, Uncle, the sun tires and soon will sleep—might we not continue? Mother is ready and hopes the same."

"We must for certe hie then, my son. Off with you. Tell your good mamie her hopes bide well for us, too."

The men guided the team along a worn path that circled the western reaches of the village and crossed the river. As they cleared the area, the broad plateau stretched before them in gentle, verdant swells; the great stones but two miles to come.

Archelaus, claiming a need for exercise, jumped down to walk beside the team, leaving the place beside his brother for Joanna. The boys he lifted onto the backs of the blacks, where they could see for miles.

Before long, the stones came into view. Edward and John sighted them first and called wildly to their father to stop. Edward slid down at once, but John's face was white and his brown eyes wide and fixed. His father, sensing his fear, lifted him down and held him against his chest.

"Papa, the stones and shades affright him; he is catching his breath again, do something!"

"Joanna, haste, take John," whispered Edward through his teeth, passing his son none too gently into the arms of his wife—"he is up to his old tricks again!" Joanna took John and tossed him, belly down, across the rump of the nearest mare. He landed with a loud gasping for breath and clung to the mare's pelt with both small hands.

"There," said Edward, smiling broadly, "we have found a remedy for this young man."

"We?" asked Joanna, giving her husband a crisp glare. "Art thou taking credit, Mr. Woodman?"

"Nay, my dear, t'would never pass my mind."

"It best pass it and not lodge, my friend," replied Joanna as she rescued her sniffling son and walked off with him toward the henge where young Edward was already running from stone to stone.

"Brother," said Edward as he stood silently watching his small family, "what thinkest thou if we alter our plans to reach Salisbury by night shade?"

"What is on your mind, Edward? Are you thinking, as I, that Joanna tires?"

"Aye, that, but just as non, I wist the lads to tarry here for a spelle of olde England. May hap their souls might imbibe its spirit to linger during the difficult days before us."

"I have no objection, brother. Indeed, I think a night in the open a benefit to both man and beast. We will arrive in the grand town fresh, and, if we move sharply, will have time to see a bit of Old Sarum, as well."

"It will be so. Tell the others we will camp the night within the henge—man, woman, and beast!"

Archelaus laughed and turned to his task. Edward ran off apace toward his treasures and the circle that held them.

The henge sat on an even section of the rolling plain in a slight depression, not far from an odd formation made from the earth itself. Grasslands extended in all directions. The horses were soon freed from service, curried, and set to graze. The boys helped Joanna select a toppled stone to serve as a table and, well-provisioned as they were, all fell to for a hearty sup.

"What think you, Joanna, if we pass the night in this balmy place? I fancy the ancient henge and find myself listening for the stones to speak," said Edward, his arm on his wife's shoulder.

"Aye, Sister," continued a smiling Archelaus, "it is probable there are scant, if any, shelters for us whence we journey. They say all of New England hast dense covering of forest, even down to the sea. Sleeping under the stars this night may hap even be a boon to ease our backs in six or eight weeks time."

"Mamie, please say it may be so! Please! John likes it here now and he is sore tired from sitting since early morn," offered young Edward.

Joanna, too, felt the enchantment of the place and opened her mouth to reply but was silenced by the distinct sound of riders approaching at a goodly gallop.

"What ho, brother!" Archelaus whispered. "Shall we show our weapons or nay?"

"Nay, but fetch them nigh. It may be naught but farm men returning from market, their purses and bellies full. Joanna, you and the lads conceal yourselves in the carriage until we are certe."

At once Joanna did as bidden and lifted the children to lie flat on the seats, unseen. But she herself stood outside and awaited the newcomers without fear.

"They'll right lather them nags if they pace this up," said one of the men.

"Fancy horseflesh for yeomen," added Archelaus.

Young Edward could contain himself no more and slipped down to join his mother in vigil, his blue eyes cautious and eager by turns.

"Mamie," he noted, "methinks thou art smiling to thyself at something. Art thou thinking a secret? Doth thee know surprises without Pappy?"

"Hush, my bright boy, thou shalt see anon."

The men rose and stood clear, armed, prepared for friend or foe. The riders took notice of their stance and, in haste, began to wave their arms in the air.

"Husband, Brother, take care," Joanna signaled, "'tis Father's new man!"

John and Edward were on the ground in a wink, running toward the slowing riders as fast as their small legs would go; Edward, reaching back to take John by the hand, urging him along.

"Return, Edward, be not so rash," his father called, to no avail. He was all set to go after them when the riders drew up and waited the lads' approach. Each man leaned, snatched up a laughing child to set before him, and walked his mount into the henge.

Shouts of "Wilhem! Wilhem!" came from the children and shouts of the same echoed back to greet Arthur's bailiff. Then Edward asked, "Why'ere are you come? What hap is this? We thought you off buying more wool!"

"Is aught well?" asked Joanna and Archelaus together.

"Ho, now, one at a time my friends! May I not first be allowed a greeting to the fair daughter of the house I serve? Best wishes to you, Mistress Woodman. I come, at your father's behest, to assist your preparations, for I have much experience in these matters. I am just now from Southhampton, knew ye not to expect me?"

"Nay," began Edward before Joanna's hand on his arm silenced him. His face coloring, he gasped in astonishment, "Joanna, you knew of this and said nothing?"

"Aye, Mister Woodman, I did indeed," she replied, giving her husband a minikin curtsy. "With two such fine heads, we need not store all counsel in but one, think ye?" She took Edward's arm and gave it a little shake and laughed to see his puzzlement. "Ah, husband mine," she confessed, "Father and I spoke long on many things yester-morn, and I happed to ask of Wilhem's quaint absence, that is all. And now we have this nice surprise!"

Edward grinned into his wife's impish face and pulled her against his side. "Tell me, are ye also aquainted with his yon siderider? I thought not. Let me present Wilhem's eldest son, newly arrived from London to share his father's labor. Dieter, Mistress Woodman."

A surprised and delighted Joanna had just welcomed the tall young man standing shyly beside his father when the boys pulled him away shouting something about the stones they must see. Wilhem smiled, shook his head and bowed to kiss Joanna's hand. "Mistress, you are looking well. I regret missing the leaving feast this morning, but my days in Southhampton have proven of great benefit. I have much to tell you."

Later, under the stars, the men talked. Edward and his brother knew they were far from alone in migrating to the western continent, but were, nevertheless, surprised at the extent of trafficking described by their visitors. The demand for ships had so increased that groups of families were pooling their funds and either hiring entire ships for themselves or buying them outright. The *James* and *Abigail* were both in the channel and expected to dock soon. The *Abigail*, fresh from London, needed time to unload its cargo; the *James* was ready for lading and would accept ninety-two passengers.

"And we are secured on one of these," asked Archelaus, "all of us together?"

"Aye, Sir, three adults and two children are now listed with the *James*, although it was a squeeze to manage for the third adult. A bartering deal did the trick and a single yeoman agreed to a better berth on the *Abigail*," Wilhem replied, a shadow of a smile betraying satisfaction with his own prowess.

"We must meet and thank this good man," noted Edward quietly. "Whence is he bound, didst say?"

"He did. He hopes to remain in the Bay Colony and take up his trade anew. He has letters from friends there who say the land is good for corn and the air clean and fresh. Nearly 4,000 are there since this decade alone and will nothing but increase. Ye are venturing at an apt moment, Mister Woodman."

"And are the prices holding to our expectations, Wilhem?" asked Archelaus. "They say £100 will carry a small family for eighteen months if well-provisioned. Is there any talk against that around the port?"

"The prices are what we anticipated: £5 for each adult with half-fares for small children; chattel and goods are £3 the ton. If you were taking animals, like horses or cows, the price would sharpen some."

"Since we are not men of bondage, as in some colonies, we go well prepared and our hard work will bring accustomed benefits in time. Joanna will need a cow immediately for the children but we may wait on our need for a horse, or team," said Edward.

"You will be wise to take a goodly sum of coin, Mister Woodman, for just such purchases. We have secured all of the provisions on your list and more; howe'er, remember, there will be no wool market on those rocky shores and a mercer's trade is a distant dream. From what I hear you will be between the sea and the forest, and since the sea cannot be moved, you must needs remove the forest. Good axes will be of great value in these early months and years."

"Think you, Wilhem, when our backs are sore and our hands worn, will we hanker for the Avon valley? Or when our food is on foot and must be hunted?"

"I do not, indeed, Mister Woodman! I have assessed the metal of each of you and expect no such regret. I see you and yours starting something over there that will go on beyond imagination! You are from this day an adventurer, Sir, and I suspect your deepest heart is ready, and that of your Mistress and lads as well."

"May you prove a prophet, Wilhem! Now, for the rest. You have listed the provisions to be taken on board?"

"Indeed, Sir, I have," replied the bailiff, handing him a sheet of foolscap, "you will find all in order. I have fairly followed the broadsheet from the catalogue, *New-Englands Plantation*, especially the recent additions offered by settlers themselves. They suggest strongly whilst you prepare well for a life at sea, be of a firmer mind to carry what is to secure yourselves upon the land. This being their earnest caution, I have provisioned you for a household of six persons."

"The list impresses me with its length of items, Wilhem. I note you list first our victuals," inserted Archelaus. "How have you arrived at these amounts; four hogsheads of meal, two hundred weight of beef, eight bushels of peas, and on so?"

"Well, Sir, first I..."

"Wilhem, please," interrupted Archelaus, "call me by name, I am a simple man and not fond of titles among brothers."

"And I feel the same," added Edward. "But, anon, the list. We have much to discuss."

"Yes, Edward, and Archelaus. I thank thee," affirmed Wilhem with a nod to each of the younger men, his cheeks flushed with pleasure. His diligence for this family being no trifling matter, their gesture came a boon and a brace to his spirit.

"As I intended to say," he resumed, "I studied the catalogue listings where victual amounts were portioned for *one adult male* and for some items tripled and for others quadrupled, counting the lads as one adult. For apparell ventured to adjust somewhat for the lads and their certain growth—shoes, boots, stockings and the like, you will find in several sizes, *par example*."

"And the chattel, considering what we sent ahead from both our holdings, was there further purchasing necessary?" asked Edward, with a glance at his brother who was frowning and reaching for the sheet.

"There you meet another matter altogether," responded the bailiff, standing and beginning to pace into the circle and back. "We need to talk most especially of these and of your goods. I heard many things in port here and there, and I was received by the lord mayor briefly. Concerns arise in two areas. The first is the land itself. I have a clearer picture to offer you of what you may expect from it. The second is related and yet more weighty by far."

"Speak up, man, and quit your confounded ins-and-outs! I sense an alarm in you for our venture and must hear it; we have no time for the King's English. Just spit it out!" Archelaus sputtered. "We needs yet sup and rest; the children already nod and Joanna is weary enow. Tell us straight what ye have learned."

"True, it is well we speak frankly, but can we not first eat and then ask Dieter and Joanna to join us? I have a sound reason for each of them to know our, er, that is, *your*, business."

"Dieter seems a fine enow lad, Wilhem, but he is yet a boy. What interest to him or worth to us is his presence?" asked Edward, his brother nodding in agreement.

"Ach, of course, let me explain. It is our thought, Master Salway's and mine, that we place Dieter to live and work at your home in Corsham, Edward, to be our eyes and ears there. He would work for Jonathon and keep a watch on your interests. Oh, I realize that there is no mistrust of your stewart on your part; howe'er, your father-in-law feels some precaution to be not amiss, and I agree."

"Wilhem, as much as I respect Arthur Salway, I differ with you both in this instance. I'll not have Jonathon spied upon like a common wastrel! He is a brother to me and I want him treated as such in my absence."

"Edward," enjoined Archelaus, "wait on this anon. I hear no accusations being laid before us, and the idea of a young man to aid in the daily work is something to be desired. Jonathon has not yet a wife and takes on much responsibility in replacing you and Joanna."

He paused to glance first at his brother and then at Wilhem. Seeing he had their attention, he continued. "I think it a wise step. And if it serves a dual purpose, I see no objection. Consider as well how Jonathon might desire the boon of access to Arthur's bailiff should the need arise. It is a balast both ways and, to me, a wise decision, and you know I am a practical man."

"You raise good points, Archelaus," responded Wilhem with enthusiasm.

"Aye, may hap, but I offer counsel only. It is Edward's decision alone."

"What is Edward's *decision alone*?" asked Joanna pertly as she and Dieter brought a a trencher of meat and jugs of soft ale to the serious-looking men. "Hast anything untoward happened? Am I not to be privy to all concerns of this venture, Edward? Archelaus? Wilhem?"

The men scurried to their feet in welcome, but, when no one answered her question, Joanna held firmly to the trencher and signaled Dieter to do the same with the ale.

"Willst have not a morsel this night. If secrets are being served, eat them!" and she turned to go, taking the food away.

Edward and Archelaus rushed to join their hands in a circle about her, preventing any move. When they began to laugh, begging her to feed them lest they falter, she still frowned and held against them. Only when they promised to tell her everything, did she relent. Trying not to smile, she sat on a turned stone, still clasping the food, and demanded her due.

In the years to come, Joanna would often remember this night, pondering again and again the portents woven through its conversation. She would recall each face, the words spoken, the eyes and expressions, and always, embracing them, the soft rising of the moon and the sweet smell of the night, the men's voices like bees in clover. But for now, it was all she could do to grasp what Wilhem was telling them.

The lad to spy on Jonathon? The port raucus and filthy? Ships' crews brawdy and foul of speech? Religious strife rampant in the Bay Colony? Pirates from as far as Turkey and as near as France waiting off their English waters? Orphans in the streets begging to be taken on shipboard? A northern passage? A new place assigned in the Colony to all those sailing the *James*? Where? What is it like? A wilderness? Our new home? The children, the babe? Joanna's head reeled with new, imagined images, and the child in her womb moved for the first time.

Dieter noticed Joanna's distress and rose from his place to offer her a biscuit and a drink from his own flagon. The men drew rein as one.

"Joanna, my dear, art thou not well? Ought we bid thee goodnight?" asked Edward, going to sit by his wife and to circle her waist with his support.

"Nay, you misread me, Edward. Dieter recognizes a 'beer and biscuit' need when he sees one, is all," laughed Joanna. "Please continue, Wilhem, I long to know what we are facing in a few days' time."

"It is prime that ye be prepared, true, but there will yet be much we cannot foresee. You may hap will find yourselves woodsmen, carpenters, inventors, explorers, physics, tanners, and justices of the peace. It may even fall to you men to muster your own militia for the protection of your people. Much is uncertain from such a distance and reports not only vary but contradict one another. You will only know when you arrive what you have conceived."

Archelaus stood and said, "You have done well by us, Wilhem, and I thank thee. While I am glad to be apprised of the stormy conflicts in Boston, by grace, in our new location, we shall be distant enow from that misfortune. But the pictures you paint of both voyaging and landfall give me pause. There is much to set our minds to and we must plan ahead; the weeks at sea will be opportune, me thinks. What say you, Edward?"

Edward looked up at his younger brother, taking a measure already known and loved. How deeply grateful he was that providence put them together precisely now. Arch was tall and well armed with natural strength;

they would be a match from the start. If troubles came, who but Archelaus would he want beside him: Edward realized this with a start and, filled with warming emotions, he replied, "This is what I think!" and he uncustomarily lifted his little brother in an enormous embrace.

"Edward," roared Archelaus, "unhand me, you villain! Wouldst tryst betides? There will be time enow!" But as his brother dropped him on command, Archelaus landed a smart wallop upside his head, returning a brief hug *ensuite*.

Turning to the bailiff, Edward asked, "Ought we go on, Wilhem, or doest suffice for this night, think you? There will be much time for planning once we sail, but we shall be well beyond your good counsel for many months to come. And what does your morrow bring? Art thou returning to Southhampton with us?"

"For the first question, Edward," replied Wilhem, "I do think it is time for rest now. I shall be again in the port before you sail, of that you may be certe. But on the morrow, I accompany Dieter to Corsham and see his position established with Jonathon. It is a fine line the lad must walk and I wist a smooth onset. Jonathon must not feel he is mistrusted; rather, that he favors us by giving work to my son."

"Good, good," said Edward and Archelaus together. "But, Wilhem, I sense there is more on your mind, something left unsaid, or do I misconceive?"

"Nay, young master, thy wit hast not failed thee. This thing that teases my mind concerns Joanna. May hap we should wait on my return?"

"No, my friend, if my wife is a worry to you, I would have it spoken now or never rest this night. What is it? Please. Is it the babe?"

"Aye, in a way, it concerns the babe and the lads as well. Sit a minute longer and I will tell you my idea."

"First I must see to a watch for the night, Wilhem, but it will not take long. Enjoy the air and we shall speak anon."

As Edward strode off, his father-in-law's bailiff stretched out in the warm grasses and stared at the stars, his mind an ocean away, his imagination challenged. If Edward be of a mind with him, Joanna's plight, at least, might be fairly eased. If not, he must needs conjure up an equally effective remedy, for the prospects were dire for a lass on her own with naught but young children and exhausted men about her. I've half a mind to ship off with them myself, I am that worried for her, he thought.

"Wilhem, Wilhem?" said Edward, shaking the older man's arm.

"Aye, Edward, aye, I merely pass the time. Is all manner of thing well?"

Giving Wilhem a hand up, Edward answered, "Very well, thank thee. The lads and wife are sleeping, Dieter is taking the first watch, I am to relieve him, and the crofters sleep and will divide the hours unto cocklight. Now, as we walk, please, what is this about my beautiful Joanna?"

"You think, may hap, it is the coming child I am concerned about, Edward. But it is not this alone. I had quiet time enroute to the coast and the thought grew upon me of Joanna's position as thrust into arduous and demanding circumstances with no one to companion her; no one, that is, but the men of the family and the lads."

"But, Wilhem, we shall be constantly together, working side by side. I shall not leave her unprotected on my very life."

"I know, I know, my lad, but what she needs, aught than thee, is another woman! To hear another female voice, to have a right-hand presence of someone like herself, who thinks as she and can cook, clean, and care for the children with her. Another woman could save Joanna many steps and divide the burden. Think ye a fresh and hale Joanna will step from the *James* onto the New England shore six or eight weeks hence?"

"Sometimes, Wilhem," said Edward, stopping and holding his head in his hands, "I think this endeavor not well contrived by half. It is seemingly full of peril and danger from the moment we board. In our scurrying, we have had little time to grasp the import of Joanna's lot. Your tempered hortation goes straight to a matter we have neglected and strikes dred in my bones!"

Dropping onto one of the nearby stones, he raised his head and asked, "Wilhem, tell me, am I, indeed, placing my fledgling family at risk? For, if so, it shadows my whole intent and draws me to rebehold our plans!"

The younger man's plight touched the bailiff and he stood before him, his hand on his shoulder. Arthur Salway's parting words rang in his ears: "Secure this venture, Wilhem, and the kingdom is thine! Above all, let no evil betide the daughter of my heart or her babes." When Edward turned his stricken face up to him, he rushed to reassure him that all was not lost by any means.

"Edward, take heart, despair follows upon your weariness. You are fatigued for many days and weeks now. I do have an idea to offer and it came to me in a flash on the docks this day morn."

"What is it, Wilhem, please—what have ye devised?"

"Joanna has been on my mind, lad, even before we met. Now the babe. But the solution was before my eyes this morne as I rode through the crowds along the dock. In spite of the hour, small groups of children and youth sat begging. It was obvious they had passed the night as they were; yea, some were sleeping yet. Orphaned by the London plague, I was informed. Later, when the mayor and I spoke of Arthur's business, I mentioned the children of the docks. To make it brief, Edward, he told me of some nuns who harbour such and who seek sponsors for them. There it was, a provident path set right before me. What do you say?"

Edward roused, grasping Wilhem's proposal with a glimmer of hope in his eyes. "Are you saying we might find a companion for Joanna with these church women, Wilhem? A young maiden of an age to be a boon? Ist your thinking this?"

"Aye, so it is. Find the nuns. They are not far off the high road entering the city."

Something flickered in Edward's eye and he turned to stare at the bailiff as at a stranger. "Wilhem, bailiff of the Salway manse, you are either knave or knight, I know not which. But of this I am certe. There is a young female in Southhampton who is even now preparing for a voyage. Am I correct? And am I correct to suppose you can not only assure me it is so, but can tell me her name, her age, her weight, her height, her coloring, and God knows what else!"

"Her pedigree," replied the older man. "Her qualities, as well," he added, a slight turn-up beginning at the corners of his mouth.

"Confound it, but you sound glib, and well you might!" shouted Edward, clasping Wilhem by his shoulders and giving him a potent shake. "What more? Doest have a name for this gift from heaven?"

"Her name is Catherine O'Malley, Edward, called Caitlin by all."

"In God's name! Irish!"

"Aye, and Catholic."

"Wilhem, good man, are ye fitting a square in a round hole, think ye, may hap?"

"There's more, Edward."

Edward slumped again to the stone seat and motioned Wilhem to join him. "Tell me nay that she be also with child, my friend. Anything betide...is she lame? foreshortened? pocked? surly? what, what, out with it!"

"No fault but one is to be found in her, Edward. She is fair of face, tall and slender, of a full spirit, good carriage, litterate, hearty..."

"Aye, so, so," interrupted Edward, "the rest or I'll not say another word but curse the ground you stand on!"

Wilhem paced a few long strides into the circle, searched the stars as for script and slowly returned. Edward rose and when they stood eye to eye, Wilhem said, in a near whisper, "Master Woodman, she comes a double blessing. She comes a twin."

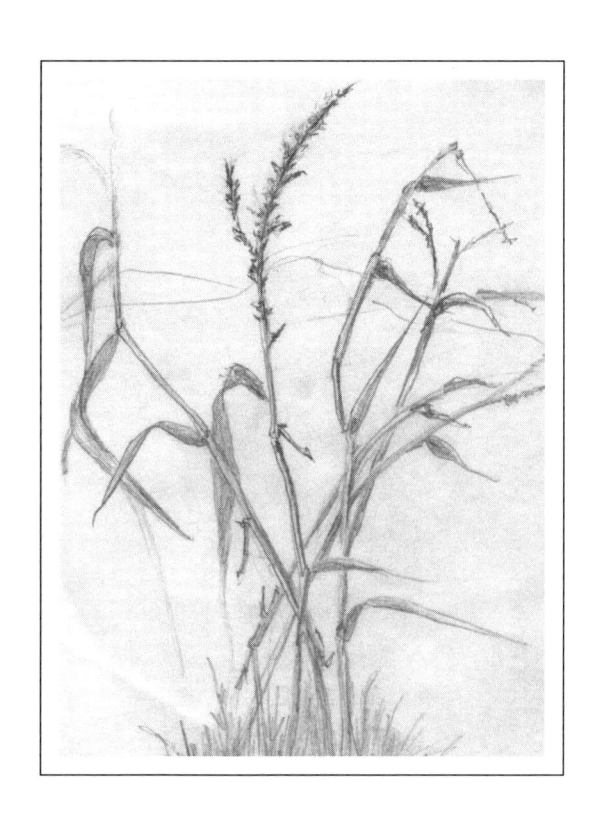

The Librarian

JACK GALLOWAY
ELAINE WAGNER

JACK GALLOWAY teaches writing and American literature.

ELAINE WAGNER writes American literature.

These characters sort of shouldered their way into our lives while we were working on some other stuff. One thing led to another, and pretty soon they were involved in some big-time corruption with a variety of genuinely scary bad guys after them, and little time for romance. So this has become a longer work in progress that we're trying to help them sort out. It's not clear right now how things are going to turn out for them, but we're working on it.

Yaz

I had seen legs like that once before. That time they were attached to a nurse in the infirmary. I remember telling her there seemed nothing infirm at all about her. She explained that I had just given her reason to write up an inmate, and if I had any other observations about her appearance I should consider keeping them to myself. I told her I didn't think that would be any fun at all because sexual innuendo was really more fun with two participants. She said she'd heard enough and got a male nurse to stitch up the gash in my arm. World-class legs and a bad attitude to go with them. Is it just me or is nobody having any fun anymore? I was the one who was locked up; you'd think I would be the one with a chip. But I'm pretty sure to this day there was a little crinkle at the corner of her mouth as she left the room. I caught it in the mirror above the sink. The male nurse had clubs for hands and I'm guessing if you saw his legs it would be tough keeping your breakfast down.

Before I went to prison I was a world-class smartass. Really subtle, ironic material rolled effortlessly off the tongue with just the right nuanced self-deprecating delivery. Women, in particular, seemed to find it intriguing. I think they sensed a keen mind behind all that dripping sarcasm. All those nineteenth-century dilettantes who sat around discussing the nature of wit would have considered me a case study. One of the things you learn right away in prison though is that nobody likes a smartass. This becomes particularly problematic because your average resident of a state penitentiary has no problem expressing himself if he doesn't like your personality. Or your hair color for that matter. So I gave up being a smarty pants, and in the year I've been out, I can't seem to get it back. The world is probably a better place for it.

On good days I like to think that my wife was getting tired of living with a wise guy, and our marriage wasn't long for the world. That's easier to live with than the notion that my wife was afraid of me. I think the way she put it was "How can I be certain all that anger won't be directed on me someday?" This from a woman I was married to and adored for six years. In the end, the only communication I had with her after I became a charge of the state was a notice of divorce action, and that actually came from her attorney. On really bad days I think a lot about how much I would still like to talk to her. I go to great lengths to avoid being overcome by those days. I don't know, maybe talking is overrated.

The librarian's legs were like the nurse's but a little longer. In retrospect I wouldn't have thought that was possible, but there it was. Most people don't realize it's reasonable to spend an entire morning thinking about women's legs. Or an afternoon or evening for that matter. It's the sort of thing I think a lot about. It's not that you think about it full-time for an entire morning, but your mind drifts back to the subject as the morning wears on. The librarian clearly had a pretty strong gene pool behind her. And as for behinds, I like to think she wouldn't feel the need to get civil authority involved if I had made some oblique reference to her also impressive behind.

These days I think less about women's legs than I did when I was in prison. But I had more time on my hands then, and in five years your mind can cover a lot of pairs of legs.

Pilar

She'd have to walk down three flights of winding marble stairs to the ground floor in three-inch spikes. She'd lost time and stayed too late. The custodian had already locked the doors and gone somewhere deep in the heart of her Italian Renaissance library to complete his chores. Hopefully, the click-click would sound through the empty building and let him know he was not alone. Some absentminded librarian had got herself locked in.

She shouldn't have worn high heels to work. But she knew they would be taking her out for a good-luck lunch and she intended her male colleagues and maybe a customer or two to remember her for her nice legs as well as her sharp mind. That mind had been her undoing, after all. If she hadn't passed on the tip-top on that last civil service test she wouldn't have been the most recently appointed Librarian II. In time of budget cuts seniority counted. But then, demotion was better than no job at all. Her mother had told everyone at Our Lady of Guadalupe that her daughter, the college graduate, was now a "libarian" and worked at the big marble library downtown. That still was true, at least.

She grew up in a family where food was always on the table, there was enough material for an Easter dress for every well-behaved daughter, and the poor were people you saved money for during Lent. In their house there was always enough loose change in the junk drawer for bus fare. Color was never lacking in their rented apartment. And as Mother always pointed out, paper flowers were brighter and lasted longer. Still, they didn't smell like a peony pulled through a picket fence so it was technically on your side of the yard, not your neighbor's.

There was that man who came to the Information Commons once a week, early Saturday morning, before the rush, and stayed a good part of the day. She wondered if he'd miss her. He always asked for a copy of the *Wall Street Journal* and took a chair at the table behind the reference desk. It had been all of three months now. He had been hard not to notice. The truth is, today wasn't the first time she had worn high heels and a shorter skirt. He was tall, broad-shouldered, and brooding. Her best friend Sally said tall men made her feel more female. She believed her hips looked trimmer when her hand was on a muscular arm. And she preferred her heroes to be unhinged by lost love like a Heathcliff, or better yet a Mr. Rochester, who lived to brood a longer time. The fact that he had gone blind in a fire only made him more interesting to Sally. Sally would be salivating over this guy, salivating and sashaying by.

But the eyes of the *Wall Street Journal* man seldom left his bible. When he did look up it was only to catch you watching him and then to dismiss you with a stare down. Even Sally would have been daunted by that stare down. Those cool green eyes seemed to see all too much and find it wanting. She simply got up and retrieved a book from the shelf just behind him. She had, of course, been looking for the *Webster's Unabridged*. Some one must have mis-shelved it. She looked up the word "misogynist" to break the spell.

Still, one day *he* actually approached *her*. He had a question, and the librarian didn't have to check a reference book or visit a web site to answer it.

"Read any good books lately?"

It was a flirty little reference interview, held promise. Now she might never see him again. It's possible he'd never venture up another flight to the Periodical Room. People often found their niches.

"Thanks, Matt. I promise not to stay so late again. Have a nice night."

Yaz

Just for fun, I waited outside the library and watched The Librarian walk those legs out and thought for a while about the first time I watched her walk in. Just for fun, I followed the progression from there to the first time I talked to her. At that time I spent most of my Saturday mornings in the library with the Friday Wall Street Journal. Actually I spent a lot of mornings at the library. Libraries are quiet, and prisons are never, ever quiet. I guess the truth is most of the world is pretty noisy, but in prisons the noise always suggests something vaguely and nonspecifically dangerous. There is always the very real possibility of random violence that may or may not involve you. Organized violence has always been with us, and in times and places of our lives serves a purpose. But the random purposelessness of prison violence is so constant it becomes almost religious. In the end it either prepares you or it destroys your sense of self, leaving you utterly unprepared for the rest of your life. On most days I feel like it prepared me.

The first time I talked to The Librarian I had to spend the better part of an hour screwing up my courage. I had been out of prison for over a year and hadn't been involved in a conversation with a woman who wasn't a clerk or a prostitute or a prison guard for six years. I asked her if she'd read any good books lately. Snappy, I know.

She laughed, "Sure, what kind of librarian would I be if I hadn't?" Her eyes left mine for a minute, but then came back, and I realized they were grey. Jesus, unbelievable legs, grey eyes, and dense black hair. Talk about out of my depth.

But I had come this far and she seemed to be possibly mistaking my insecurity and unease for depth and mystery. Some days even Irish guys get lucky.

"Well can you recommend one to me?" I was clearly on a roll now. If I got any wittier how could she possibly keep up?

"But you might not like my kind of book. Tell me what you read last that you really liked, and maybe I can recommend something. It's an old librarian's formula; usually works like a charm."

I was quickly reaching the point of nonsustainability. The ability to carry on any sort of conversation with a beautiful woman is a skill that needs daily prac-

tice. And come on, it had been six years. "But then you might know more about me than you would want to." Christ.

She looked at me for a moment and actually tilted her head just a bit, and her hair moved around the side of her face, and that was it for me. I thought about feigning a seizure and then thought I might actually have one and she finally ended the misery, "Well let me show you the new releases, maybe you'll find something there you like."

I managed a grunt of some sort and followed her to the new fiction section. Her hair reached almost to the place where her legs started, and it sort of moved like liquid sand on her back when she walked. I followed her, strong of heart, and hardly drooling at all.

Pilar

There was a maleness about him you could smell when he walked by and it wasn't Armani. There was a presence, a lethal combination of strength, sinew, and confidence. God, these days her hormones protested too much. She couldn't really blame them. They were just demanding what they thought was their due. She was a long time between boyfriends she couldn't remember why she had liked, but they had served their purpose with some regularity. Jesus, Mary, and Joseph, she was starting to think like a man. Perhaps, she was just a little bored in her new assignment. It didn't take much training to learn the materials. They were magazines and newspapers, after all. And the indexes to them were on the computer. Between customers she played and replayed a new "she said, he said" scenario. She might actually use it, should he come in. By four in the afternoon it was edited to perfection. She'd walk up behind him, look at what he was reading, and then casually ask, "Got any good stock tips lately?" She'd toss her hair as if she didn't really care.

"What kind of an investor would I be if I didn't?" He would, of course, get the joke.

"Any you'd like to recommend to me?"

"You might not be the kind of investor that I am. Are you looking for a safe bet or do you like to take risks?"

"If I told you that, you might learn more about me than I'm willing to tell." She'd get up quickly but not before he got the last word.

"The younger you are the more time you have to take risks."

"The more you've got to lose. But thank you, I'll keep that in mind." She would be wearing tight jeans under her short tweed jacket. There would be no way to modestly pull the jacket down over her derriere, the way she always did when she got up and walked away, whether she was wearing skirt, slacks, or too-tight jeans. But she wouldn't have pulled down anyway, not while he was watching. She wouldn't let him know that it mattered to her.

The daydream was starting to unravel. A librarian didn't usually wear jeans except when she was weeding the stacks and certainly not on a busy Saturday. Still she went on to imagine his low whistle. She couldn't be offended. This was her imagination after all.

Yaz

It was a warm side-lit summer evening, and this time I watched from the coffee shop across the street as she walked down the steps. She stopped while three neighborhood kids rolled by on noisy skateboards. She watched them roll by and then turned to look at the building. Clearly there was no way I could top my dazzling performance last time we talked, but my heart was strong and pride was no longer in my vocabulary, so I planned my trajectory, crossed the street, and was casually strolling down the sidewalk as she turned and started walking.

"Nice evening what?" I said without even spilling any coffee. I had on a pair of jeans and a white t-shirt that probably belonged in a Frankie Avalon movie, but she recognized me right off. She was making a designer skirt and heels look even better than the designer would have imagined. The sun was behind her and it caught some of the red in her dark hair that was pulled together in an artful gathering at the back of her head.

"It's absolutely perfect. Mr. New Fiction, did you find anything you liked?"

"Not really. I tried the new Philip Roth, but it was a little self-important and east-coasty for me I think. Us hayseeds don't do well with all that relativism. We like our stories to have a point." I could keep this repartee up for a good five or six more seconds. I tried to smile enigmatically.

She tilted her head again. Why did she do that? "You're right, you never feel real satisfied with any of those guys who can't seem to stand for anything."

"That's it, isn't it. I wouldn't care if they were fascists, if they just stood for something; anything." This was getting easier.

She seemed to think about that for a minute, so I decided I'd better fill the space while I was rolling. "But I started Larry Brown's new one. That man could tell a story."

"Oh yeah," she said, and her eyes seemed to spark just a bit. "Like he wasn't even trying. Like he was just telling it to you sitting on the porch. I love that."

My God, she read Larry Brown. I had no idea what to do then, so I said, "How about I buy you a coffee and we talk about who likes Larry Brown more." Hard to imagine wit like that, I know.

"But you already have a coffee." She laughed.

"Which seems to have gone a bit cold on me." I looked at the coffee in my hand for a moment before I forged on, "So you could buy me a refill."

"But a refill is a lot less than a regular coffee, so then I'd owe you the difference." She smiled with one corner of her mouth, and I remained upright, but had to stand very still to avoid what once might have been called a swoon. I wondered what happened when she smiled with her whole mouth.

She watched me for a minute. "What, no snappy comeback?"

I watched over her shoulder while a young family crossed the street. They were pretty casual about the whole affair, and traffic came to a stop as if this was just what went on in this neighborhood, families just wandered out into traffic. St. Paul wasn't Boston. I focused back on those grey eyes. "No comeback. I think I'm a little out of practice. But you better say yes to the coffee, because in about a half an hour I'm going to give up and go away."

She seemed to have made up her mind. "OK, Mr. Wall Street Journal, new fiction guy, let's have some coffee. But sooner or later you're going to have to tell me your real name."

I turned to cross the street and sort of motioned for her to go first. Like I always do I kind of said it under my breath, "Yaz." I couldn't see if she laughed, but at least she didn't laugh out loud.

Inside, the coffee shop was mostly downtown J Crew types who each spent about ten minutes ordering what must be extravagantly complex concoctions. Sometime while I was in prison ordering coffee became a process akin to sorting out the double helix. We waited quietly in line and then each spent exactly four seconds ordering a small cup of coffee. Exchanging the currency added another fifteen seconds, and the staff seemed utterly clueless about what to do with the remaining time. I think The Librarian looked at me a couple times, but it seemed like if I returned the look she might see the fear in my eyes, so I watched the fifteen-year-old produce our coffee.

"How about that table in the corner?" I asked.

She looked around at the rest of the patrons and said, "How about we walk? It's such a glorious afternoon, and I've been inside all day."

Walking was good, I thought, less chance to see the terror in my eyes. The fear of making a fool of yourself in front of a beautiful woman is even worse than the fear of getting caught driving a minivan, but not as bad as the fear of running into your old prison cellmate on the street. I reminded myself of that simple fact and my heart rate slowed noticeably.

We walked out into the late-day sun and I watched the long shadows it made on the street and sidewalk. "So how does it seem to be going so far?" I asked.

"Well, I'm not sure. Are we talking about the day or the week, or the year, or my entire life to date?" She did that thing at the side of her mouth again. I could see it from the corner of my eye. It was disarmingly cute and sexy at the same time.

"I actually meant the coffee, but pick any of the others."

"Let's talk about your day instead. How's your day going so far?" She took a sip of coffee and shook the hair off her face. Then she handed me her cup to hold while she gathered her hair up behind her head and re-tied it up with a barrette that looked like tortoiseshell. She had a lot of hair and it made a big statement. I don't think anyone would have even noticed my knees wobbling. Stout lads us Irish.

"Actually, my day so far has been like most of my days."

"And what would most of your days be like?" We stopped at a corner and she turned to look at me.

"Well, probably pretty exciting stuff to your average urbanite, I guess. There's breakfast, of course. And then I like to look at the paper for awhile. And I like to get some exercise before lunch. And then after lunch there's high tea, of course, with a party of favorites and other swells. Then there's the whole matter of picking out an outfit for dinner, and from there I'm sure you can imagine the anxiety that goes into the actual dinner prep. And, well, you get the idea."

She wasn't smiling. Shit. "Does patter like this work with most women?"

I had to think about that for a moment and then tried unsuccessfully to look her in the eyes. "Some, I guess, if they haven't been around much. How's it working for you?"

"Pretty lame so far."

"How did I know that?"

"Because you're a smart guy. And smart guys know beautiful women don't like smartasses—they're usually covering up stunningly bad toilet training."

I was so far out of my depth I should have just gone home, but my work ethic kicked in. "And you're a beautiful woman."

"Yup."

"And that's a problem because you're also smart."

"Yup." *This time she laughed, just quickly.*

"And I'm way out of my league here right?"

She thought about that one for a moment. "Can't tell yet, but it's not looking good."

"Let's walk some more," *I said.* "I thought I was doing pretty well at that."

"Let's walk." *She smiled while she said it. Hope sprang up in my heart.*

We crossed a busy four-lane street and walked a couple blocks down to a park that ran along the bank of the Mississippi. The shadows were getting longer, but it was still warm, especially for an early June evening in Minnesota. The river still smelled of stone and sand and water, and it seemed that maybe some of the work of the various environmental groups out to restore the river was paying off. A decade ago by June the river smelled more of human waste, and by August the smell could make your eyes water on bad days. We sat on a bench and watched people wandering across the Wabasha Bridge while we made small talk about the condo explosion along the river. She told me her name was Pilar and we talked for awhile about the subtle importance of names in our lives.

"So is Yaz your given name or a nickname?"

"Yaz McCandless is what it says on my birth certificate. Born 1967, Boston Mass. My father took his loyalty to the Red Sox very seriously."

"I'm going to go out on a limb and guess there is something here I should be getting." *She raised both dark eyebrows. I enjoyed that for a moment.*

"Carl Yastrzemski played left field for the Sox from 1961 to 1983. Actually played first base for the last few years, but you get the idea. His nickname was

Yaz. In 1967 he won the triple crown, so my father really had no choice in the matter. I've always thought it was fortunate I wasn't a girl."

She thought about that for a minute. It seemed to be something she did when she sensed the subject was important; she let things be quiet for a moment before responding. It gave you the sense she was really paying attention. It felt nice. This was a complicated woman. "So what was it your father liked so much about this Yastrzemski?"

Absolutely the right question, I thought. I didn't ask her to marry me, but it crossed my mind. "He loved his work ethic. Yaz showed up every day, played hurt, and could do pretty much everything there was to do on a baseball field."

"Cool," Pilar said. Way, way out of my league.

We walked back toward the library and she asked me what I did for a living now that we knew I had a good work ethic.

"I'm a day trader. I used to be a teacher, but now I pick stocks and watch markets and events and try to buy and sell them at just the right times."

"And you can make a living doing that?"

"I had a good mentor, so the short answer is yes. The longer answer is, you have to pay attention to events more than finances. The stock market these days is primarily about perceptions."

She crinkled the corner of her mouth again. "Good to know. I may need some advice in the near future if the library budget cuts don't ease up."

We found ourselves back at the coffee shop as the sun sank below the trees and turned the horizon orange. "This has been pleasant, Yaz. Maybe I'll see you around the library again. Or maybe we could get another coffee."

"Or maybe we could get some dinner." It was out before I could get it back. "Jesus, I'm sorry. I'm not usually given to overexuberance. You can ignore the adolescence."

She narrowed one of those grey eyes at me for a moment. "Dinner would be nice." She finally said. And then she pulled out a pen and paper from her bag and wrote down Pilar Peres and her number. There it was. The answer I wasn't expecting that left me only one place to go. A long time ago I had decided no woman would have to go to dinner with me without the story in advance. Or at least part of the story.

She said, "Call me." Then there was a big smile as she turned to go.

I stood for a moment looking like a thirteen-year-old, but then stuck to the plan I had made several years ago, a plan that I had made the center point of my life. "Pilar, before you go..." I wasn't sure if she could detect the trembling in my voice or not, but it didn't seem important. "I'd really like to call you. And I'd really like to have dinner with you. And I'd really like to get to know you. But before we even think about anything like that you should know that the reason I'm so out of practice is that I was in prison for five years." It came out in a rush and it hurt like hell, but it was my life, and Pilar was, as best I could tell, a really decent person.

She looked at me for a long moment. Twice she started to say something, but stopped to reconsider it. I stood there pretty much with no idea what to do. Finally she asked, "Is it fair to ask why?"

"It's fair." I tried to smile. "It's just hard to talk about."

"Try." This was a serious moment in the company of a smart, serious, beautiful woman.

"Because I killed a man."

"Jesus."

"I know."

"I don't know what to say. Was it an accident?"

"No. I tried to intervene in something and it got out of control and I didn't have many options. Or at least I didn't believe I did."

"Jesus." She said again.

"I know." I said again.

"Can I think about this?" she asked.

"Of course."

She looked across the street at nothing. Her hair was a dense gorgeous mess at the back of her head. "Tell you what," she finally said. "Give me your number and I'll see if I can call you."

I did, and she turned and walked away. I tried to watch anything but the silhouette of her against the sun. I felt absolutely holy. And absolutely alone.

Pilar

It was a hard call. A man respected her enough to confess a crime before she might become emotionally involved. That was a good thing, but not so much if he expected just as much honesty in return. She found out the rest of his story easily enough. He'd killed someone. It was in the public record.

Over appetizers she could distract him with what she'd learned about him. Through the entrée he'd still be reeling. She'd hit him with the hard questions after dessert, a dense chocolate that sharpens one sense as it deadens the others. As they walked to their cars she'd let him know another date was not out of the question. Another day, another date, another time to consider her own night of the soul.

She hadn't really thought about if or when or where she would tell anyone about her own relationship with grace. In her religion all you really needed to do was tell your confessor, but under her circumstances a priest would be the most difficult person to tell. She'd put herself on a spiritual island once she walked through the door of the rectory and asked Father Paolo for a private consultation. She could tell by the wary look in his eyes and he certainly could tell from the flame in her cheeks that this meeting was not about absolution. They had known each other since they were ten years old. He taught her chess on a picnic table in his backyard. She taught him how to catch carp in the river on her grandfather's boat. When they were old enough to start dating they practiced kissing on each other. It seemed a practical, safe experiment till they got too good at it.

For a little while after that surprise they stopped meeting for chess and carp. It was all a little too confusing. He started hanging out more with her brothers. She went to the library and got books from the Young Adult Room fiction section, romance novels written for girls just like her, eager for their first real boyfriend, but not sure how it worked.

By sophomore year, they both knew enough to realize it might be okay to be more than friends. Maybe they didn't know. Maybe they just came to feel. It felt good holding hands in a movie. It was exciting parking at the lookout and letting your mouths stay open for the first time. Paulie, as she always called him, knew his commandments, and when they should stop short of confession. An altar boy, the priests knew his voice even in a confessional whisper. And he didn't dare not receive communion at the Mass he served. And so, she stayed a virgin and he stayed a server, and they both had a date for every high school dance.

She was looking forward to the junior/senior prom. She was thinking of wearing black. Black was grown-up and sophisticated. Black was the most dramatic choice for mascara and the bravest choice in nail polish.

Everyone had to have a little black dress. And, of course, her hair was black, black as night, luminous as the moon. And, come to think of it, when she played chess she always won playing black. Black was becoming her color.

One summer night, parked on Harriet Island, she snuggled into his shoulder, and asked him what he thought of black.

"You'd look beautiful in any color." He kissed her forehead.

"I had thought of white. It's also dramatic. But I'll save it for my wedding day. Unless you think I should defy tradition."

"You'll look just as beautiful in defiance as tradition."

"But you must have a preference? And it's important that you of all people like my choice."

"Pilar, I think we need to talk."

"Of course we do. Like about how many children? My parents and yours had way too many. Wouldn't it be nice if at least the girls had their own room?"

"You wouldn't wish one of your brothers or sisters to not be here, would you?"

"Don't tell me you buy all that stuff about birth control and hell fire?"

"Pilar, you must know how I feel about the church."

"Well, I know from experience you obey all the commandments."

"I've been talking with Father Santiago."

"Not about us, I hope."

"About me. About me and the priesthood."

She might as well have told him to take her home then and there, because from that moment on he didn't kiss her again except on the forehead or in her palm. Maybe then would have been the time to press her breasts against him. She knew he felt the same things she felt. His fingers went to her buttons and fingered them way too long. She would have opened them herself if his hand hadn't stopped. Once his hand went lower than her back. More and more and more they both came up breathless and wanting more. Letting go was becoming impossible. She thought it would eventually happen. She only had to wait for his lead.

His face came out of his hands, he started up the car, and she went to the prom with someone else. She dated a football player, a baseball player, a basketball player, whatever was in season. She watched to see if he was watching, but it seemed God had won. She didn't realize you could fight God until later.

College was a distraction. The first two years she struggled trying to find a major. She almost wished she too had a vocation and knew with such certainty what she wanted to do. And then there he was, being introduced to their congregation as a visiting deacon. She saw his eyes search the church and find hers. And she knew Paulie's God still existed, but then so did she and the rectory was not on the moon.

She didn't really have to throw herself at him. He was the one who closed the door to the reconciliation room. He was the one who pulled her out of her kneeling position on the prie-dieu. She only had to wet her lips and touch his cheek. She was glad he was inexperienced enough not to know she was no longer a virgin. Or perhaps he didn't care. She didn't feel like one. A virgin wouldn't have known just how good this moment was. A virgin might have thought this was holy, a sacrament. She knew it wasn't and she saw to it that he wouldn't be confused. By the time they pulled apart he would feel the sacrilege, would know he had no right to be a priest.

Sadly, he also seemed to decide he had no right to be hers. He left her as she was pulling the sweater back over her head. He didn't put his Roman collar back on. And no one to this day was sure where he went.

She had every right to claim his love. He was hers before he was God's. She felt no guilt. Only anger that God had somehow claimed him anyway or worse yet, consigned him to the devil.

She never went to church again. The encounters after Paulie came in what felt like a tumbling, falling rush, each enjoyed less for itself than for the black mark smeared on her soul. Black, as it turned out, was her color.

But you can't make a career of being bad. Somehow you have to make your way out of your mother's house, especially when she saw you go into the rectory that day before Father Paolo disappeared. Mothers know these things, mothers never forget, although they may keep your secret so no one else knows about the disgrace you share.

Yaz may never need to know. At this stage she could probably let him assume a librarian had no interesting secrets. If he poked around she might say something romantic like, "Let's pretend our lives began when we met."

Nah, that would only make him more curious. And God, it was the worst line she ever heard. Who knows if this would even get to that stage. He could mess up any time. She kind of hoped he wouldn't.

Yaz

By the second week of June unseasonable heat and humidity settled into Minnesota, and the local descendants of hearty German and Scandinavian settlers looked utterly confused and complained at length about it. Minnesotans don't know quite what to do when summer feels like summer. In a broader way they just seem to have an uneasy relationship with the outdoors in general. They spend a lot of time asking each other, "What's it like out there today?" And they're a little more comfortable if the answer gives them a reason to stay inside. So despite the long hot days, a lot of my favorite haunts were pretty deserted. Parks and bike paths were often there for my private use.

I didn't miss the things I expected to miss while I was incarcerated. A glass of good wine, or the feel of a woman's hair, or an evening at the theater never really lingered on my mind as acute losses. But the absence of the fragrance that comes with the natural world was unbearable. I made myself crazy trying to recall the smell of a spruce forest or a simple backyard flower garden. The human mind doesn't seem to be organized in a way that allows for the recollection of those remembered smells. You can close your eyes and pull up visual images of important sunsets, and you can even remember the texture and taste of favorite foods and drink, but the smell of new-mown grass or a dog's fur always resides just outside human reach. Prison smells just like you'd think it would; concrete and metal and industrial disinfectants are always there, but it is the literal and metaphoric stench of wasted humanity that pervades and ultimately overwhelms the senses. I have been living outside of the walls for over a year, and that combination of smells still seems a part of my being.

I stopped going to the library so Pilar wouldn't feel uncomfortable. And I pretty much stayed away from the neighborhood altogether. One day was pretty much the same as the one before it. I watched the markets in the morning and talked on the phone with my friend Morgan who served as my stock trading mentor. Morgan was still in prison and would be there for at least five more years. He was sixty-five years old and his health was failing, so there was a pretty good chance he would die there. It wasn't so much that he was sick in any specific way, but more that he had just given up. Life had been devilishly cruel to Morgan. He was a brown-shoe accountant who had spent most of his working life managing pension assets for large unions. He was recognized as one of the best money managers in the Twin Cities, but he was so socially insecure that he was destined to always be a backroom guy. His insecurities were particularly problematic around women and, as a result, he had gone through four wives. The first three had been kind, thoughtful women who saw his basic decency, but ultimately couldn't find a way to live with his relentless peculiarities and eccentricities and desperate need for order. So, had given them all generous settlements and wished them well, somehow seeming to understand that they really shouldn't have to put up with him. The last wife, though, got him when he was looking at sixty, desperately lonely and completely vulnerable. She was thirty-five or so, surgically enhanced and dyed and augmented and liposuctioned and manipulative. He never saw her coming, but she saw him from miles away. She loved to travel, and really liked expensive houses and cars and jewelry, and pretty soon Morgan had stolen an enormous amount of money from the pension plan he ran. They caught up with him in almost no time and sent him away for a minimum of ten years. He paid back most of the money, and could have made it all back in a year, but the District Attorney really wanted to be a U.S. Senator, and this looked like the case to get him there.

So now Morgan coached me on timing the markets and watching the peripheral factors that most people didn't realize influenced stock performance. If I was careful, and prudent, and listened to Morgan I could live comfortably without losing my stomach lining. So I did my trading in the morning and spent my afternoons exercising beyond reasonable limits until I was too tired to think about how my life could have turned out. I spent the evenings reading and looking for new and interesting places to watch the sunset.

The week after the Fourth of July the winds shifted to the south and added even more humidity to the hottest summer Minneapolis had enjoyed in fifty years. On Wednesday evening I was sitting on my front porch waiting for the sun to turn orange and then red in all the humidity when my cell phone rang and the name Pilar Peres appeared on the screen. I hadn't thought about The Librarian more than two or three times that day. "Who is this really?" I picked up after the fourth ring. Tasteful.

She hesitated for a moment before, "It's Pilar, the librarian. But you knew that didn't you?"

"I did. Sorry, once a smartass, always annoying. It's a complex skill." I rolled my eyes at my stunning lack of creativity.

She was quiet for a long moment. "Are you done?"

"Yes."

"You don't make it easy do you?"

"I'm trying to make it exactly that. I guess I'm just surprised to hear from you. Actually, I'm just really pleased to hear from you and I seem to be having trouble saying so."

"Wow, that almost sounded sincere."

"Now who's the smartass?" I was quiet for a moment. "Really, it's nice to hear from you."

"How do you feel about buying me dinner?"

"Love to." I think I sort of croaked it out.

She suggested Friday night and I croaked out agreement. "I could pick you up at about eight and I can make a reservation at Lucia's if you'd like."

"I'd like. But I'll meet you there. Eight it is. I'll wear my librarian glasses so you'll know it's me."

"Cool." God, I have to get some new material.

On Friday evening I was standing in front of Lucia's at five minutes to eight with a linen jacket over my arm and a smile on my face. It was still eighty-five degrees at 8:00 and I think I probably looked as overeager as a fifteen-year-old on his first date. But I figured screw it, at least eager was sincere, and I had the feeling for whatever reason that Pilar had little time for phonies. I saw her come around the corner out of the corner of my eye, and I turned to watch her with the same idiot smile on my face. Sincerely idiotic that is. She was wearing slender white summer wool slacks and a light green sleeveless blouse, all of which seemed designed to downplay her sensuality, but I still thought about reaching out a hand to steady myself on the building. All that dark hair was pulled back in a severe bun at the back of her head, and as best I could tell she wasn't wearing any makeup at all. But she was stunning all the same, and I got that feeling of being out of my depth again. As she approached me she pulled out a pair of tortoiseshell glasses and put them on.

"Oh, it's you," I said. "I never would have recognized you without the glasses."

We sat at a small corner table by the front window. I ordered an Irish whiskey and she thought about it for a minute and had the same. We talked about restaurants and the weather and cities and books, and the conversation just sort of moved from one subject to the next. She was easy to talk to and her education served her well. I managed most of this without thinking about her with her hair down and some of her clothing missing. Maturity.

We had crab cakes, and while we waited for our dinners I asked her if she would like to talk about my time as a ward of the state.

"Sure," she said without smiling. "Would you?"

"I guess I'd like you to know the details."

She did that head tilt thing again, and said, "Well, I know most of the details. I guess what I don't know is the you behind the details." I was quiet and she went on, "Librarians have lots of resources. So I know that you were a high school English teacher who went to a student's house to investigate what you thought was a case of child abuse, more specifically incest. I know that this broke a number of school policies and you should have reported it to social services, but chose to deal with it yourself. I know you have a history of dealing with things yourself, and you seem to have more confidence in your own ability to deal with, shall we say, difficult situations than you do in the system. I know that you got to the house, in a pretty rough neighborhood, and confronted the father who may or may not have been drinking with several, shall we call them, colleagues? And I know that several of those colleagues tried to subdue you, but you proved to be difficult to subdue." She looked thoughtful for a moment. "How am I doing so far?"

I looked out the window and then back at her. Her grey eyes were bright and liquid and intense. "You have most of the facts right, so far."

"Should I go on?"

I had to think about that for a bit, but finally said that I thought she should.

"Well, it seems that somewhere in the process of attempting to subdue you a gun appeared. Later, those same colleagues suggested that you brought the gun with you, a fact you denied. But whatever the source of the gun, it did eventually, as Chekhov would tell us, go off. And one of those colleagues died. There was powder residue on you as well as some of the others, although you were adamant about not having fired the gun. In fact, you said you were trying to wrestle it away from one of the men. There was an additional problem that involved the father of the girl you had chosen to go and protect. Apparently he has several broken vertebrae, is unable to turn his head from side to side, and one of his knees was, I think the report said, pulverized. At trial, the investigating officers said you created an enormous amount of mayhem, my word, for one average-size male. Somehow, I have this feeling if I looked into the rest of your background I'd find other places you have created mayhem. In any event you went to jail for manslaughter, served your time, and now, I'm guessing, would like me and others to believe you are rehabilitated."

We sat quietly for a full two minutes, and I finally said, "I guess I don't really care too much what others think, but I'm keenly interested in what you think."

"I think I'd like to know if you brought the gun with you."

"I did not."

She held my eyes for a long time. "Fair enough," she finally said.

I asked, "Will you have more questions later?"

"Probably, but that's enough for now."

"Fair enough."

We ate our dinners and talked our way through two cups of coffee. We walked out into the still warm evening and I asked her if she would like to go for a nightcap.

She put the glasses back on and looked at me as though she had known me forever. "Another time. I'm tired and feel like going home to bed."

I smiled and said that I hoped there would be another time.

"There will. Thanks for dinner." She turned and walked down the street and around the corner without looking back.

I stood in the hazy humid light of the streetlight and tried not to tremble. And as I walked to my car I felt just a little less alone in the world.

Pilar

How brand-new was the guy? Nobody is really brand-new after thirty. And after prison? She wished she couldn't imagine it, but the trouble was she could.

And here she was fresh from a date, wondering about another, still rationalizing. She thought she was past that. She had stopped reasoning why this or that wasn't so bad when she stopped going to confession. She figured it was all just between her and her deformed little conscience. A man entering her life might not agree.

She took the Summit Avenue way home. She loved Summit enough to overshoot by one block Grand Avenue, the street where she lived. She drove slowly past homes that got older, more majestic and architecturally diverse as the avenue meandered east. She no longer dreamed she would some day live in one of those mansions, walk down winding staircases, look through lead glass windows. That would take a Prince Charming and she'd learned that less is better if you earn it yourself.

Summit Avenue ended at the cathedral, which stood on a hill overlooking downtown St. Paul. She never forgot her first visit to the cathedral. It was for the First Communion of cousin Esthela. From the perspective of a ten-year-old the steps that led to the great front marble entrance were like a stairway to heaven. It seemed as if there were thousands and every step made it a little easier to make out the marble figures over the big bronze doors. She wasn't sure at first if she was seeing Christ and his apostles or God and his archangels. It was a celestial assembly either way. And interestingly enough it appeared that she was sneaking up on them. Jesus, God, et al. were totally engrossed in themselves.

But at the moment she was engrossed in sharing the wind with the maples bending over her and the avenue. It had been a hot day, but a full moon, now in charge, was encouraging the cool draft coming through her open car windows. She had been right to skip the blusher and concentrate on a light dusting of powder. She wanted to appear as professional as possible as she laid down the facts of his life—as much for him as for herself. Although the facts took the edge off his crime, they also pointed out the depths of his anger. There was no way of knowing if those demons were beaten down or only in remission.

At Lexington she turned south towards her Grand Avenue condo. The brownstone was a conversion of a conversion. Originally there had been four Pullman apartments that ran the whole length of the building. Then they had each been divided in two, the more profitable to rent. Now they were back to full length, and sold outright. She was proud of hers, proud of owning her own place, second story north. She could walk to the prestigious Lexington Restaurant. She could grab a cone at the ice cream shop on the corner. She could buy a birthday gift for a friend or the latest in cookery or a bridesmaid dress that she wouldn't mind being caught dead in. There were specialty shops after specialty shops with striped or scalloped awnings. Sidewalk cafes were popping up as fast as the zoning laws could be amended. Grand Avenue was a little town, complete with its own movie theatre, one screen downstairs, one screen upstairs. No churches, but that was okay too.

She just wasn't sure what Yaz would make of it, of her, once he knew more. A West Side Hispanic girl should invest in her own community and not behave like any other young upwardly mobile young professional and predictably flee to an up-and-coming neighborhood. Actually, Grand Avenue had already arrived! Yuppie. What exactly did those initials mean? The Y she got. Young. The U she got. Upwardly. The first P was Professional. The second? She didn't have a clue. And was it Yuppy or Yuppie? A quick Google would erase the mystery. But other mysteries were more pressing.

Out on her wrought-iron balcony she sipped lemonade, enjoyed a little more breeze, and thought about their first real date. Thinking was easier in bare feet with red tiles cooling her soles. The antique streetlights put a nice glow on things. The ice in her glass sparkled. Her nails gleamed with her pearl-polish pedicure. She wriggled her toes as she rewound and played back.

She had known he was there waiting before she even rounded the corner. Anticipation was in the air, hers as well as his. A shaggy poodle had looked back at her as he led his master towards Lucia's. There was a tease in his uplifted snoot as if he were saying, "I spied him first! I might even give him a whiff."

She hadn't remembered Yaz being so blond. He may have spent more time under the sun since she last saw him. He certainly hadn't been in her dark, dim library. If he meant for her to notice his absence, even miss him, it had worked. He had a jacket over his arm. Frank Sinatra would have draped it over his shoulder. Was it because Yaz didn't have a pose in him or was he just too cool to imitate?

She almost forgot to pop on her glasses. But putting them on right then and there was even more fun.

"The Librarian! I almost didn't recognize you without the glasses."

They started on the light note she had been hoping for. The appetizers and the small talk prolonged the light. By the crab cakes he felt comfortable enough to broach The Subject that was breathing down their lightness. It was time to go into her reporting librarian mode.

His eyes never left hers, never looked away as she told him the facts as she knew them. She liked that and she returned the courtesy, only stopping to look deeper as she asked how he thought she was doing and if she should go on. He didn't wince when she mentioned *the gun*. He didn't flinch at *pulverized knee*. *Pulverized* is a brutal word, dense with meaning. He didn't seem to like *rehabilitated*. That was the one time he looked down. Why? Did he already feel beyond that sort of thing? Or were there dark deeds yet to do? It was important for her to know he hadn't brought the gun. He said no with just the right speed, not sputtered out in defensive anger, or sliding out like a well-rehearsed lie. It was a-matter-of-fact of course.

And it was enough for one evening. She'd probably think of something else to ask, but for now she wanted it to rest on that "of course." She made a joke of putting her glasses back on as she left. They had come off after the menu left the table. Not that she was vain. She just didn't want anything between them. She promised they would do it again, but she carefully kept any urgency out of her voice. Keep it light.

She walked away feeling his eyes on her. She was tempted to take the barrette out of her hair and let him see her hair slide down her back. But this was too soon for a provocative head toss. There were more questions to ask, on both sides. She could feel her hips doing their natural swing but stopping them now would make too much of it. If only she had brought a jacket or a sweater to pull down over them. The best she could do was not look back. She knew he was still looking. It was as if she who didn't know him at all had known him forever.

Yaz

Do the best you can, and that won't go unrecognized. That's what my grandfather told me anyway, and it seemed to be good enough for him. But things were simpler in western Kansas in the early part of the twentieth century. There are lots of days I'm not so sure it's good enough in Minneapolis in the early twenty-first century. I think about my grandfather a lot, particularly when I'm restless and there are snakes in the corners of my thoughts. He was born at the beginning of the twentieth century, almost made it to the end, worked with his hands all his life, the last twenty-five years in his own auto repair shop, and had the most nimble and subtle sense of humor I've ever encountered. I'm pretty certain there was always a little Jameson in his morning coffee, and maybe that's why he lived to ninety-six. More likely it was because his view of the world had little to do with his importance in it. He worked, and ate, and slept, and told stories that on the surface were ironic and funny, but when you thought about them later you found the layers you missed at first.

These days I find myself wishing I could remember all his stories I've forgotten. I think he understood that I was wired differently than he was and he worried about it. I remember him tilting the cowboy hat he always wore off of his forehead and telling me, "Boy, you've got to try not to get quite so many knots in your rope." Of course this is the same man who always set his cowboy hat down with the brim up, and told me it was because the two most important things a man has in life he stores upside-down until he needs them. You don't get life advice like that just every day.

After my dinner with Pilar I went home to my bungalow and sat on the front porch with a tumbler of Jameson and ice. Sleep seemed unlikely, so I sat quietly and listened to the sounds of my neighborhood on a warm July night. There was a full moon that looked like damaged crystal, and it lit up my street putting bright edges on the houses and cars. My little house was built when my grandfather was twenty-five, and it is still straight and tight at all the seams. I bought it with cash, mostly from profits realized from Morgan's advice that Google stock had peaked at 600. I got out when he told me to, sunk the profits into the house, and watched Google go right on up to 700. "Christ, even I'm wrong once in a while," Morgan said. "But what are you complaining about; you still cleared a couple hundred large after taxes. You would have just spent the rest on something you didn't need anyway."

I don't think of myself as a hedonist, but on most days I'm not sure how I would identify myself. When I was released from prison I looked around at a laundry list of options that all looked like a slow slog through a hand-to-mouth existence culminating in a different form of incarceration in a state-run nursing facility. I had already been to prison, and once was enough. I couldn't go back to teaching, criminal record or not. That race was about over for reasons unrelated to a manslaughter conviction. Public school teachers are expected to parent, not teach. Before they can even approach a true curriculum they have to teach manners and respect and some notion of a work ethic, and an array of social traits they didn't sign on for and don't have the tools to impart. Changing that dynamic involves politics, an arena reserved for the self-absorbed and the venal, and the shameless. I had lost my stomach for it.

My friendship with Morgan had provided several side benefits; most importantly it had given me an understanding that our capital markets system had become a casino run by a cabal of perfected capitalists who were beyond regulation or oversight because too much depends on the status quo of that system. If the American economy doesn't grow at something like three or four percent a year, everything collapses. We need that much growth just to provide jobs for the growing population. Our capital markets provide the money to sustain that growth, and if you pay attention to that casino, all you have to do is learn how to count cards and know when to stay in and know when to fold. Bulls make money, bears make money, and pigs lose. So I became a pretty good card counter.

But being a good card counter doesn't make for much of an interior life. Sitting on your front porch on a Saturday night when it's still eighty degrees at midnight brings you face-to-face with the loneliness of your life. For a while there were a few carefully chosen professional women provided a measure of relief, but in the end the erosion of dignity that comes with that charade becomes too demeaning. For a while a form of self-imposed celibacy seemed like the more high-minded way to live, but spiritual and dignified is still lonely. I wasn't monastic, and really found that I couldn't quite imagine how anyone could be.

The moon was moving across the sky giving light to new stars, buttressing my confidence in the romantic possibility of life. Or maybe it was the Jameson. In any event, I called Pilar sometime after one.

She answered after five rings, "It's after one."

I chose to believe she was smiling. "Are you smiling when you say that?"

"No."

I stood up and looked to the moon for support that suddenly wasn't forthcoming. "Did I wake you?"

"None of your business." She was quiet for a moment and I had no idea what to say. Finally she asked, "Did you call for a reason?"

I felt pretty sure I had, but it was hard to just come out and say you were desperately lonely. But I tried. "I think I just wanted to tell you how much I enjoyed your company tonight."

"That was actually last night. Technically it's Sunday morning."

"You're not going to make this easy are you?" I grinned while I said, it hoping she'd hear the grin.

"Are you drunk?"

"Define drunk."

"You're drunk."

"Yup."

"Go to bed"

"OK."

"And one more thing."

"OK."

"You're right, I'm not going to make it easy."

"Good to know, but I'm stout of heart."

"You'll need to be."

She hung up, and I went to bed and finally slept at about four and dreamed of discarded barrettes on the floor of my bedroom.

Pilar

He had called in the middle of the night and asked if she were awake. She could have simply answered yes. Her nipples were certainly up and about after that last sneaky little breeze. "None of your business!" was what she said. And that was true enough. She hadn't opened herself to him—not yet, maybe never. But her imagination was certainly engaged, remembering and mulling over. There were his hands on the menu, running up and down the edges, strong fingers curling and uncurling, edgy fingers. She liked edgy in a man if it meant she was responsible for the tension. If a man was tense enough, wobbly enough, he could tip over. That was when a woman had power. But the truth is a man on the edge could fall either way.

Falling in love, that's the way it's always described. It's never a practiced dive or a deliberate free fall. It's more like a wind knocking you over or a tidal wave sucking you in. The only choice you have is not getting too close to that edge when you can see it coming. She still had a choice. He could be plummeting or he could want her to think he was. A man can toy with it, waver, teeter, make a woman think he's about to go down head first. And then when he sees her fall past him he can so very easily tilt back. But I thought you knew we were only friends. You had to know I already have this commitment, this duty, this important thing I have to do, more important than us, bigger than us. Yada, yada, yada.

"None of your business!" She wished she could have been more original talking to a man who liked Larry Brown and who was critical of Phillip Roth. She herself never questioned the authors she read, felt they knew what they were trying to do and were better at achieving it than the ordinary souls that read them. She did know which authors spoke to her and she read them till their books ran out. With the others she simply didn't waste any more reading time.

Small minds pick apart and search for flaws. I find fault, therefore I am intelligent, maybe even creative, if I really wanted to be. They are kindred spirits with the photographers who follow a beautiful woman till they get that money shot, a patch of cellulite on the back of her thigh. Not Yaz, not him. He'd be searching for a well-turned phrase, a fully-realized character, a setting that can be seen, tasted, smelled, and heard. He'd be disappointed not finding at least one of these elements. He would not be the one to show off with cutting words or a clever dismissal. How did she know that about him? She just did.

He said he'd enjoyed her company. She knew that. Still, she should have paused and let him say more. With any other man she might have. Well, any man whose opinion she respected. Instead she cut him off like some proper schoolmarm or some stuffy librarian. Why? Because it was late? Because she was tired? Because she had been thinking of him, had hoped it was him before she picked up the phone, had almost been afraid she'd let it ring too long and he would not be there? Some of that, but most of all because accepting compliments would make it too easy for him.

She wouldn't make it easy for him or for her. It was too easy to slip into something that you couldn't slip out of. Late-night drinking may have made it easier for him to call. Daydreaming was her drug of choice. Thinking of someone, thinking of your hands on the back of his neck, of his hands wanting more than your peripherals, could be intoxicating. It was so easy to get drunk on dreams and want still another round.

Yaz

July went by like we were living in Miami. The dew point hovered close to seventy on many days and the daytime temperature didn't drop below eighty-five. Miami. In the evenings I sat on my porch and watched the sun flatten into a red and orange horizon that seemed out of place. Minnesotans looked dazed and confused, and outdoor activities went begging. I watched my trades and started putting a bathroom in my basement. Actually I started the demolition process on some half-assed effort the previous owners had made. It was slow going, but rewarding work. The going was slow too with Pilar Peres. We had lunch a couple times and at the end of July I asked her how she'd feel about driving up to the shore of Lake Superior for a weekend getaway. We were sitting outside a little sandwich shop in my neighborhood watching shoppers slowly navigate through the heat. The only ones who seemed unfazed were the children. They seemed to understand that this was summer, and it was to be embraced.

"With you?" She gave me that head tilt thing that I had become pretty certain was the most provocatively innocent gesture I'd encountered. It was like watching a feral animal consider you with no sense of self-awareness.

"No, I was asking for Bill Clinton. He'll meet you there."

"Yuk. I'm eating here do you mind?"

I laughed out loud, and watched her eat some more of a sandwich. I had come to realize that the world seemed to gather itself up around her, at least my world did. But she seemed to have found a pace that she was comfortable with for us, and it was, at least for now, decidedly non-romantic. I lived with it. It was killing me, but I lived with it. Living with limitations was something I knew a lot about.

She ate and thought for a minute and then looked me in the eye, "It's too early for that, Yaz. I'm sorry."

"Don't be sorry, I've been turned down by a lot hotter babes than you."

She laughed, "I doubt it tough guy." We both thought about the double meaning floating in that response while I gathered my strength.

I started twice, coughed both times, and finally said, "Do you think there will ever be a place for something more for us?"

The head tilt came and then that look deep into the eyes. God, I could get used to seeing that every day, maybe every hour. "I don't know, Yaz. Does it matter right now?"

"No, not right now, but I think it may matter at some point."

She didn't seem to need to think about that, and she did that corner of her mouth thing, "Yes, I suspect it will."

At first it seemed like I would need to live with just that for now. But there was more that came in an uncharacteristic rush, "I haven't always treated romance in exactly the way I really want to." She fiddled with the gathered-up hair at the back of her head for a while. I sat and thought about her hair and realized I had only seen it down once, at the library. She looked at me and I tried to pretend I wasn't thinking about her with her hair down. Tough to conceal.

She went on, "A romantic involvement has become very important to me in the abstract. But at this point in my life I'm not sure I know how to square up the real with the abstraction."

"You've thought about this a fair amount." I didn't know what else to say.

"Yes." She smiled and put her hand on top of mine. I sat very still. It was either that or convulse, and that's hard to pull off with any style.

"And I'm also trying to help a good friend through what is becoming a kind of troubling incident, or problem, or I'm not quite sure what, but it's taking some time."

I let that sit for a moment. "I understand. I think. Or maybe I don't, but it's okay either way. Your friend's situation sounds troubling."

"It is, I think. It's actually becoming more than a little unsettling for her, and therefore for me."

"Is there anything I can help with?"

She narrowed her eyes and thought about that. After a bit she seemed to decide something. "Tell you what, let's walk and I'll tell you about it. I'd actually like another opinion."

I paid for the lunch and we got up to walk. Her tank top stuck to her back with sweat, and there were curls of damp hair at her neck. I didn't tackle her, but gee whiz.

Ava's Story

JOAN PORITSKY

JOAN PORITSKY grew up in upstate New York, where she liked to play on her grandmother's front porch. These days she lives in south Minneapolis and works on her back porch.

There was a time when soot and solvent fumes shrouded the small town of Mohawk Falls in upstate New York. In those days, factory whistles raveled the predawn wintry air. Searchlights shivered over tracks of freight cars, weighted with coal and scrap metal. Throughout the night billows of white smoke rose and disappeared above the river and its snow-covered banks. Drifts of snow scattered across the near frozen water and glimmered like black stars.

By morning, the air would clear. Across the bridge, to the north and east, just beyond the flats of the old towpath, the business district came to life. Canary yellow trolleys with frosted windows moved like metronomes up and down the main street, showering the air overhead with a cascade of sparks. In those years, the downtown was only a few blocks long. There was a row of narrow brick buildings darkened by centuries of weather and decades of coal tar. It was a somber street, faithful to its roots as an early Dutch settlement. Each building had its tiny storefront and stood without ornamentation. They were built to last forever.

Hannah Frier's childhood memories of the downtown always came back to the fabric shop. It was on a narrow side street between repair shops for clocks and shoes. Nearby there was a barber's pole that would spin like a giant stick of candy, a temptation cemented forever in the sidewalk. Once inside the fabric shop, Hannah wandered aisles crowded with bolts of cloth while she waited for her mother to plumb remnant bins for bargains.

"I won't be too long," her mother would promise. She'd fix her pocketbook under her arm and slowly make her way through tables piled high with varying lengths of cloth. She rummaged in search of the few she could afford. Hannah remembers watching her mother touch these drab finds with such satisfaction and an unexpected delicacy. In all the hours she stood and waited, she never saw her mother's thick, reddened hands linger over a frivolous remnant or too-costly one. She remembers holding that against her. Like many children of immigrants, Hannah felt burdened by her mother's daily sacrifices. Her mother's willing acceptance of life's demands and limitations kindled her anger and left her with the uneasy and unwelcome sense that she was somehow obligated to make her mother's unprotested fate worthwhile. She scowled at the sale sign and stepped away from her mother's side.

"Stay where I can see you, Hannah," her mother said. It was as if she could read her daughter's mind. Hannah nodded, and waited until her mother's attention returned to the sale bin, before she turned to leave. Her face brightened as she found her way in and out of little aisles, narrowed by displays of sequined fabrics and bolts of velvet, to a small alcove, her favorite place in the shop. There, tall, thin bolts of silk leaned in solitary and elegant languor. Even in the pale light of an overhead chandelier, their watery colors were luminous and soft. She liked to just stand there and look at them for awhile. Sooner or later she'd move as close to them as she dared and half close her eyes until all the colors vanished into shimmers. For Hannah, not yet overtaken by the restraints of adolescence, these were lyrical moments. Her face flushed with shy pleasure. She marveled at the way these colors disappeared as if suddenly hidden beneath sunlit rainwater. Such elusive wonders fed her daydreams and her belief that such mysteries were portals to life's possibilities.

Ava Munson had taken note of the plain little girl who, she had to admit, wore a winter coat that was both well tailored and splendidly mended. She had little experience or interest in young children and, even though Hannah seemed well brought up, her ventures into her department made her uneasy. More as a precaution, or so she told herself, she kept a watchful eye on the nine-year-old, especially when she neared the glass case. It had been a long time since Ava felt the energy she needed to keep up with a nine-year-old. In fact, she could seldom recall any enthusiasm for much in her life anymore. She wasn't sure if it had slipped away, perhaps so slowly and with so little resistance that she had simply failed to notice it was gone. She thought about that for a while and shook her head. She knew better. That was not the way it had happened.

Ava rubbed her hand over her swollen knuckles. "Your mother doesn't know you are back here, does she?" she asked. She stood just outside the alcove and waited.

Hannah studied the shiny buckles on her red rubber boots and shook her head.

Ava carried herself like the beautiful woman she once was. She normally stood behind the the glass-cased display of fine laces and beaded trim. She was, of course, the most senior sales clerk, and in that role greeted and assisted the more affluent patrons of the shop. Like the other clerks, she wore a tailored black dress and pearls. Unlike theirs, Miss Munson's pearls were real. They grew more luminous with daily wear and over time, a poignant contrast to the faint maze of powdered wrinkles that had overtaken her once fine complexion.

The wall clock chimed the late morning hour. Soon, patrons in their fur-trimmed coats would hurry off to keep their luncheon engagements. Meanwhile they browsed the newest collections, pausing from time to time to whisper, and share looks and slanted smiles behind their gloved hands. They seemed to glide back and forth leaving faint and fading scents of their perfumes among the floral prints of spring. On a particularly clear morning a pearl gray Packard eased into a parking space in front of the fabric shop door.

"Thank you, dear," Mrs. Van Vliet said. Arthur took his mother's arm as she lowered herself into the passenger seat of the Packard. Once she was settled, he made his way around the back of the car. His step slowed as he glanced back at the fabric shop they'd just left.

"I'm so sorry I have wasted your morning, Arthur," his mother said. She raised a gloved hand and touched her brow as if to uncrease it. "I can't remember when I've seen a more dismal collection of spring fabrics." She shook her head. "Poor Mildred Frier. She'll not be getting any dressmaking orders from me any time soon, I'm afraid."

Arthur had started the car, and after he'd adjusted the rear view mirror, slowly wheeled the Packard away from the curb. The traffic was light. It was a clear day, but that time of year when small-town shops decorated their display windows with paper snowflakes and metallic icicles.

As they drove along Erie Street, Mrs. Van Vliet looked out her window. Shoppers hurried along the sidewalks. Others crowded in sheltering doorways willing trolleys to arrive on time. "I suppose I could make do with what I wore last spring," she said. She sat quietly for a moment, then looked over at Arthur. "It's such a pity Capital City is so far away. Their fabric shops have such a fine selection, much better than here, you know."

Arthur nodded. "Of course, Mother." He nodded again. I'll take you there tomorrow."

"Are you sure you are not too busy?" she asked.

Arthur shook his head.

Mrs. Van Vliet reached over and patted his arm. "You are such a dear, Arthur." She sat back in her seat and smiled. Across the street, swarthy workmen in heavy boots and thick woolen jackets chopped ice and shoveled snow into idling trucks whose drivers smoked cigarettes and stood around drinking coffee from silver thermos bottles. Mrs. Van Vliet pulled her fur coat around her lap. She glanced to make sure the doors were locked and the windows closed before she opened her pocketbook.

Arthur slowed the car to make his way around the desolate public square at the edge of the downtown. In the fall, groundskeepers had heaped straw on the perennial beds along its brick sidewalks, and put burlap wrappings around the small trees and bushes that framed its perimeter. Even the gazebo had been boarded to protect it from the winds and deep snow. Arthur leaned over and raised the setting on the heater.

Mrs. Van Vliet drew a small hand mirror from her pocketbook. She did this often to assure herself that her once-blond hair remained presentably tucked beneath her hat. "I hope you won't be too bored tomorrow, dear, having to wait again in another fabric shop," she said. She looked over at him and smiled. "Who knows, perhaps there will be another attractive sales clerk to distract you while I shop?" She looked at her reflection and adjusted the brim across her forehead. "Not another one wearing real pearls though, I am certain of that!" When she was satisfied with how she looked, she returned the mirror to her pocketbook and snapped it shut. "You do know that that clerk, Ava or Ada or whatever her name was, was wearing real pearls, don't you?"

Arthur obliged her with an uncertain silence. He checked the rear view window and after signaling a left-hand turn, made his way along a residential street lined with elm trees and sprawling grounds.

"Must have been a gift, wouldn't you say?" his mother asked. "She was certainly an attractive enough woman for that," she added. Mrs. Van Vliet gazed out the window at a large Victorian house, one with fretted porches that she remembered filled with large wicker furniture that would be hidden in summer by awnings and hanging planters filled with flowers. "It seems unlikely she could afford to buy them for herself, not on a clerk's wages."

Arthur lowered the visor above his mother's head and touched her hand.

"Oh, Arthur," his mother said, "I cannot tell you how grateful I am that you are not one of those foolish men, dear." She sat quietly for a while as they drove beneath an arch of leafless elms, then closed her eyes and before long drifted into a light sleep.

By the time Ava Munson closed the shop, Erie Street was almost empty. What little warmth the sun had offered earlier in the day had fled. The air was cold. Gusts of wind rifled down the icy sidewalk. Windows in darkened storefronts rattled in the pewter light of late afternoon. She made her way across the street, a specter in the yellow glow of headlights. Waiting cars stuttered in swirls of exhaust fumes, their drivers and passengers impatient for any relief from the heavy set of midwinter. The arc of porch lights and warm kitchens with simmering pots of soup marked the end of these long days for families.

Once she turned the corner and out of the freezing wind, her step slowed. She was too tired to think of supper. She pressed her face in her coat collar, imagining the warmth of the hot bath she would draw as soon as she reached home. Her apartment was only a block away. It was a distance magnified by snow, quarried from the street and steeply piled along the curb and rutted sidewalk.

Ava's apartment building was a three-story brick building that fronted on a small enclosed circle at the end of the street. At its center was a bronze statue of young Indian, his face lifted to the last rays of the daylight. Ava discovered it years ago when she returned to Mohawk Falls. It had been a late afternoon in August when she met its gaze from a second-story window of a vacant apartment. She decided to rent it even though it was small and too expensive. In those days it didn't seem the extravagance it had now become.

These days it was her downstairs neighbor, not the snow-covered warrior, who welcomed her return from the fabric shop. Every late afternoon Henry would watch for Ava from his window. He'd listen to hear her push the heavy front door shut, then hurry from his apartment to unlock the main entrance.

"You're very late tonight," he said. Henry had the quiet habits and small courtesies of the bank teller he once was. He was man who missed the daily pleasures of work, the overheard bits of petty gossip, the unfiltered hints of scandal that seeped from boardrooms and closed doors. Ava looked up and nodded. He stood by the door, mildly disappointed as he waited for her to remove her gloves. Her fingers, stiff from cold and years of handwork, were slow to unzip her overshoes and unlock her mailbox to confirm its emptiness.

"Thank you, Henry," she said as he closed the door behind them. He took her smile as encouragement.

"I don't suppose you'd join me for a little brandy, Ava?" he asked.

Ava glanced at the stairs and shook her head. "Another time, Henry. Thank you."

Henry shifted his weight lightly from one slippered foot to another. "Of course," he said, watching her closely. "I was thinking it might warm you up a bit. But if you haven't had your supper yet...well, we could have a glass later." He paused. "Maybe we could play a hand or two of cards too." He patted his vest pocket and smiled, "Give me a chance to increase my winnings, eh?" he added with an awkward modesty, as if he had made a small but witty joke.

"Not tonight, I'm afraid," she answered, but softened her reply by feigning a touch to his arm before she turned away.

The hallway was quiet. The air was stale, heavy with smells of burnt toast and cabbage. As Ava made her way up the stairs, familiar with its every creak, she heard Henry's door quietly click shut once she reached the landing and was out of sight.

By the time she reached her own apartment, exhausted relief shielded her from giving his disappointment a second thought.

Ava's apartment was not without elegant touches. Most front rooms were clutters of furniture, of prickly mohair sofas and heavy chairs swathed in antimacassars. Dark shades shuttered lace-covered windows. Hers took on a different sensibility. Her sitting room was light and spare. A few years earlier, she had sold off her silver tea set, leaving the small cart empty. More recently, she had parted with one of a pair of pencil sketches by Degas and centered the remaining one above a small writing table. Unopened bills were stacked behind a wooden box. Ava felt the room, like good bone structure or breeding, suggested an appropriate sense of refinement. Two loveseats covered in well-mended apricot silk were arranged by a low marble table. Their small pillows matched drapery that framed the tall front window. In bright sunlight, these furnishings had the look of elegance and ease, a reminder of what they once were in another place at an earlier time.

Ava removed her pearls and placed them in a velvet case before she turned on the hot water tap in the bathtub. Radiator pipes banged with efforts to force heat, but on windy nights her apartment was cold. She undressed quickly, grateful for the familiar comfort and warmth of her robe and slippers. Steam rose from the filling tub and fogged the medicine cabinet mirror. She leaned into its heat and poured Epsom salts into the hot water. On this night, it wasn't an anticipated relief that welled in her but waves of memory of fragrant oils and soaps. She turned off the water and made her way into the kitchen where she poured herself a small glass of Scotch.

Below her window, the statue stood in drifts of snow. Its upturned face was barely visible. Ava raised her glass to the young warrior and took a sip. She stood looking at the empty street, the pools of light under street lamps as if to fathom the vagaries of its silence. It wasn't until she returned to the kitchen to refill her glass that she realized she'd forgotten to have supper.

The long, insistent rings of the public telephone had roused her neighbor who hurried to answer it. Ava could hear Clare's familiar footsteps. Like the rest of the tenants in the building, she took advantage of Clare's constant longing to disguise her loneliness with the small gratitudes of others. A few minutes later she tapped softly on Ava's door.

"Ava?" she said. She tapped again. "It's Arthur. He asked to talk to you."

Ava leaned against the closed door. "Yes, Clare," she said. "Thank you." She cradled her head with her hand as if to plead for a relief, however momentary, from the room's slight but insistent sways. "Please tell him I'm sorry, will you? I can't take his call," she said, finally. "I have a headache."

"Are you sure, Ava?" Clare asked. She gave a worried glance down the corridor, reassured that it was empty and without prying light from unlatched doors. "You had a headache last night, remember?" she added. Clare pulled her sweater closer, wrapping it tightly around her chest. She waited for what seemed to her a long time. Finally she tapped on the door again. "Ava?" she asked.

The furnace had been banked for the night and the hallway was cold. The amber light beside Ava's door was weak and did little to add even an illusion of warmth or welcome. Long before Clare could retreat to her own apartment, Ava had already fallen into a dreamless sleep. By then, the water in her bathtub, like her moonlit bedroom, had lost its heat.

Across town Arthur had walked the few blocks from his office to the club. Even though his wool coat and homburg could not keep out the chill of that January night, he hadn't hurried. Earlier he had driven to the bank to call Ava. She had stopped taking his calls a while ago. Still, he phoned her as often as he could manage, usually from his office on his way to the Mohawk Club after dinner. Some evenings he drove by her apartment, reassured to see light from her window. He had rehearsed as he drove what he might do if she looked out and saw his car, what he might say if they should happen to meet on the street. In time, his wishful musings gave way to irritation. The last time she did this to him it took her a few weeks to relent, but she came around then, and she certainly would again.

By the time Arthur arrived at his club, the Fireplace Room was almost empty. All the regulars who met to reminisce and play cribbage had long since made their way home.

Most of the club's residents had gone to their rooms, some to fill their evenings with a book, others to escape it in sleep. A few, for whom habits of a lifetime were not easily abandoned, dozed in the firelight, their heads bowed over the too-fine print of the evening paper. Except for an occasional and snuffled sound, the room was quiet. On weeknights, especially during the winter months, the club closed early. Freezing winds and snowstorms kept even its younger members from lingering over their after dinner smoke and drinks.

Arthur settled himself in one of the larger leather chairs close to the fire's warmth. Late that afternoon the heavy draperies had been drawn, sealing the room from fading light and cold drafts. As he had in the past, he felt comfortable near the well tended fire, among the familiar surroundings in the lamp lit room. Like many regulars, Arthur took little notice of the room's polished floors and furnishings, the immaculate white linens, or the well watered and pruned ferns that stood in decorous pots at doorways. For him, the Mohawk Club was a place free of minor discomforts and inconveniences, a place beyond reach of disquieting intrusions.

His waiter welcomed him with a cognac, then returned with a large cedar box filled with a selection of hand wrapped cigars, fragrant and arranged with a practiced care.

"The Cubans are fresh, Mr. Van Vliet," Carl assured him.

Arthur nodded and reached for a Havana. On this night he lit it without ritual or his usual relish. The smoke rose in slow and careless drifts, at odds or at least in seeming contrast with his present mood. He drained his drink and wanted another. Carl cleared Arthur's empty glass, and replaced it with a full one.

Arthur leaned his head against the back of his chair. From across the room he had the look of a relaxed club member, savoring a good cigar on a quiet winter night. Whatever second thoughts or regrets he might have had about hanging up on Clare earlier in the evening had dissipated. The drink had relaxed him. He puffed on his cigar and watched the smoke disappear. He was pleased with himself for refusing to listen to that woman stutter another one of Ava's excuses. He tamped the cigar ash along the edge of the ashtray and decided he would wait weeks before he called her again. He sat for a long time, imagining the distress his resolve might cause her. That warmed him, even raised his spirits. He finished his drink and looked around the room, disappointed to discover he was alone. He'd have liked to play a game or two of cards. But the room had emptied. He'd read the paper, so he sat watching the fire and finally decided that what he really wanted was another cognac. It was not long before his mouth went dry and a headache set in.

Carl looked at him. "Are you unwell, sir?" Arthur's eyes had been closed for some time. His face flushed. He seemed barely aware of the pulses of heat rising in his body, the prickly warmth from the fireplace on his legs.

And Arthur shifted his weight and sat up in his chair. "No. No, of course not. I am fine, Carl, thank you," he said. "I'm just a bit off my game tonight that's all."

"Yes, Sir," Carl answered, "I'm sure you're fine."

The two men smiled at each other. "It's nothing that another cognac won't cure." Arthur looked over at his empty glass with a small laugh.

"I'm sorry, Mr. Van Vliet," he said. "The bar has closed. The Club will be closing in a few minutes." He paused. "Would you like me to arrange for you to stay here tonight?" Carl took his arm to steady him as he helped Arthur to his feet. He watched as Arthur brushed specks of ash from his vest and buttoned his jacket. "Or perhaps you'd like me to call a taxicab to take you home, Sir."

"No," Arthur said. "A short walk in the fresh air is just what I need tonight." He turned to leave but not before he patted Carl's shoulder with a nod of thanks. Arthur was a bit unsteady as he made his way to his car, but the world felt orderly and he was satisfied with himself. He could leave thoughts of Ava for now. Like many things, she would just take time.

Ava awakened early and went out to buy herself a newspaper. Usually she waited to read Henry's. She couldn't remember a Sunday when he didn't leave his copy, neatly folded at her door, but always without its business section. Henry liked to reread the stock market reports throughout the week. He kept track of them in notebooks neatly stacked on his writing table. In its drawer he'd arranged wooden compartments where he stored his sharpened pencils, pocket knife and eraser, and a metal edged ruler he'd had for over forty years.

She poured cold water in the kettle, and spooned the last of a French tea she'd saved into a small sieve. More than two weeks had gone by since Arthur had last tried to call her. For some reason she didn't understand, the relief she felt seemed weighted by a vague unease. She tried not to think about it. It was his silence that troubled her. And more than that it was his patience. His patience was relentless.

Ava struck a match and lit the working front burner. After she adjusted the flame, she set the kettle on the stove to heat. She rubbed her hands above it and cupped them to take in a little more of its warmth. The warmth reminded her of one of the first times she and Arthur had been together. It was one of those Sundays in early September when the sun was high and its light yielded all the textures of an August day. As was his custom, he'd called her from his office one night and asked her to spend the following Sunday afternoon with him. She assumed they'd go across the river for a late afternoon dinner at Leon's. It was a small place with knotty pine walls crowded with fish plaques and shelves lined with dusty trophies. On that Sunday he'd taken her for a drive in the country.

That summer had seemed to stretch on and on. One sultry day followed another with little or no relief. Every evening she'd return home from work to a cool bath in a room swagged with still damp towels. Most nights she had to make do with only a few hours of fitful and dreamless sleep before it was time to get up and dress for work. Often she spent her Sunday afternoons alone. She'd walk or take a trolley to one of town's vest-pocket parks with fountains and shade trees to read or just sit, and escape her airless apartment for a few hours.

The outskirts of Mohawk Falls opened to fields dotted with barns and grazing cows. Small truck farms fringed back country roads. If you looked closely you could see their makeshift chicken coops and meandering beds of late summer vegetables. Soothing worlds of meadow grass gave way to well-tended apple orchards, their branches bent with shiny fruit. Roads banked and curved around hilly woodlands tinted with reds and oranges, and light flecked shadows. It was one of those late afternoons when the air breathed in the ripening, sun soaked earth. Ava found herself appraising Arthur with a stirring she'd not felt for a long time.

Arthur had slowed the Packard and turned down a gravel lane. It was marked by a cast-iron gate. A canopy of vines and bramble had overtaken its archway and weathered sign. Beyond its entry, thickets of overgrown brush had narrowed the lane. Arthur drove slowly as they made their way in silence for what seemed to Ava a long time. She gave him a mild look of surprised disappointment and crossed her legs. If he noticed her slight but distancing shift, he didn't show it.

"I'm taking you to see my new horse," he said at last. "It's a seven-year-old gelding."

Weeds swept the Packard's fenders. Their whispery arcs were a sharp contrast to the crushed bits of loose gravel, grinding beneath its weight. Arthur braked to slow the car.

"I just bought it from the widow of one of the best horse trainers in this part of the country," he told her. "Probably the best," Arthur looked over at her finally and smiled. "I paid a small fortune for this horse, I can tell you, but it is worth every penny." He took his hand off the steering wheel and adjusted his tie in the rear view mirror.

Ava nodded.

When they reached the clearing at the end of the lane, he parked the car under a shade tree. He hurried around the car to open her door but slowed as he reached for her hand. "Quality never comes cheap, now does it?" he said as he watched her step out of the car.

Ava stepped across her small kitchen to remove a serving tray from the shallow drawer beneath the counter. She traced its oval rim with her fingers, remembering those times when she'd used it for small tea cakes and buttery scones. She opened a small tin of peaches and forked a few slices into a bowl, careful to first drain them of their sugary juices. She poured the rest into a glass container and wrapped it in waxed paper before storing it in the refrigerator. She rinsed the sticky wetness from her fingers, and waited for the water in the kettle to come to a boil.

She remembered the grey and white stable. It was small, privately owned, and freshly painted. There was a border of rose bushes that just a few weeks earlier must have skirted the building in ruffles of scented pink. A once elegant hunting lodge stood beneath a distant rise of elm and cottonwoods. It was half hidden by an untended hedge spread with drying work clothes in patches of sunlight. Off to the east, beyond equipment buildings and storage sheds, a path disappeared through a stand of white and burr oak. Ava slowed to admire its cloistered shade. She wondered who had imagined such an enticing entry into the woodland hills. The path curved up a small rise and gave way to trails that wandered beneath the chatter of nuthatches and chickadees, and slate-colored juncos. In the distance crows hectored from their high nests and orioles voiced their sad laments from sacks that swayed in the transparent wind. For all its busy and bright noises, these woods seemed to Ava like a place where she might gather herself and be taken away.

It had been a long time since she'd imagined what it might be like to live a life of such lightness and ease. These days she tended to fill the empty and difficult spaces of her daily life with remnants of the past. She shaded her eyes as if to catch a glimpse of herself, splashing across a shallow autumn stream, silver still in the first yellowing of goldenrod along its distant banks. Ava gave Arthur a long speculative look. It was hard to imagine him in the woods. He was an attractive enough looking man whose hand-tailored suit and erect carriage drew attention to his propriety and away from his girdled paunch. She watched as a dragonfly hovered above a wild blackberry bush and disappeared into its shadowy weeds. In the distance sun baked outcroppings of granite, like felled ledges of the sky, glinted in the slowed rhythms of the rolling hills as vees of geese curved and vanished beyond piney slopes.

Inside the stable, Ava made no effort to keep up with Arthur. She moved slowly and with care along the wood planks. Even so, her high heels were soon caked with dirt and straw. It was an airless place, thick with black flies and the pungent smells of horse leavings. A thin, unfriendly cat menaced an unseen prey and chased it into the shadows. When she finally reached its stall, Arthur's prized horse turned out to be a big, jittery animal. Its white coat was a mottle of sooty grays and spatterings of black. She stood outside its stall watching as Arthur slapped its flanks with obvious pride. Neither the apples he offered nor his touch did much to calm its skittish, almost desperate restlessness.

"He's just spirited, high strung," he reassured her. "Just how I like them," he added. Later, after they had finished their dinner, and in the days to come she would come back again and again to that moment. She wasn't at all sure what it meant but it had chilled her and made her more cautious when she remembered it.

They had eaten at an out of the way place, one with faded green and white striped awnings fronted by a small bed of marigolds. Someone had planted them within a circle of rocks and painted them white. Next to the parking lot was an old picnic table, carved with initials and charred by careless smokers. Except for the few men sitting alone at the bar, the roadhouse was almost empty.

After a time their waitress cleared the dinner plates, and Arthur lit a cigar. He waved aside the smoke that had momentarily drifted across the table. Ava was often taken by small gestures, but Arthur's unsettled her. There was something too studied about his mannerisms, and, in the end, it made him seem self-serving. She wasn't sure what it was and wished she felt differently, but there it was. Outside the screened window and beyond the white washed rocks, the countryside had turned to the color of eggplant. The chant of crickets seemed to blanket the cooling land.

"It took me a long time to get the widow to sell me Ovid," he told her.

"Ovid?"

"That's what her late husband had named the gelding. Ovid."

Lillian came to their table with a water pitcher and refilled their glasses. She wore a hairnet that matched the large pink handkerchief she'd plumped like a flower in the breast pocket of her aproned uniform.

"We've a Boston cream pie for dessert this evening," she said to Ava with a smile freighted with enthusiasm. "Fresh made today."

Ava looked over at the bar. "I'll have another Manhattan," Ava said.

"And you, Sir?" she said.

"Bring me a Scotch and water, will you?" he said. "I can't let this lady drink all by herself, now can I?"

Ava took a sip of her water. "So," she asked, "was this widow unhappy with your offer?"

Arthur shook his head. "I offered her a fair price, right from the start," he began. "A very fair price, but she refused it." He brushed an ash from his vest. "So, I made her better and better ones. She refused those too." He paused for a moment, then leaned across the table as if to speak out of turn. "She was one stubborn lady, I can tell you," he said. "But I must admit, I admired her for that." He gave the Formica table a swiping slap.

Lillian returned with their drinks and placed them on small paper doilies.

Ava stirred her drink with the candied cherry before removing it. "What changed her mind then?"

Arthur leaned back in his chair, templing his hands under his chin. "Well," he began, " as I am sure you may know, I am not without contacts or influence."

He paused and stroked the side of his face with the back of his hand. "I happened to mention my interest in the gelding to a few people. Turns out the widow's son was behind in his mortgage payments."

Ava took a sip of her drink. She took care to replace it on the paper doily.

"So," Arthur continued, "I just offered her a chance to save his home, that's all."

They finished their drinks, and after Arthur had paid the bill, he took Ava's arm and they made their way to the parking area. It had a been long day and the Manhattans had left her feeling a bit muddled, even low. She thought about that horse, tethered in its stall, its fragile ankles in frenetic motion as if by some accident or grace, it might set itself free.

"It was just business, Ava," Arthur had told her, as he helped her into the Packard.

Outside her kitchen window, the sun's faltering hold on the morning gave way and dimmed the room. Ava poured herself a cup of well steeped tea. She placed it on a tray alongside the small bowl of peaches and cloth napkin. As she often did on Sunday mornings, she carried it to her sitting room and lowered it onto the marble table. On this morning she'd promised herself she'd look through newspaper listings for a room to rent at a boarding house in or near downtown. She would read the business section too. But it turned out, as it often did with Ava, that she found herself staring out the window at the young Indian warrior, believing his roped arms and upturned face offered her promises of a better time.

Winter that year had been one people in Mohawk Falls would remember and talk about for a long time. Old-timers say it began during the holidays with a heavy snowstorm. Blizzard winds stranded cars in drifts and downed power lines. On New Year's Eve the temperature dropped below freezing and January turned out to be the coldest month on record. People wore extra layers of clothing, some bundled up indoors. They took to sealing drafty windows and doors with cardboard or blankets and towels only to have them stiffen with frost and thicknesses of ice. As the weeks went by, hardware store owners and other small businessmen grumbled about heating bills and worried about empty cash boxes. Corner grocers lugged bins of perishable fruits and vegetables away from doorways and sudden rushes of cold air. Young boys, eager to earn extra pocket money, delivered food to old and ill people and families with young children.

By mid February, the temperature rose above freezing. The ice and snow began to melt, and after a few of these seemingly balmy days, people began to believe that the worst was finally over. But an overnight ice storm turned a typically busy Saturday morning into one of near idleness. By early afternoon, when Erie Street's glassy sidewalks had become islands of caked sand, the department store and specialty shops remained almost empty.

The fabric shop was quiet. Ava looked around for something to do.

The listless sales clerk, a round shouldered woman in her late twenties, sat by the cash register. To pass the time she thumbed through old movie magazines. Only a photograph of Rita Hayworth in a red gown seemed to take her interest, though her eyes did fix on Clark Gable's hooded ones for a much longer time.

Ava found herself looking for the old Zenith radio she'd once noticed in a storage room. It was dusty and its tubes were loose, but she managed to improvise replacements for lost knobs and actually got it to work. Even with its occasional crackles of static, it seemed to take the edge off her worry and offer a distraction from the tedious task she'd set for herself. For most of the morning and early afternoon, Ava measured, priced, and bundled remnants of cloth to prepare for the shop's upcoming winter sale. Among these were a few silks. They reminded her of the way young Hannah was drawn to the alcove. She stood and thought about the little girl for a long moment before shrugging and tossing the overlooked silks into the pile. When she finished she sat and rested for a while. Her hands and neck were tired and sore. The store was still empty. The young sales clerk by the cash register sat chewing a candy bar, then pocketed its red and white wrapper, careful to leave no telltale sign in a wastebasket.

Ava went into the office and closed the door. She withdrew a small piece of paper from her pocketbook. She felt cold and wished she'd thought to bring a thermos of tea to work that morning. She knew a cup of tea couldn't lift the weight of the call she had to make, but it might have helped her ease into it. Over the last week, she'd walked by the rooming house on Canal Street several times. Each time she hoped to find something she could like about it. In the end it was just a grey house, with a sagged porch and a welcome mat that did little to overcome the dreariness of peeling paint and a badly repaired railing. She'd planned to look at a vacant room, one with dark green shades drawn against the street's neon lights and loitering men smoking near the corner. Across the street was a shoebox of a diner with a row of six red leatherette stools and a menu chalked on a board above a black grill. The smell of grease seemed to attach itself to everything along Canal Street like an invisible stain.

Ava unfolded the paper and dialed the penciled number she'd kept for a long time.

"Mr. Rosen? This is Ava Munson calling," she said.

"Ah, yes," he said, "the lady with that fine Degas sketch, of course. How can I help you, Miss Munson?"

"Well, you may recall I had a pair of Degas drawings, Mr. Rosen," she began, "and I wonder if you might be interested in the other one." Ava closed her eyes. "I'm finding myself a little short these days."

"Of course," he answered. Mr. Rosen, like his father and grandfather before him, owned the pawnshop in the town's immigrant neighborhood crowded between its two largest factories. As a boy and young man, he had no time for the weepy widows, fumbling to unclasp their gold crosses, as they too often did, to pay for a proper burial. And he'd been impatient with working men who were regulars. They'd arrive just before closing and before payday to pawn their fathers' watches for a bottle of cheap whiskey that couldn't wait until Friday. He'd seen people come and go, even the wealthy matrons who hurried in and out of his father's shop, exchanging jewels for money to pay gambling debts that would have embarrassed and enraged their prominent husbands. But the years passed and as his own life unraveled from time to time, he spent more time with the stories and secrets of those cut off from banks and too easily exploited by loan sharks.

"Of course," he repeated. "I'd be glad to arrange something for you." He paused. "I must tell you, though, Miss Munson, the market for art... sadly even for such an exquisite piece as your Degas, is never as good as jewelry."

"No, I don't suppose it is," she said.

"But I promise, I will do the best I can for you."

He waited, hoping she would not be ready to discuss its value, certain it was much lower than she needed.

"Thank you, Mr. Rosen. Would it be fair to assume this Degas might be a little more valuable that the other one?"

"I'm afraid not," he said. "I am certain, though, I could offer you a very large sum for your pearls, that is, if you'd want to consider it. It's just a thought, Miss Munson."

Ava touched her pearls beneath the collar of her dress.

"I seldom have inquiries for high quality pearls. But as it happens, just the other day a gentleman called and asked me to be on the lookout for a valuable strand. I assume he'd pay a fair price if they suited him. You may want to give it some thought."

She thanked him and though she didn't want to think about it, she could think of nothing else.

Charlie Veeder, the Mohawk Club's star squash player, looked up from the medical chart he'd been reading and grinned.

"You're a lucky man, Arthur," he said, tapping the papers on his clipboard.

Arthur opened and closed his eyes.

"No broken bones, fortunately," he continued, "but you must have taken one hell of a fall." He took off his reading glasses and in a single deft motion, dropped them in the breast pocket of his white coat. "No need to worry though, Sport. We'll have you fixed up good as new." He patted Arthur's shoulder and nodded at the nurse who had followed him into the room. "Loretta here is going to take very good care of you."

Loretta was short and sturdy. Her white uniform was freshly starched, and her white stockings made a distinct brushing sound as she moved efficiently around Arthur's bed. He felt the soft weight of her fingers as she slid her hand beneath his wrist. When she'd finished monitoring the wall clock, she steadied his elbow to keep his bandaged arm still before she withdrew her hand. It seemed a small gesture, but to Arthur, whose pain thresholds were spent, it was a palpable relief.

"The neck brace is just a precaution, Arthur," Charlie explained. He checked the IV drip and made a small adjustment. "Seems you got a pretty good whack on your head. Lucky, you didn't land on any rock." He gave Arthur a long look. His face was pale and rendered by exhaustion. His eyes were closed in sunken circles of darkness, his neck sheathed in a thick collar of milky plaster. "We're going to keep you around here for a few days, just to make sure you are A-OK." He paused and drew in a breath. "I'm sure you are going to be fine. Sore for a while," he added with a little laugh, "but fine."

Charlie handed Loretta the chart to put away, and turned to leave. "You've contacted his mother?"

She shook her head. "No, Doctor, not yet. I've tried several times, both yesterday and today. There has been no answer, no housekeeper..." she caught herself. "I'll keep trying."

After he left, Loretta turned to Arthur and smoothed his light blanket. "Are you warm enough, Mr. Van Vleit?" she asked. She waited, wondering if he'd heard her.

"Is it Saturday?" he asked.

"It's Sunday," she told him. She touched his hand. It felt dry and very cold. She opened the large metal storage cabinet against the far wall and found more blankets.

The room itself was warm. It was one of the largest private rooms on the second floor of the hospital's newest wing. Outside the sweep of thin green curtain that encircled the bed was a pair of upholstered chairs covered in a fashionable plaid. The windows looked down on a forlorn courtyard of wintered plantings framed by a rectangle of concrete and four empty benches. Venetian blinds with thick wooden slats covered the windows but did little to block the drone of daily traffic from the street, much less the whine of ambulance sirens that worried the days and nights.

"We've not been able to reach your mother, Mr. Van Vliet," Loretta told him as she folded the bedsheet over his blankets and drew it to cover his shoulders. She rested her hand on Arthur's chest and leaned toward him. "Is there someone else you'd like me to call?" she asked.

Arthur's breath was slow and shallow. "Why no." He'd been drifting in and out of an agitated sleep. As it happened, the air held the faint scent of her powder. It seemed familiar and it calmed him. His breath lengthened as if the remembered fragrance and Loretta's quiet hand on his chest had suffused his fitful drowsiness with a soothing tonic.

"Is my horse okay?" he asked.

"I don't know, Sir. Would you like me to see if I can find out?" she replied.

"Yes. Please."

Loretta placed the call button near his hand under the blankets and lowered the Venetian blinds. She closed the door behind her and looked down the corridor toward the brightly lit nurses' station where there were telephones and a directory. She decided to make herself a cup of tea and headed toward the nurses' lounge. By now someone would know where his mother had gone and what had happened to Arthur's horse.

Arthur's days and nights had been a seamless blur of nurses. They came and went, their skirts rustling, their white oxfords quiet on the tiled floor. Often they hovered with paper cups filled with coin-sized pills and long silvered needles. He listened for the voices that promised sleep and relief from pain.

Word spread of his accident. Bank and club associates and old family friends hurried off cards of well wishes and grand bouquets of flowers. His mother, stranded in Chicago by a March snowstorm, missed her train connection and arrived days later at her brother's West Coast villa. Waiting there for her was a fistful of reassuring telephone messages left by Loretta, Arthur's hospital nurse. As it happened it was Charlie Veeder's practiced reassurances and her own very bad cold that kept Mrs. Van Vliet from boarding the next train home.

By the end of the second week, most of the flowers in Arthur's room had lost their splashes of color. He had given them little notice. It wasn't long before petals withered and fell in haphazard circles on window sills and tabletops. Outside his north-faced windows, the sky was overcast. Not even the bright interior lights could overcome the bleakness of a late afternoon Sunday or Arthur's brooding mood.

In time his wounds began to heal, the swelling subsided, and Arthur found himself more alone. The long and empty stretches of time weighed on him. During the day he sat in a wheelchair, his cane propped against its side. More often than not he took his aches and pains as omens of loss. Charlie Veeder tried to assure him he'd regain the use of his left leg. He did admit, when pressed, that it would take some time and probably never be quite the same again.

The brief, early evening visits by his colleagues did little to distract him. Their trifling banter and bits of gossip wore thin. Often they seemed ill at ease and eager to be on their way just as Arthur himself had been so many times in the past. And so they glanced at their watches and with a flurry of awkward excuses left Arthur tethered to a place that stirred their dread and had sharpened his own. In the end it was the lingering smells of cigar smoke and shoe polish that deepened his worry and bothered him the most.

He had come to look forward to the hour when Loretta greeted him with her warm hands and lotions, offering a back rub to help him sleep. She always took her time massaging the soreness in his shoulders and his stiffened neck. The long rhythmic strokes of her hands seemed to lighten and slow over all the tender and still tight places. Eventually his eyes closed in the quiet rocking of her touch. His breath deepened and slowed as his body relaxed, taking in the slight drifts of her familiar fragrance, releasing unspent tensions and pain.

Loretta poured more lotion on her hands and rubbed them together to warm it. "A lady called to ask about you a little while ago," she told him. "She'd just heard about your accident."

Arthur grunted in disinterest. "Rub my arms tonight will you? And my left leg?"

Loretta pulled the blankets over his back and uncovered his left arm. She turned her attention to bruises and scarring along Arthur's arm, careful to touch, not rub mended wounds. "She asked about your horse too," she added quietly. "Ovid, I think she actually said." Loretta rested her hand on his and looked at him.

Arthur turned and lifted his head off the pillow to look at her. "What did you tell her?"

"Nothing," she assured him. "Except that your doctor says you are making a fine recovery." She smiled as if to put an end to the conversation and busied herself straightening Arthur's gown over his damaged left leg.

"About the horse!" he insisted. "She wanted to know about my horse, right?" His face darkened. "What was her name?" Arthur dropped his head back on the pillow. Fully awake now he stared up at the ceiling trying to bring back the name of that horse trainer's widow. The more he pressed, the deeper it slipped from his memory.

"She didn't leave her name, Mr. Van Vliet," Loretta answered. She went about her business, but she'd been a nurse for a long time, long enough to see the many ways the pain of loss can skitter and crash on a patient. She knew his night would be a restless one and had to admit that her own would not be without its own regrets.

Sometime before dawn Arthur was jolted awake with a sharp pain in his left hip. He told himself he'd just had a bad dream. It didn't take long to discover that his hip hurt whenever he moved a certain way. Shortly after seven o'clock Charlie Veeder hurried into Arthur's room and picked up his chart. His presence made Arthur feel even more anxious. His usual way of masking his anxiety seemed to be failing him.

"What the hell is happening, Charlie?" Arthur demanded. "What's the matter with me?"

"That's what we're going to find out, Sport." Charlie Veeder examined Arthur's left leg and hip for red streaks and any telltale swelling. "No sign of infection." He looked relieved. "That's a good sign, a very good sign," he told Arthur. He ordered a second set of x-rays and left to begin his morning rounds. Whatever doubts or suspicions he might have had, he took with him.

It wasn't long before Arthur found himself wheeled off to the x-ray lab, down an elevator to the hospital basement. He was left to wait in the corridor near its closed double doors. Arthur was not accustomed to waiting for service, but this would be a day of long waits, one that he wouldn't be able to rearrange.

Later that morning a young radiologist trailed Charlie Veeder into Arthur's room. By then Arthur's face had taken on the hardened look of a man braced for bad news. Charlie cleared his throat and tapped the x-rays in his hand. "You didn't break any bones when you fell, Arthur, but the fall did damage your hip joint." He paused to give Arthur a little time to take in this unexpected information.

The younger doctor pulled at the cuff of his white coat in an effort to hide his wrinkled shirt sleeve. "When we compared the first x-rays we took when you first arrived with the ones you had today, we can see there has been a slight deterioration of your femur," the radiologist explained. "It's something we call avascular necrosis."

Arthur looked at Charlie.

"We can talk more about this later," Charlie said, "but basically it means your bone isn't getting quite the amount of blood that it needs. I assure you we are going to do everything we can to keep that pain under control."

By the end of the day word spread quickly that Arthur had summoned a specialist from Capitol City. His visit confirmed Charlie Veeder's grim diagnosis. Word of this made its way into bits of overheard information in elevators and lounges. Nurses understood Arthur would eventually be confined to a wheelchair. For some this news fed an unspoken satisfaction that the long reach of Van Vliet money and influence had its limits after all.

That evening Loretta prepared all her other patients for the night before she went into Arthur's room to give him his back rub. She expected his care would take more time than usual and be more difficult. Others warned her of the impact the specialist's visit had had on his mood and temper. He'd refused food and medication and ordered nurses to leave him alone. He shouted at aides to get out and stay out of his room.

"You're late," he grunted, without looking at her.

"Yes," she said, "but I am here now." Loretta rested her hand near his head and looked at him. He'd paled. His face had gone slack, especially around the mouth, the way it often does when children are about to cry and old people sleep. It was no surprise that this unexpected turn had exhausted his body, but it was too soon to know what it might ignite in him. She wondered about that as she watched the shallow rise and fall of his chest.

"I want to go home," he said finally. "Tomorrow."

"Once we strengthen your upper body, you will be able to use crutches and go anywhere you want," she told him.

Arthur frowned. "No. I want to go home tomorrow."

She touched his shoulder and rubbed it with her fingers. "It will hurt some to get in and out of bed or chair," she added, "and you will need to have someone there to help you." She watched as his jaw tightened. "It might be worth thinking about."

"I have," he said. "I want you to be my private nurse."

"Leave the hospital?" she asked. "You mean leave the hospital?"

"Why not? I'll make it worth your while. I promise you that."

She shook her head. "I can't do that." She smiled. "I'm sorry," she added. "This is what I do, Mr. Van Vliet. I'm a hospital nurse." She smiled again at him. "Besides, you won't have any need for a nurse when you return home. A companion or housekeeper, perhaps? But not a nurse."

Loretta uncapped the lotion and poured a circle of its milky contents into the palm of her hand. She hoped it might ease the sudden and terrible news that had already begun to change his life. Over the years she'd come to believe that these small comforts made a difference, if only for a few minutes.

Ava seated herself in the armchair Mr. Rosen offered her away from the draft and watched as he locked the shop door and drew down its window shade. He usually closed the pawnshop earlier on Friday evenings, but when she called, he'd offered to stay late so they could meet after she came from work.

"Would you care for a cup of coffee, Miss Munson?" he asked. He raised a somewhat battered aluminum pot from a hot plate plugged in on the counter behind his chair. "It's not freshly made, I'm afraid, but it is warm."

Ava looked up and shook her head. "No, thank you," she said. "The walk here wasn't as cold as I expected it to be."

He nodded and reached to pull the plug from an extension cord that connected the hot plate and an old radio to a single wall outlet. "That wind must have died down. Makes a big difference, doesn't it," he added. "Especially when it is that damp wind we get this time of year."

He settled himself in his desk chair and adjusted the tie he wore under a brown wool sweater. "I took the liberty of discussing your Degas with a friend of mine," he began. "He owns an art gallery downstate." He rummaged through the scraps of paper tucked in the corners of the large green blotter in front him, but couldn't find what he was looking for. "He told me he'd be interested in buying it. Of course it would have to be authenticated." Mr. Rosen shifted in his chair and opened his desk drawer. Inside was a battered manila envelope crammed with unsorted mail, business cards, and clippings from the newspaper he'd meant to read or keep. It seemed an unlikely place for the information he'd saved for her. He promised himself he'd look for it later, that is, if there was any hope of proving her drawing's value. He felt he owed her that. "Perhaps you have a bill of sale for it?"

Quickly she shook her head and waved her hand. "It was a gift," Ava said. "A long time ago."

Mr. Rosen nodded. He started to say something, started again and finally asked, "Is there someone who can verify its provenance?" He looked at her. "An art dealer needs to be certain it's an original. I'm sure you understand," he added after a moment.

Ava found herself unable to meet his eyes. She touched her pearls, her eyes held on a spindle of papers. Quietly she asked, "And if I have no proof?"

Mr. Rosen leaned across his desk and folded his hands. He seemed to consult them before he spoke. "Well," he began, "you could hire an expert. It would take time and money." His voice too became quieter. "In the end, you might get a very handsome price for the drawing. But it would be a risk."

Ava nodded and while Mr. Rosen waited, her mind went to the scrawled note she'd kept that TK had written. He'd enclosed it with the drawing when he'd sent it more than twenty-five years ago. She remembered that time. It was the spring he took his wife to Europe on the Queen Mary and missed her birthday. Weeks had gone by and she hadn't heard from him. At first she worried he'd been in an accident or taken ill. There was no way to find out what might have happened. Time passed more slowly at night, and it was at those times she thought of nothing but of him in the cold sheets of a double bed warmed by his wife.

She remembered how she felt when he telephoned her from a noisy train station in Paris. Somehow, over the din of an impatient crowd near him and the bad connection that too often broke his voice, he managed to make her wandering anxieties disappear. TK had always been able to draw her close. Later she'd lain awake the rest of the night, and at dawn she brushed out her hair and watched as the darkness fell away and the light slowly made its way across her room.

"Are you suggesting it is a fake, Mr. Rosen?" Ava's words came out in a rush. She seemed to freeze in her chair in anxious disbelief.

Mr. Rosen's neck reddened. "Of course not. Of course not," he assured her. He looked around for something to do. Finally, he patted his sweater pockets for matches and relit the pipe left in an old metal ashtray on his desk. "Most likely the drawing is authentic and has remained in private hands all these years." He looked at her. "That would explain its lack of markings but unfortunately this makes it almost impossible to trace."

Rosen's tobacco was the kind that old men on pensions often smoked over chessboards in public parks. It was sold in bulk and coarsely cut, which gave it a strong, almost stale smell. Even in open air and in passing, it had made Ava queasy. She found herself willingly distracted by Rosen's frugal choice. She wondered why he would deprive himself of such a small pleasure. In some way it reminded her of women who were once overweight but who forever avoid small or fragile chairs.

"What is it you suggest I do, Mr. Rosen?" she asked. The room had cooled, and sharpened the draft around her legs and feet. She felt the chill more keenly than she might have if she'd had more than tea for lunch and not had such a restless night.

She shifted in her chair and pulled her coat around her shoulders and lap, more to suggest it needed rearranging than to call attention to her discomfort.

Sam Rosen took off his glasses and rubbed his eyes with the palms of his hands. "May I speak plainly to you, Ava? Do you mind if I call you Ava?" he asked.

"Please," she answered.

He nodded. "I know this is a difficult time for you," he began, "and I am sorry, Ava. I wish things were different. I wish there was a way I could spare you the hard choices you face right now." He shook his head. "Seems all of us have to make hard decisions from time to time. It's never easy." He smiled and stared for a moment at his hands. "Doesn't get any easier, does it?" he asked finally. "All I know is we need to do what we need to do and get on with our lives the best we can. That's what I think, anyway."

Ava nodded.

He looked older without his glasses, and more tired. "I lost my home a while ago and have been living here, in the back rooms, ever since." He shrugged. "It takes a while to get used to, you know, but we can and do." He looked at her. "What I can offer you, Ava," he said softly, "is a good sum for your pearls, possibly enough to settle your accounts and have a bit to live on for a little while." He gave a slight cough and cleared his throat. "You'd have been careful, of course, but it might give you a little more time to find a living arrangement that is more suitable, given your circumstances."

"Yes, given my circumstances," she repeated. Her voice had gone flat and surprised him. There was no trace of the self pity or bitterness that Rosen had come to expect from women like Ava. They sat for a little while as strangers sometimes do in a bus depot or doctor's waiting room, lost in their own thoughts.

"This has been a long day," he said finally. "I'd be glad to come by your apartment on Sunday. We can settle all this then, if you like."

He waited for her to tell him she needed more time, as she had in the past. Instead she shrugged on her coat and stood up. "Sunday afternoon would be fine, Mr. Rosen," she answered. He rose, and after they shook hands, he unlocked the shop door. As he stood watching her leave he noticed that wind had picked up and scattered litter along the curb.

His meeting with Ava on that Sunday didn't go as he expected. He arrived at two o'clock and she met him at her door. He remembered he glanced at her sitting room, and waited for her to invite him in, offer him a cup of tea or coffee. She didn't. Instead she excused herself for a few minutes and left him standing in his winter coat, his hat in hand. When she returned she had the pearls in her hand and gave them to him. It was an awkward moment he would not soon forget. In the end he handed her an envelope and left with her pearls. As he made his way down the stairs of her apartment building he found himself too preoccupied to notice the quiet click of doors in the hallway behind him.

It was later in the afternoon before Sam Rosen stepped off the elevator in the hospital's new wing. He checked his pockets for the scrap of paper with the room number, and took a moment to smooth down his hair before he knocked on the closed door.

"Well, Rosen," Arthur greeted him, looking neither pleased nor displeased to see him. "That took you long enough." He wheeled himself around and faced his visitor.

"I'm afraid some things take more time," Sam Rosen replied. He removed the black and cream jewelry case from an inside pocket of his coat and opened its worn velvet lid to arrange and center the strand before he offered it to Arthur. The pearls had lost her body's warmth, but not their luster or her scent. Sam could not recall when he'd last seen anything more beautiful or more forlorn, unless it had been Ava herself.

"I had these appraised a while ago, you know," Arthur told him. "All it took was the experienced eye of a jewelry store clerk posing as a shopper in the fabric store." He looked pleased. "I've waited for these for months."

"Take this to the bank first thing tomorrow morning," Arthur said, handing him a folded piece of paper. "Ask for Malcolm. He's my secretary and has the authority to pay you for the pearls, and for your trouble, of course." For the first time since his accident more than month ago Arthur felt like his old self again. He'd lost a lot of weight, a fact even his thick dark wool robe couldn't hide, but his appetite for his life had come back.

"About those code violations," Rosen asked, "on my shop?"

Arthur shook his head. "I wouldn't worry about those complaints, Sam," he assured him. "Probably just a mistake. Building inspectors do make them now and then, you know." He slipped Ava's pearl's into his monogrammed pocket and patted it. "I'll see what I can do to help you out."

Ruby Lupino toweled off Loretta's hair and stared at the kinky wet mass that sprang out from beneath the weight of her hand. "For god sakes, Loretta, how could you let that sister-in-law of yours get her hands on you again? I've seen some awful home permanents, but this one is a doozy."

Loretta looked at herself in the mirror. "Well," she laughed, turning her head from side to side, "you have to admit it's good for your business."

Ruby frowned. "I'm going to have to cut at least a half inch off all over. The ends are burnt. Frazzled. What did she do, leave it in all day?" Ruby looked at Loretta's reflection in the mirror and shook her comb at it, "Wouldn't surprise me in the least if she did it on purpose, that one."

"I've got to be back at the hospital in twenty minutes, Ruby," Loretta reminded her, hoping to side step her old neighbor's familiar grievance. As far as she could tell, this one-sided rivalry began in high school with Ruby's very public crush on her older brother. Ruby had never forgiven her best friend for flirting with him near the boys' locker room. "I promised one of my patients I'd find someone to take care of him after he goes home in a week or so."

Ruby fastened several hair clips to the sleeve of her pink smock. "Oh, yeah," she said, pinning back fistfuls of damp ringlets, "that's that banker, what's his name, who had that accident." She shrugged. "I haven't heard too much about him lately." She gave Loretta's hair a hard look. "I hate to tell you this but it is going to take forever for this mess to grow out." She shook her head and reached for a pair of scissors. "One thing I can tell you, though, all that talk about him being thrown by his horse and all? That never lit up this place like the gossip about them did."

"Them?" Loretta asked.

"Uh huh." Ruby's attention shifted as she slowly trimmed the singed hair behind Loretta's left ear. When she finished she stood up to check its length. "You know, him and that shop clerk." Ruby looked at Loretta in the mirror. "She used to be a regular customer here, but I haven't seen her in months." Ruby thought for a moment. "I liked her. She was generous tipper too." She shrugged. "Too bad he dumped her."

"How do you know he did?" Loretta asked. She looked down at her white shoes, as if someone had reminded her to watch her step.

"Well, she didn't leave him for a richer guy, that's for sure. I hear she can't even pay her grocery bills these days. Seems to me only a fool would make that choice. It's simple arithmetic." Ruby wrapped a hairnet around Loretta's head and settled her in a red leatherette chair under the hair dryer. "Five minutes, at least," she shouted over its loud noise, "can't have you leaving here with wet hair. You catch a cold and your mother would kill me."

Loretta laughed. She sat under the huge silver dryer blasting warm air and watched as Ruby swept the floor and tidied her station. The trip to the beauty salon was just another chore for Loretta. She felt out of place with all the small talk and gossip. It reminded her of high school. She had to admit Ruby's offhand remarks about Arthur Van Vliet had stirred something up in her though. It seemed to be about more than just her professional interest. She wasn't sure what it was, and that nagged her even more.

Loretta paid her bill and for no reason she could explain to herself later, gave Ruby more than her usual fair, but modest tip. That was when it came to her.

"What was her name, Ruby?" Loretta asked as she buttoned up her coat, her face still flushed from the dryer's heat.

"Who?"

"That, uh, friend of Arthur Van Vliet's. You know, that former customer of yours."

"Munson. Ava Munson." She pushed the bouquet of fake flowers aside to make more room by the telephone for her appointment book. "Why?"

"Do you know where she works?"

Ruby gave her old friend a sideways look. "Now why would you want to know that?" she asked. She folded her arms and watched as Loretta tied her woolen hat under her chin.

Loretta stood by the door and waited.

"I know what you're thinking, Loretta," Ruby warned. "Don't. Don't do it. It's none of your business. Besides," she added lightly, "I have personal experience of your matchmaking talents and believe me," she said, "they're pitiful."

Loretta's rueful expression was in comic contrast to her round and bundled appearance. "He needs someone to look after him and she needs a roof over her head," Loretta said. "It's not about matchmaking, Ruby," she added. "It's about arithmetic."

Ruby shook her head. "That fabric shop, just off Erie Street," she said. "And put on your gloves. It's cold out there."

The Dutch Reformed Church was a felt presence in Mohawk Falls. It stood on a wooded rise not far from the river on a street arched by elm trees and marked by historic plaques within the gated church grounds. Some say the original building had been torched by displaced Indians late one Sunday night during Advent. Others claim it was destroyed by fire caused by a cache of gunpowder hidden in its sanctuary by hard drinking fur traders. These days all that is left of that first church is a small cemetery. Its worn stones lean in doubtful rows behind bushes of wild dogwood, weathered and bent like frail old women in precarious, if not everlasting, prayer. Over the years its small but established congregation did little to call attention to itself. Members lived in closed circles, marrying whenever possible into families with comparable wealth or more distinction. On Sunday mornings they gathered in the modest pews once occupied by their ancestors, just as they assumed the burdens and privileges of their birth in local board rooms, social circles and at family gatherings. It was no small matter to Arthur or his mother that the Van Vliet family had occupied a front pew in this church since the early 1720s.

It wasn't until Arthur had been home for a while and his tailor had altered his dark but lighter weight suits that he was ready to resume the comfortable habits of his life and began accompanying his mother to Sunday morning services again. Church deacons stood ready to offer their help to him and his mother, as were valet attendants at his club. In this way he was able to preserve a weekly ritual that was important to them both. Following church services on Sunday mornings, Arthur drove his mother to the Mohawk Club where its most senior waiter seated and served them brunch. Theirs was always a well placed table some distance from those occupied by families with restless children. It was no accident that they were given tables near the fireplace during the winter months, and ones that overlooked the club's prized tulip garden every Sunday throughout the month of April.

On a warm but overcast Sunday in mid May, after the French lilacs had come and gone and the flowering crab trees had lost most of their lingering fragrance, Ava knelt on the window seat and pushed aside the swag of curtain to open her sitting room window. The room itself was a small space that had once served as a nursery. It opened into a bedroom and bath large enough to accommodate a nursemaid and whatever belongings she might be able to fit into a wardrobe and chest of drawers. Someone had papered its walls with a large landscape print, no doubt in an effort to use up rolls of wallpaper left over from matching its pattern in a much larger and more public room in the house a long time ago.

She sat in an old rocker, her hair still damp from her bath, half listening for the Packard in the driveway below her window. Arthur would be returning home soon and need her help getting out of the car. She rubbed her forehead as if to clear her mind. Lately she'd found herself distracted and often tense. There seemed to be no specific cause but the chair's slow, rhythmic motion seemed to calm her. She leaned her head against its high cushioned back and closed her eyes. She remembered those first days, after she'd arrived by taxicab with her suitcase and a few boxes.

Arthur had greeted her as if she were an obliging guest. "Come in, Ava. Come in," he said smiling. "Take the lady's belongings to her room," he instructed the driver as he helped Ava remove her coat, "it's on the second floor, the last door on your right." He smiled at her again and gave her a long look. "No need for you to trouble yourself in this house, Ava," he had told her. Back then he'd offered her chocolates and later a fine dry sherry. She remembered sitting across from him in the parlor for the first time. He looked much thinner and seemed to lack some of the fulsome mannerisms she had found so off-putting in the past. They sipped their sherry and made small talk for a little while, managing somehow to get through those first small, but awkward silences. Neither of them spoke of the past and she took that to be a promising sign.

Later, though, when he asked her to help him out of his chair, she was surprised and perhaps even a little alarmed by the way he gripped her arm. He held it longer and tighter than she'd expected. She remembered reassuring herself that there was nothing more to it than her inexperience and his awkwardness. "Come," he said to her, "let me show you around the first floor." Ava nodded. "I know you will be quite comfortable here, Ava. Very comfortable." He patted her arm and smiled again. "I've a few habits I hope you won't find too tiresome." He gave a small laugh. "And I will need a little help now and then," he added. Arthur smoothed his hair and looked at her. "We'll get on splendidly, you and me." Ava touched the blue scarf she'd taken to wearing around her neck. "Pretty scarf," he told her. "The color suits you," he said as he led her through the pocket doors and out of the parlor.

Ava stood by the open window and took in the quiet and the fresh air. A small creek disappeared into the ravine beyond the low fieldstone wall that bordered the grounds. She passed her days quietly in Arthur's old Victorian house. She had three small rooms to herself, and she spent most of her time there, although Arthur had explained she could come and go in the rest of the house as she wanted. When she first arrived, she had given some thought to replacing the tired, cast-off furnishings with something more to her taste, but she never really found the right time to approach Arthur about it, and as time passed the existing furniture seemed comfortable enough. The only memory that seemed to interrupt the passing of the days was the young Indian warrior. She often remembered his reassuring presence in the circle below the front window of her old apartment. Every once in a while she promised herself she would visit the old neighborhood, but the effort seemed more than she had time for. Tending to Arthur's needs took much of her attention, and the time she had to herself she usually spent in the quiet of her room.

The rain began soon after Arthur returned from brunch with his mother. It was a slow, steady rain that farmers and gardeners wish for early in the season, but one that confined Arthur first to his bed for a nap and later to his study for a cigar and a neglected pile of financial reports he had put off reading the previous Sunday afternoon. Ava had put out a change of clothes for him but instead he chose to wear pajamas and his bathrobe. He put on a pair of moccasins he'd promised Charlie Veeder he wouldn't wear again and scowled when Ava reminded him of his doctor's warning. It would be a long Sunday afternoon and evening, one without visitors whose presence gave her respite from his attentions and demands. These long days, when she was home alone with Arthur, were the ones she dreaded the most.

"Ava?" Arthur called out. Ava lowered the flame under the tea kettle on the stove and hurried through the butler's pantry and down a carpeted hallway to his study.

"Yes, Arthur?" she asked. He'd seated himself on the leather couch, his feet up on a hassock, with his papers strewn on the floor, the cushions, and the table behind him. It had been a while since he'd sat in the big chair behind his desk even though it was much easier for her to help him get to his feet than from the soft and slippery couch.

He reached for his lit cigar and held it above his ashtray. "I hope I haven't taken you from something important. What were you doing?" he said.

Ava shook her head. "Why, nothing, really. I was about to make a cup of tea." She glanced at the journals and reports scattered around him. "I thought I'd go upstairs and read a magazine for a little while." She waited a moment. "May I get you something?" she asked.

Arthur looked at her and smiled. "Yes," he said. He pushed aside the papers on the cushion beside him and patted it. "Why don't you get your magazine and read it in here, Ava?" Arthur put out his cigar and smoothed back his hair. "A cup of tea would be fine," he said, "unless, of course, I could convince you to join me in having a glass of sherry." He nodded toward the cherry liquor cabinet in front of the book lined wall on which his collection of bronzed horse statues was prominently displayed. "That does sound the perfect way to spend a rainy afternoon, don't you think?" Outside the study windows rain slid down the panes of glass, sealing the room in a glaze of silvery drizzle.

Ava nodded and turned to leave.

"There is one more thing, if you wouldn't mind, Ava?" he said lightly.

"Yes?" she answered.

"I wonder if you would humor me a bit? It's been a long time since you've worn that lovely scent. Or is it a powder?" he asked. "Would you mind wearing it this afternoon?" He shook his head, "Unless you'd rather not...?"

"No," Ava said. "Of course I don't mind."